WHISPERS IN THE WIND

WHISPERS IN THE WIND

Janet Woods

This first world edition published 2017
in Great Britain and the USA by
SEVERN HOUSE PUBLISHERS LTD of
19 Cedar Road, Sutton, Surrey, England, SM2 5DA.
Trade paperback edition first published
in Great Britain and the USA 2017 by
SEVERN HOUSE PUBLISHERS LTD

British Library Cataloguing in Publication Data
A CIP catalogue record for this title is available from the British Library.

ISBN-13: 978-0-7278-8692-7 (cased)
ISBN-13: 978-1-84751-796-8 (trade paper)
ISBN-13: 978-1-78010-863-6 (e-book)

This is a work of fiction. Names, characters, places and incidents
are either the product of the author's imagination or are used fictitiously.
Except where actual historical events and characters are being described
for the storyline of this novel, all situations in this publication are
fictitious and any resemblance to actual persons, living or dead,
business establishments, events or locales is purely coincidental.

All Severn House titles are printed on acid-free paper.

Severn House Publishers support the Forest Stewardship Council™ [FSC™],
the leading international forest certification organisation.
All our titles that are printed on FSC certified paper carry the FSC logo.

MIX
Paper from
responsible sources
FSC® C013056

Typeset by Palimpsest Book Production Ltd.,
Falkirk, Stirlingshire, Scotland.
Printed and bound in Great Britain by
TJ International, Padstow, Cornwall.

One

December 1816 – Winter.

Adele was hot and sticky. Her body ached, her throat felt raw and pain throbbed inside her head.

She struggled to breathe as she tried to rid herself of the remaining shreds of her dream. Somewhere below her a man emptied his last breath into the sea . . . a lone cry of despair encased in a bubble. She slid into the deep, fighting for her life – her hair tangled like seaweed between his fingers. A net of rope captured her body, tore them apart and pulled her into the light. Hauled over the side of the ship she flopped, face down, on the hard wooden deck. There was a shadow, hunched down low. Air swooped harshly into her lungs as the sea was pumped out by a strong span of hands.

The ship's watchman gazed down at her. 'You'll be all right now, missus, but the sea has taken your man.'

Gone! Edgar was gone. The pitch and toss of the sea calmed. The shadow had gone too. She was saved . . . but what would she do with such freedom?

A light was burning. Adele turned her head towards it to encounter the soft, uncertain sputter of a solitary candle.

Beneath her the bed was as soft as a baby's cradle. Four posts supported dusty-smelling hangings. Beyond, a fireplace cradled the remains of a fire that coiled ashy breath into the maw of the chimney. A clock measured the seconds on the mantelpiece with a muted tick. Adele couldn't see the hands mark the passage of time but she could hear it, each second unable to be retrieved. There were few ornaments, the most noticeable being a heroic bronze – a man on a horse, its mane flowing in the wind. She had seen one like it before and it struck her that the room had a mannish feel to it with its leather chair.

She was safe. Edgar was drowned. She drew in a breath, whispered, 'Where am I?'

A prolonged sigh drew her attention to the chair. A man occupied it, if the pair of long legs stretched to their limit was any indication. The wing of the chair concealed half of his face and the other half was hidden under an untidy abundance of hair.

Perhaps he was a doctor. She tried to attract his attention with a greeting, but it was quiet and unintelligible . . . more like a squeak from a mouse than a sensible word from a fellow human. As quiet as it was, the murmur of sound registered in his ears, and he woke.

Head now withdrawn from her sight he stood, enclosed within his own shadow, blending into his background and perfectly still. Not a noise could be heard as he waited for a second confirmation of life within the tension she'd created.

Who was he . . . where was she? She could hold her breath no longer and it huffed painfully from her.

'Ah . . .'

Splaying his hands against his back he stretched his spine, giving such a pleasurable and prolonged groan that Adele almost experienced it with him. Then he pushed a log from the hearthstone into the grate with his foot. The ashes glowed red and spat aggressive sparks. Tiny blue flames licked around the log and he gave a satisfied grunt. Only then did he turn his attention her way.

Adele recalled being on a horse, held intimately against his body so they were almost one. His horse? Then she remembered Sarah, and with some alarm. What if she was lost on the heath! 'Sarah . . . she went to find help.'

'Rest easy. The girl is safe. Reverend Bryson has taken her under his roof. He lives in Brackenhurst .'

Relief rushed through her, leaving a yawning hole in her stomach. Reverend Bryson. She knew that name, knew him to be trustworthy. He was a church cleric, after all. 'Where am I, sir? How did I get here?'

He came to stand at the end of the bed. His face was dark, shadowed with several days' beard. The log flared up and the fire began to crackle, causing his shadow to dance on the wall in a rather menacing manner.

After a short silence he said, 'A young lady raised the alarm and I came to look for you. The snow became too heavy to take you back into town, so I brought you to my home, which was the closest shelter. I was the only one in the tavern prepared to look for you in this weather and I found you on the heath, frozen to the bone and half-dead.'

Fatigue filled her body. 'I'm grateful for your assistance. I feel . . . unwell, and I'm thirsty.'

'You've caught a chill and you're suffering from a fever and a cough, I believe.' He crossed to the dresser. Taking the cover from a stone jug he poured liquid into a tumbler and brought it to where she lay. He slid his arm behind her shoulders and gently lifted her from the pillows, holding the tumbler to her mouth. 'It's a tot of brandy mixed with water, and has honey to sweeten it . . . a concoction guaranteed to cure any cough. After you've finished it you must try to get some more rest. What's your name?'

After a moment of hesitation she murmured, 'Mrs Pelham.'

'And the girl who was with you?'

'Sarah is my . . . stepdaughter.' She took a sip of the liquid and shuddered, though it was soothing. 'Are you a physician?'

'I'm no physician, Mrs Pelham, but out of necessity I've done some doctoring in my time. It looks as though you must trust yourself to my soldierly medical skills for the time being.'

His heart beat against her shoulder and there was a moment when she felt as though they'd known each other in another life. 'I remember that.'

'Remember what?'

'Your heartbeat . . . we were on a horse and it beat against my ear, keeping me alive. I was counting the beats and when I could no longer hear them I thought I'd died.'

'Your mind is wandering, Mrs Pelham. It was not that romantic an event. You were a dead weight and my horse grumbled, and as you can see, you've survived your ordeal on the heath. Now you must recover so you can be on your way.'

Adele felt as weak as a kitten when he lowered her onto the pillow and drew away. 'What time is it?'

He placed a little bell within her reach. 'It's only first light so try and sleep for an hour or so longer. Where were you going?'

'Home . . . I was going home.' She yawned and turned on her side, her eyes beginning to close. 'I'm so tired.'

'You might feel a little better when you've rested more. If you need anything ring the bell.'

He was a kind man, she thought, as she closed her eyes.

Despite the early hour Ryder went downstairs, greeting Hal Stover with a smile. An attorney by profession, Hal had been with him since they first met. They'd become brothers in arms. Since Ryder had handed in his commission their friendship had strengthened. Only a few weeks ago the pair had shared a comfortable billet in London, waiting for official news of their discharge. Now the war with Napoleon was over their soldiering days had also come to an end.

Hal had beaten him to the kitchen and he'd got a fire roaring in the stove. The cast-iron kettle steamed and the lid clattered away on top.

'You're up early, Sergeant Stover.'

'I'd forgotten how suffocating snow is when it comes to deadening sound. It was too quiet to sleep for long and the bivouac was more comfortable than I'm used to. I guess I'll adjust eventually.'

'I've spent better nights with a woman occupying my bed. The invalid's name is Mrs Pelham, by the way.'

They grinned at each other.

'As for my quarters, they were passing clean and the bed had sheets, thanks to your dubious domestic skills.'

'I'm an attorney, not a chamber maid.'

'And inept at both.'

'True . . . How did you sleep, Captain?'

'I spent the night in the chair. Mrs Pelham survived the night, though she's weak with fever. She was travelling with her stepdaughter, apparently. We must bring the girl here since Mrs Pelham needs a female to look after her.'

'How old is she?'

He shrugged. 'Old enough to send off across the heath to fetch help. Her name is Sarah. That would have taken some guts. Having her here will bring Mrs Pelham peace of mind, if nothing else. I'll take the pack horse and if I can get through to the rectory I'll bring the girl back with me.'

His glance lit on the recently washed table and to the contents of their saddlebags spread out there – half a stale loaf, a chunk of cheese, a thick slice of ham and a wad of fat that provided the grease for cooking. A piece of unsalted fish housed a colony of pests. Hal fed it to a small dog that had followed him in and was lurking under the table.'

'Where did the ratter come from?'

'It came charging at me from the barn and would have torn my leg off if I hadn't been wearing boots. He's a gutsy little bugger, a stray, I think.'

'It looks calm enough now.' Ryder put his hand down to fondle the creature and the dog offered him a rattling snarl.

'Sit!' Ryder said and it rolled on its back and presented its belly to be fondled.

Hal laughed. 'I'm glad someone likes you.'

There was also some tea in a tin-lined box. 'You've been busy, Hal.'

'The food won't last long.'

Ryder sighed. 'And is not the kind of food we should offer a sick woman . . . especially one as emaciated as our guest. I'm hoping the agent delivers the list of provisions I ordered on the way through. I told him it was urgent.'

'I'll go and see what I can scrounge from the garden and I thought the smokehouse showed signs of use.' Hal reached for his greatcoat, hanging over the back of a chair. 'Some chickens have been wintering in the barn so there might be eggs. Use has been made of the kitchen garden in your absence, so there will also be winter vegetables under the snow. I'll neck one of the older hens and we can make a broth.'

Hal was nothing if not resourceful. He reconnoitred their immediate surrounds thoroughly and a little while later he came back with some onions and turnips, a couple of thick pork rashers and a chicken he'd already plucked. He hung the fowl upside down over a bucket to bleed, so the flesh would be white and tender.

'You made a good haul,' Ryder said when Hal carefully

transferred half a dozen frail eggs from his pocket to a bowl of cold water.

Hal grunted with satisfaction when they sank to the bottom. 'These are freshly laid; if they'd been old they would have floated.'

The sergeant's seemingly trivial remarks never ceased to amaze Ryder, for invariably he was proved right. 'Where did you find the pig?'

'The smokehouse. It might interest you to know that the kitchen garden is in use and the smokehouse has a quartered porker hanging in it. I cut us some rashers. Someone seems to be making use of the land and outbuildings. I found a couple of turnips going begging, and some potatoes. The well has been kept free of debris so the water is sweet. The lid will stop it from freezing over. It will make a change from drinking melted snow.'

'Take care if there are signs of my estate being used illegally, though I see no signs of the house being occupied. I imagine someone local is taking advantage of the situation. We'll get to the bottom of it eventually. In the meantime we'll profit from their hard work, and thank them. They might abandon it once they know the house is occupied. After breakfast I'll leave you to look after my guest while I chase the rector up. I doubt if the woman will eat anything, but she might enjoy something warm in her stomach, tea perhaps. Mrs Pelham sounds like a lady down on her luck, so use the best china, if you can find any.' He ignored Hal's grin. 'God knows, the caretakers I left in charge might have taken the china with them.'

'The house doesn't seem to have been ransacked and its condition is sound considering the amount of time it's been unlived in.'

Ryder shrugged. 'For me it feels like I never left. I spent much of my childhood here, and was twenty-one when I departed. You know the rest.'

Hal grinned. 'It wasn't hard to figure out it was woman trouble.'

'I got over it.'

'Once you stopped feeling sorry for yourself you became a

passable soldier, but tell me you're over the woman in a day or two.'

'I can always find another. As for you, I can safely say you're the worst companion I've ever had.' Ryder took the bent and battered coin from his pocket and spun it in the air. 'I still have my lucky shilling. Who'd have thought it would come between me and a bullet?'

'No one in their right mind.'

'That event was a turning point for me. The word duty took on a new meaning . . . and it included a future.'

'It sounds as if you're contemplating marriage, Captain. Not to me, I hope.'

An image of a young woman stabbed into Ryder's mind, and with such a bright clarity that he narrowed his eyes against the shine of it. She'd captivated his heart with her smile and her innocence, and then, to his mortification and shame, she'd left him − left him standing at the altar. There was a moment of yawning heartsickness, as though he stood on the edge of a deep, dark void, then he shrugged it off. He was through pining for what might have been.

There had been women since her, physical encounters he'd enjoyed for what they were and for as long as they'd lasted. Mostly they were discreet women who played the game and asked for nothing more than the temporary comfort of a man's arms around them, otherwise he'd avoided thinking her about since that day she'd walked away from him without explanation. He was twenty-seven . . . not too old to change his way of life. Why had he come back here with the intention of making a living from the estate if he had nobody to leave it to?

'You could be right, Hal,' he murmured, and then he laughed. 'Marriage is not a bloody impossibility, you know.'

'Marriage to me is? It's not going to happen.'

Ryder threw a tin mug at him.

Ryder's journey into town was uneventful. He passed a team of wagons heading for the Madigan estate. One was piled high with bales of hay and sacks of oats and the other with the provisions they'd need for winter.

When Ryder pulled his horses to one side to let the wagons

through, he introduced himself. The driver touched his hat with a grimy forefinger. 'Good day, my lord.'

'What's the road like closer to Poole?'

'We got stuck in a drift a mile back and had to shovel our way out of it. The wagons are heavy and the horses have tramped a path through it so it should be open for the time being. We'll be coming and going all day and the livestock will come through last. We've been up all night getting this organized, but we should be all right for a day or two, I reckon.'

After a short conversation about the weather they moved on.

When Ryder reached Poole he went to the workhouse and hired a housekeeper, a cook and two maids of all work.

He arranged for the cartage company to take them out to Madigan House. It would do until the snow had passed and he could reorganize his life. On the way back he went into the church, which was situated just inside the village of Brackenhurst . . . not to pray or seek solace, but to look for the rector.

The place hadn't changed. The ancient dusty smell of it gave him a cruel kick that tore open his wound. He hadn't been inside a church since that day. He remembered standing before the altar, a faintly derisive smile on his face as if he didn't care that the congregation was whispering behind his back. As that awful day had progressed they'd begun to leave one by one. When the soft evening light had turned into darkness the Reverend Bryson had extinguished the candles on the altar. 'Go home, my lord. Your bride will not be coming now.'

He'd gone, only to pack his travelling bag. He'd stopped in Poole long enough to inform his attorney of his departure and to sign the papers necessary to run the Madigan estate before he headed for London.

Oliver Bryson looked up at him now and smiled. 'I thought that might've been you in the inn.'

'I was too tired to be sociable. You should have said something.'

'You had an unapproachable air about you, as though you were sizing things up. But I wasn't sure, since the beard has changed your appearance considerably. Besides, I was more interested in trying to stir up a search party for the woman traveller.'

'Nobody was going to leave that fireside and a cup of hot toddy to risk their lives for a lost woman, not even you, Oliver.'

'You did.'

'Because it was on my way home. Besides, I'd sent my companion on ahead and had to check that he'd arrived safely.'

'You've been a long time gone and there had been no correspondence from you. We were discussing the preparation of papers to put before the court and have you pronounced dead *in absentia.*'

'We?'

'Stephen Tessler and myself. He came across an article stating that a snake had struck at you on a riverbank and you'd died, and had been buried in a cave in India. How are you, my lord?'

'I'm well enough for someone who's dead and buried. The snake had no venom. You'll be pleased to hear I found the woman alive, though she's suffering from a fever and a cough.'

'Surprised would be a better word. She must have a strong constitution to have survived exposure for several hours on the heath in such weather. She's ill, you say. Will she live?'

Ryder nodded. 'After spending half the night on the heath in the snow, I can only say that she certainly has the will. I thought it would do her good to have her companion with her so she doesn't worry about her. I've come to collect the young lady.'

The reverend looked troubled. 'They found room for Sarah Pelham in the workhouse.'

'Oh . . . I see.' Ryder was puzzled. 'I thought you had offered her your hospitality. You acted rather quickly considering they have the same surname. They are obviously related. I would have thought you'd have waited until you'd heard from me. Now they'll have to let her out again.'

'Are you sure that's wise, my lord?'

'I don't know what's wise and what isn't, but I'm certainly of an age where advice is unwelcome unless it's asked for.'

'Then I won't inflict any more on you, unless asked.'

Ryder sighed. He'd upset him. 'You seem to have an objection, Reverend. May I ask what it is?'

The man shrugged. 'My wife said the girl had too much to say for herself and she turned out to be rude and ungrateful. I was surprised, because they seemed to be getting on at first. Mary gave her some clean clothes and some breakfast, and then she got a ride on one of the wagons and took her into Poole, to the workhouse. My wife thought they might be able to find her employment as a scullery maid. A girl of her age would probably work hard for little more than a roof over her head and a meal in her stomach.'

'The ethics of which hardly bears thinking about,' Ryder said. 'She might be forced to do more if the wrong employer got hold of her.'

'Ethics, is it? That's all right for you, my lord. You were born with a silver spoon in your hand and never wondered where the next meal was coming from to dip it into.'

Ryder hadn't pondered on his privileged position in a long time. He'd learned it wasn't relevant in the face of death. 'Most people prefer to work than accept outright charity. It allows them to keep their pride intact.'

'They could be picking oakum or packing pins in the workhouse instead. What's the difference?'

'My pardon, Reverend, you are right, of course, and I retract my words if you'll allow me. Right now the girl has employment waiting, looking after her mistress . . . sister . . . daughter, whatever the girl's position is?'

The reverend shuffled from one foot to the other. 'Sarah Pelham is the stepdaughter of Mrs Pelham, I believe. Her father—'

'Spare me the family history, Oliver. I don't give a fig whose loins these women sprang from. Both need help, and for the time being, at least, I can provide it. My home will need staffing from the ground up, so I'll probably be able to fit the pair of them into my household if they need employment and have nowhere else to go.'

The reverend frowned for a moment, then he straightened, ironic amusement captured in his eyes. 'May I just say, if you act in haste you're likely to repent at leisure. Yes . . . you could employ them, I suppose, but it remains to be seen. There really is something you should be made aware—'

'Save it for later, Reverend. I have no time to stand and chat since at the moment I'm trying to rustle up some stores and some house staff before the weather closes in. There's nothing colder and more unwelcoming than a house that's been left empty for some time.'

'As you wish, my lord. May I just enquire if your intention is to remain in the district?'

'My intention is to make the estate productive. Do you know what happened to my caretakers?'

'They were old. They died about three years ago, within weeks of each other. They were grateful to have somewhere to spend their last few years together in comfort. I consulted with Stephen Tessler and we decided that rather than hire a stranger we'd simply employ an enterprising young man, a relation who was known to us, and who lived a short distance away, to keep an eye on the place for a fee.'

'His name?'

'Luke Ashburn.'

Ryder searched his mind. 'Ashburn . . .?' He couldn't put a face to the name. 'I didn't think you had any relations, except me.'

Oliver smiled. 'He came as a surprise to us too. Luke is . . . well, you could say he's my wife's nephew. He's good with figures and works in an accountancy office in Dorchester at present. Luke recently came of age and into his legacy, but has been running his own household since he was seventeen . . . some four years since. I can guarantee his honesty. The attorney who represents us both looks after his legal affairs. I trust you approve.'

Ryder didn't entirely approve. Close kin could turn minor disputes into wars, especially if money was involved. However, he recognized that the fault was on his own head, since he'd neglected the Madigan estate. To be fair, he'd be just as guilty at offering work to a needy relative if he had one.

Now he was home he would need a manager for the estate, and at least the young man had kept it in some sort of order. But if he was adequately housed and could afford to hire an attorney for his own affairs, it seemed to Ryder that those who were unemployed and also suitably qualified should be offered the position.

Ryder felt ashamed of his curt manner. The reverend had gone beyond what most people would expect. 'Thank you, and please accept my apology for being so churlish earlier. I got very little sleep last night. Perhaps you would tell Mr Ashburn to come and see me when the snow has cleared.'

A wry smile twisted the man's mouth. 'He's another soul who doesn't take advice kindly and insists on learning from his own mistakes. He'll probably make himself known to you before too long, and when it pleases him. Now I must go. I have a lot to get through today in case it starts to snow again . . . and I think it's more than likely.'

Ryder smarted a little from the comparison, and was annoyed to think that Ashburn would come only at his own convenience. 'Make it clear to your wife's nephew that the time and place will suit me, not the other way around. Good day to you.'

As he turned to ride away the reverend called after him, 'Miss Pelham told Mary they were on their way to Brackenhurst. They have relations there, apparently.'

Pelham . . . the name wasn't uncommon. The wine merchant in Poole was called Pelham, so was a family of potters and brick makers in Verwood.

Brackenhurst was a large village populated mostly by wealthy tradesmen. There was a small church and vicarage on the outskirts. It provided a living for the Reverend Bryson. Then there were the usual shops and a bakery, plus a physician. Mrs Pelham and her stepdaughter didn't show any outward signs of wealth. Perhaps her relatives were shopkeepers.

So why had the reverend mentioned it?

The idea his mind threw at him was just too coincidental to entertain.

Hah! He threw back at himself and put it from his mind.

Adele came out of sleep, her body bathed in perspiration again. Murmuring with distress she threw the covers off. The crumpled chemise she wore stuck to her flesh and her mouth was so dry there was barely any moisture left in it.

A man approached the bed carrying a tumbler, his form a tall dark shape against the light streaming through the window. When he got closer she saw a handsome if slightly weatherworn face, and grey eyes.

She gulped down the contents of the tumbler held to her cracked lips, shuddering at its sharpness. She murmured, 'I'm too warm.'

'You must try and keep the covers over you, Mrs Pelham. I've just given you some willow bark. It will help bring your temperature down.' The voice was gruff. 'Would you like me to cool you down a little? I could wash your face, and then brush your hair and braid it. After that you might like to take some tea. We have to make sure you drink plenty. I can make you some breakfast if you think you can manage it. We have fresh eggs and some ham, and we're waiting for a cow to arrive with a delivery of fresh milk.'

She managed a smile, but it felt more like a grimace. 'I'm not hungry, but thank you . . . I forget your name.'

'I haven't told you it.'

When she'd met him the previous night she'd formed the impression he'd been a younger man with blue eyes. But it had been dark, and her mind had been rambling. 'Will you introduce yourself, then?'

'It's Halifax Stover. Most people call me Hal.'

When she struggled to sit and see what lay beyond the window, for there was something familiar about the room, her head spun.

'Stay there, Mrs Pelham. I'll put a towel under your head so the pillow doesn't soak up the excess water. If you need to get out of bed for any reason let me know and I'll make sure you have privacy.'

'I don't . . . not yet.'

'Because you have a fever and you're perspiring.'

The water was wonderfully cool as he carefully bathed her face, neck and hands, and as impersonally as if she were a child. Goosebumps crawled over her body like ants and she began to shake. 'I'm shivering.'

'The fever is the cause of that. You will go from one extreme to the other for a while, I'm afraid.' He gently brushed the knots from her hair and loosely braided it before hanging the plait over her shoulder. 'There . . . that's better.'

The tea was sweetened with honey and she appreciated its flavour as she sipped it, her teeth chattering against the lip of the cup as she said, 'I've got to get to Brackenhurst. I have property there . . . and relatives.'

'Are they expecting you?'

'No.'

'So your relatives will still be there when you're fit enough to travel, will they not?'

'Yes . . . but . . .'

'But nothing, Mrs Pelham, and I can't stress this enough. You are seriously ill as well as being undernourished. The young woman you were with will be here soon to look after you. We will send your relatives at Brackenhurst a note when the snow clears, so they'll expect you.'

'May I ask you something, Hal?' she said, when he moved away – and her blush added to the flush of fever now firing her cheeks. 'My clothing . . . who . . . undressed me?'

'I removed your boots and you managed the rest by yourself. Don't you remember?'

She most certainly didn't remember – she didn't remember anything – and must thank him for sparing her feelings when she recovered, she thought, and said when he moved to gaze out of the window, 'Is this your home?'

'Where I lay my head to rest on any given day is usually my home. However, I can't lay claim to this house since it belongs to Lord Madigan, who is also my friend. It was the earl who saved your life and brought you in from the heath.'

She gave a cry of anguish. 'No wonder it seemed familiar. This cannot be . . . Ryder is dead. He died from snakebite in India two years ago. It was reported in a news-sheet and I saw it with my own eyes.'

'Rumour, that's all. It wasn't a venomous snake and he recovered.'

'You mustn't let him see me . . . I can't face him, not like this. I must leave at once . . . where is my clothing?' She struggled to fight off the damp and twisted rope of sheets that seemed to be trying to bind her body to the bed. 'I must go

. . . I feel sick. I thought he was dead and I mourned for him.' She retched, but nothing came up and the effort fatigued her. She gave a little groan.

'Hush, don't agitate yourself, my dear. The earl has already seen you . . . in fact, he rescued you from a blizzard.' Gently, he pushed her back on the pillow, his voice soft and reassuring. 'You are going nowhere at the moment.'

'I doubt if I could even walk to the door without assistance.'

He gazed down at her, his eyes sharp as they scrutinized her features. 'Ryder is not here at the moment. He showed no sign of recognizing you before, though it was dark and there is no reason why he should wish to see you on his return. As for your garments, you had only those you wore on your back with you and they're hanging in the wardrobe.'

A chill hit her, a mind-numbing cold that made her shake and shiver. Her teeth began to chatter and words tumbled out of the befuddled maze of her mind. 'I left him there . . . poor Ryder. I couldn't face him.'

Hal soothed her, pulling the bed covers up under her chin. 'The fever is making your mind wander and you've had a shock.'

Yes, that was it. Her mind was at odds because of the fever. She would go to sleep and when she woke everything would be as it once was before. She plucked at his sleeve. 'You won't let him hurt me, will you?'

'Calm yourself now and rest. Nobody here is going to hurt you. I can hear a wagon and must see to the provisions. Sleep now and don't worry about anything.'

As if she were a child and he her father, she told herself, except her father had closed the door against her. 'You no longer exist,' he'd said.

Perhaps it had been a mistake to return. She willed herself to die and the room conveniently faded to a suffocating darkness.

The next time Adele woke it was to discover a female figure gazing down at her. She stood in a white light that poured through the window. Adele screwed her eyes up against its glare. 'Are you an angel?'

'Dear me, now there's an odd notion and I certainly hope I haven't reached that state yet. I'm Mrs Betts . . . the house-keeper. Mr Stover has explained your circumstances and has asked me to see to your needs, Mrs Pelham. I've stoked up the fire.'

So she still wasn't dead. Disappointment stabbed at her. 'Would you pull the curtain across please; the light hurts my eyes.'

'It stopped snowing earlier and the sun is reflecting off the snow. It's bitterly cold though and I reckon it will snow again tonight, since there's a big band of low cloud on the horizon.'

Mrs Betts' face took on a form when she approached. She was about forty-five, angular and thin-faced, but in a pleasant sort of way. Adele placed a hand over the woman's as she went to straighten the bed covers. 'Have you worked here for a long time?'

'No, Mrs Pelham . . . we, that is Amy and Edith and Bessie the cook, used to work together at our previous positions. Our mistress upped and died, God rest her soul, and we were turned out. We heard there was some work going here in Dorset, but it wasn't true . . . not at first, anyway. Then along comes the earl and says he'd be prepared to employ us, on account that he owned a house that had been closed up for years. He said he'd understand if we didn't want the job because the place needed a good clean and would take a while to set straight. But if we suited each other the positions would become perma-nent . . . as if we'd ignore an offer of employment. Beggars can't be choosers, I always say.'

Her mouth parched, Adele hoped the woman would soon stop her chatter as she reached for the glass of water with shaking hands.

'There, there . . . it's weak you are.' Mrs Betts reached it first and held it to her lips. 'A nice young man is the master of the house . . . very polite. You could tell he was above the salt. If there's any lifting to do there will be at least two men to help out until we get adequate help, myself and Mr Stover, he says,' and Mrs Betts' head went to one side like an inquisi-tive bird. 'If you don't mind me asking, Mrs Pelham, are you a relative?'

Something inside Adele's head briefly flared, like the first shining beam of sunlight on earth, then it extinguished. She gave a faint smile. The lack of a few heartfelt words had prevented herself and Ryder from becoming relations. Circumstance had left them unsaid and they would remain that way. Besides, it wouldn't be long before word reached the housekeeper's ears and she learned the truth.

'No, Mrs Betts, I'm not a relation. I'm nobody – nobody at all and will be moving on as soon as I've recovered.'

Two

Ryder made his way over to West Street. It was his second visit to the workhouse in Poole that day. Having hired the minimum of staff for the Madigan estate he'd packed them off on a hay cart, along with their baggage and some livestock.

Ryder promised to return for more servants when the snow had cleared. 'I'll need two men of all work. One of them can be a lad. It would be an ideal father-and-son position. I'll also need a coachman and stable hand, a laundry maid, and . . .?' He ran his hand ruefully over the growth on his chin. 'A personal servant wouldn't go amiss, perhaps you know of someone suitable.'

The warden smiled. 'I do know of an experienced manservant. His master left the district a few years ago, though he gave the man a generous bonus.'

Ryder gave a faint grin, suspecting he might know the man more intimately than most. 'Tell me it's John Moore. I thought he was moving in with his son and I gave him a cottage and an allowance to carry him over. What's he doing in the workhouse?'

'The son married four years ago and the pair sold the cottage from under John and took off. He lived at Madigan House for a short time but was turned out when the caretakers died.'

'Who turned him out?'

'Them who took charge,' the warden said darkly. 'I'm not one for tittle-tattle. Be that as it may, John wasn't doing any harm there and he offered to take on the task of caretaking for no reward. Instead, the Reverend Bryson slid his wife's nephew into the position, name of Luke Ashburn. The reverend gave John's allowance to Ashburn, as recompense for the work he was doing. The reverend reckoned he was your next of kin, and that gave him the authority. Greed if you asks me.'

While it was true that the reverend was a distant relation and was his legal heir, the man had been presumptuous in thinking he could step into Ryder's shoes and just take over.

'It sounds as though Ashburn is overzealous.' Guilt filled him for neglecting his estate for such a long time. 'John must be getting on for fifty, is he still able?'

'That he is. He's a little on the sedate side, though.'

'John was always a little on the sedate side but he'll do me nicely. If he's not too proud to take his former position send him out to the house on the next wagon.'

'I'm sure he'd be delighted. I'll go through the books to see who might be suitable for the other positions. Most of them will appreciate being offered the chance to work. Do you need nursery staff?'

Ryder laughed, because the nursery at the top of the house would accommodate a dozen offspring as well as matching nursemaids. 'Not at the moment, but you never know what the future will bring.'

The Pelham girl appeared and after a moment of scrutiny, bobbed him a curtsey. She stood quietly while her release was obtained, holding tightly to two hessian bags that were little more than sacks with straps attached. There was an air about her, as if she were expecting bad news. It made him feel uncomfortable.

Eventually, she asked, and in a voice so soft he could hardly hear it, 'Have you found my stepmother?' Her calmness belied the dread in her eyes.

'I have. Mrs Pelham has a fever and needs some care and attention. She will be my guest until her health improves enough for her to move.'

A smile instantly transformed her grave face into one of charm and the words rushed out of her. 'Adele has survived, then . . . thank goodness. I was so worried, especially when

Mrs Bryson at the rectory said she wouldn't have survived the heath.'

Adele! The name punched Ryder in the heart with some considerable force. Surely it couldn't be *his* Adele – not after all this time.

He dismissed the thought but it stole into his mind again as possibilities arose. Could it be her – his lost love? The rector had told him the pair had relatives at Brackenhurst. He would have had said more had Ryder not cut him off, making it clear he had neither time nor inclination to stand and gossip.

Dare he ask the girl?

No . . . it would be a coincidence for them to have returned to the district at the same time – and too much of one to find himself in the position of having saved her life and being obliged to take her under his roof. He would look like a fool if it were someone with the same name.

It wouldn't be the first time he'd looked like a fool, so did that matter?

He took in a breath. 'I understand you have relatives hereabouts. What are they called?'

'They're not my relatives, they're Adele's. I don't know their names, but they are two aunts who live in a cottage she owns in Brackenhurst.'

His heart soared, then flopped, and then soared again, but cautiously before it sank again. He trod carefully, flattened by dread. 'I'm given to understand your father died recently.'

'We were on our way by ship when he fell overboard and drowned. He was drunk.' It was a matter-of-fact, unemotional statement.

'I'm sorry.'

'Thank you, my lord. Our trunks were mislaid in Bridport while we were looking for a carter willing to cross the heath with them. We're left with what we stand up in.'

Which wasn't much. The woman in his home was thin to the point of being skeletal. Her face was gaunt . . . yet there was something about her. Surely that wreck of a woman sleeping in his bed was not his Adele . . . no, she looked nothing like her. She must be another of that name. He resolved to put *his* Adele from his mind. 'There's a dressmaker's establishment up the road a ways. We'll stop there and I'll kit you both out.'

'Adele will not like it.'

He lost patience. 'I'm weary of being informed of what other people like and dislike. Mrs Pelham will have no choice in the matter, since you both must have clothing unless you want to freeze . . . and if that was your intention, why didn't the pair of you stay on the heath and make a quick job of it instead of cluttering up my home like a couple of twittering magpies? Only fools would go on the heath in this weather.'

His tirade was met by a steady look, and then her lips twitched. 'May I point out that you did exactly that, my lord . . . and with a good result.'

He opened his mouth, and then shut it again, robbed of breath by her impudence. He began to laugh. She had really called his bluff. 'You have me there, Sarah Pelham. So I did. Thank you for pointing it out.'

A grin licked the corner of her mouth. 'I'm sorry if my words seemed to criticize. I was thinking of the expense to you, when we have adequate garments for our needs in our trunks. They are in the shipping office, I imagine.'

'If they were left on the shore they will have ended up on a market stall. I'll make enquiries when the weather has cleared, but don't hold out any hope. Where have you journeyed from?'

'Boston. My father worked for a relative, but he lost his employment.'

'For what reason?'

'He never said, but I understood he was accused of being . . . sometimes he couldn't concentrate and anger got the better of him. Then it began to happen too often.'

A delicate way of saying he drank too much. Ryder supposed. He liked this young woman. So that's where they'd gone, and it accounted for the girl's accent. He'd had enquiries made, of course. He had wanted revenge on the man who'd stolen Adele from him – had wanted to kill Edgar Pelham. Now the man was dead and Ryder's chance for revenge was gone. He recalled how angry and humiliated he'd been – still was. How could she have left him and gone off with that fancy lout? To add insult to injury it appeared that this girl was Pelham's daughter.

He could feel his ire, a slow churning sensation deep inside him. He should take Adele back to the heath, watch the snow cover her up and then walk away from her and forget she ever existed. Or he could throw both of them into one of the flooded clay pits, or a stagnant pool. The ice would crack open, allowing entry of the bodies before the jagged shards healed like skin over a wound. They wouldn't be found until spring, if ever.

But the wound she'd dealt him would never be healed.

He looked up at Sarah Pelham and discovered her gaze on him. It was guarded, her eyes were steady and dark as though she could read his thoughts. If that were possible she would have learned that his thoughts were hot air, for he wouldn't harm a hair on Adele's head, or hers.

Sarah's father's sin was not hers. 'You've just realized who I am,' he said, and it was a statement, not a question.

She nodded, and then gazed at him as though she had something to say and didn't know quite how to go about it. He would get to the bottom of this – and now. 'If there's something you need to say to me, do so now. I won't chastise you.'

Pelham's daughter didn't flinch at his harsh tone. 'Please don't hurt her.'

Astonished by the unexpectedness of it, he said, 'Hurt her? Of course I won't. Once she is recovered from her illness sufficiently I'll place you both in the care of her aunts. Tell me one thing, Miss Pelham, and please be truthful. Was she happy with . . . him . . . your father?'

The weary droop of the girl's shoulders told its own tale and was embellished with, 'I love Adele dearly. I will not answer on her behalf, or break any confidence she might share. Neither will I judge the amount of suffering another person endures because the pain is theirs.'

She girl was wise beyond her years, as though she'd never been a child at all. Tears seeping into her eyes told him what he wanted to know. The thought that Adele had got what she'd deserved gave him an unworthy sense of satisfaction. It was overtaken by an anger so dense and dangerous he knew he'd put a bullet through the man's head were he still alive.

The girl was loyal, and for that alone he could grow to like her, Ryder thought as he unhitched Henry's rein. Clicking his tongue he walked towards the dressmaker with the horses following.

Ryder knew nothing about women's apparel, though he'd undressed one or two on occasion and found them a tease of buttons and laces. There were several women in the establishment and all of them turned to gaze at him. One bobbed a curtsey. 'Good afternoon, my lord.'

He didn't know her but she recognized him, despite the beard. Her eyes were avid with curiosity. He inclined his head before turning to the dressmaker. 'I require four warm gowns, two shawls, capes and any other garments women need for their comfort.'

When somebody tittered, warmth crept into his cheeks. 'My companion here will inform you of the size and colours. Send the account to Stephen Tessler's office. Do you have somewhere I can wait?'

'I was about to close the shop . . . the snow will only get worse.'

'Then you'd better fill my order quickly, because I need to get home.'

'We have a private room for gentlemen who are inclined to wait for their ladies, or wish to be consulted. It's through that curtain. You will find the latest news sheet there and I'll send an assistant through with some coffee. Is there a limit to what you wish to spend, sir?'

'Please address me as my lord.'

'Yes, sir . . . my lord.'

There was a collective intake of breath and the women froze into position, their eyes wide with anticipation, so he felt like a rogue rooster in a hen house.

He tried not to smile at his fancy and had no intention of satisfying their curiosity. 'I'll expect to spend a reasonable amount on a basic wardrobe and a female frippery or two.' He turned to Sarah. 'You have half an hour in which to make your purchases, young lady, and I'd rather you didn't consult me. There are several ladies who can act as adviser if you need one, I imagine.'

Sarah's eyes narrowed slightly at the thought of anyone advising her, but Ryder left her to it while he relaxed with his coffee and news sheet, grinning at the verbal, but mild, skirmish that came to his ear. She was certainly an independently minded young woman.

A world of yearning entered Sarah's voice when she asked, 'What's the cost of that bonnet with the pretty blue ribbons and silk forget-me-nots?'

'It's expensive, miss. I doubt if Lord Madigan would appreciate me selling it to a ragamuffin. Basic wardrobe, the earl said, and that's too good a bonnet for the likes of you.'

The blades were coming out, and Ryder burned for her when someone laughed, and said, 'The very idea.'

He was about to remind them of his presence when Sarah said, 'I'm not interested in your opinion of me, just in the price of the bonnet.'

The shopkeeper named an outrageous price.

'The hat is not worth that much and I could decorate one better myself.'

The shopkeeper snorted. 'Then go ahead.'

Sarah Pelham finished spending his money in the time he'd allotted her. It had become apparent to Ryder that she had an inclination to barter. When she quietly suggested a fifteen per cent discount might be appreciated he wasn't surprised. The amount was outrageous, and he chuckled.

'Certainly not,' the shopkeeper said, and with justifiable outrage. 'I will offer you five per cent and no more.'

'I will accept the five per cent and an extra two for the insults suffered at the hands of you and your customers, that's seven—'

'I know what the sum of two and five is,' the woman snapped. 'What does a chit of a girl like you know about commerce?'

'Enough to cancel the order and go to the salon further up the street.'

The woman's voice changed at the thought she might lose their custom. 'There is no need for that.'

Oh, well done, Sarah Pelham. Ryder grinned to himself.

She knew a damned sight more than the dressmaker did by the sounds of it, Ryder thought, and with some satisfaction. A trader who insulted their customers deserved to lose them.

Ryder scraped his chair back and emerged from behind the curtain in case she needed help. 'It's time we left, Miss Pelham. I hope you've completed our purchases?'

'Yes, my lord. The price awaits your approval. The proprietor has discounted her fee on account of the fact that she's sold me several garments that are no longer fashionable.' She turned to the woman. 'We were just about to agree on a percentage, were we not?'

The woman's mouth opened, then she shut it again and shrugged. 'Seven per cent, and not a penny less.'

Ryder tied the parcels on to Sarah's horse and lifted her onto its back. The girl had impressed him. Telling her to wait he went back in the shop. As before, the noise of collective female voices quieted and all eyes swivelled his way.

He purchased two plain bonnets, a variety of silk flowers, ribbons in several colours and a box containing sewing imple-ments, silks and cotton threads. On impulse he bought a couple of feathery plumes, saying, 'Add the cost of these to the account if you would, and present it to Mr Tessler.'

'Yes, my lord.'

'I was disgusted by the animosity shown to my acquaintance in this establishment. The only reason I didn't cancel the order was because the trunks containing their goods were stolen and they needed something to wear. We will not shop here again. Good day, ladies.'

He strode from the shop, leaving silence in his wake. Joining the hat boxes with a length of rope he hung them across Henry's back like a couple of drums, then mounted. 'I've bought you a bonnet apiece, and you can decorate them to your liking. It will give you something to occupy your time with. And if you like to read you can borrow books from my library as long as you look after them.'

Her eyes shone for a moment and then she said bluntly, 'Thank you, my lord. May I ask, why are you being so kind to us? You didn't have to purchase the bonnets.'

'Firstly because you're a female who wanted something pretty in her life, and it's a way of thanking you for the amusement you afforded me. Going into that establishment was like walking into a den of feral cats. You may call the bonnets your two per cent.'

Her mouth softened. 'You know they will talk and things will be exaggerated out of all proportion.'

'You don't seem to mind.'

'There's no point in minding since I can't put a stop to it. Adele told me the best way to extinguish a fire is to starve it of fuel.'

He laughed. 'It's too late for that.'

'Adele might think so despite the gift of a bonnet,' she said.

He remembered, and his laughter stopped. 'Perhaps Adele shouldn't have returned home since there was nothing to gain.'

'She had no expectations.'

Ryder mulled that over in his mind for a moment or two. 'Tell me something; did she ever mention me?'

'Now and again, when she thought she would perish on the heath she said it was a fitting punishment for her because of the wrong she'd done you. Though she sent me to get help I know she didn't expect me to bring any. She thought you were dead.'

'But you knew who I was . . . how?'

'Adele has a locket with a painted miniature of you. Since my father died she wears it around her neck. I recognized you from your eyes and your forehead and hair. Plus there was the idle talk.'

Mrs Bryson, Ryder imagined. The rector's wife had always possessed a vivid imagination, a busy tongue and an inclination to preach to others in a hectoring manner. For that reason alone he'd never liked her, and she knew it. Adele had believed she was a witch because of her frightening stare.

He urged Henry to a faster pace. Like Sarah, Ryder didn't want to talk about Adele. He would rather pretend she'd never existed, as he had tried to for the past few years. He put her at the back of his mind, closed the door to his heart and locked it.

Then he recalled the damp flame of her hair lying against her pale skin. Her eyes were greenish grey and darkly myste-rious like the needles on the pine trees. He didn't want to forget her! He needed to see her again, and soon. He needed to make her account for her treachery – make her suffer, as she'd made him suffer.

Two empty wagons approached from the opposite direction and Ryder stopped to ask the driver, 'Is there much more?'

'Two more loads after we get back to Poole.' The man gazed up at the sky. The sun that had made the landscape glisten so prettily that morning was being absorbed by a mist slowly drifting in from the sea. 'Your man is making hisself useful lifting the heavy stuff and we should finish just as darkness sets in, I reckon. It's going to come down hard tonight, sir. You were lucky to get all your provisions in time.'

Ryder took some coins from his pocket and handed them over. 'Buy yourself and your handlers a jug or two for your efforts, and give them my thanks. Pick up John Moore from the workhouse with your next load if you would. He should be ready and waiting.'

The man touched his hat. 'That I will.'

Sarah caught up to him. She was out of breath. He'd forgotten she was behind him. 'Sorry, did I go too fast?'

She nodded.

'It's not much further, Henry,' and he patted his horse, wondering if he would recognize his stable after all this time. 'We're nearly home.'

Ten minutes later they were about to pass under the ornate rusting archway that supported the gates. Although the gates hung open he stopped to give the bell pull a vigorous shake to announce his arrival. The metal pull came off in his hand. He threw it aside with a snort of disgust. It had about as much pride left as he did. He gazed up at the arch where the words 'Madigan House' were fashioned in rusting wrought iron. He was the last of the Madigan family and had inherited the earldom from his father when he was quite young.

He must do something about the gate and its arch, he thought. Five years ago he'd ridden out through it, his heart broken into pieces. He'd painted the gate himself to welcome his bride to her new home. It had been as black and glossy as a raven's wing, the letters were picked out in gold, and the cartouche in the middle of the gates bore the family coat of arms of three arrows in red and gold.

Now it was all one colour . . . rust brown.

'Welcome to Madigan House,' he said to the young woman, who was waiting patiently beside him. After all, she was barely a child and nothing was her fault. She seemed older than he'd been led to believe.

'Sixteen,' she said when he asked. 'Thank you, my lord, I'll try not to get in your way.'

He left the horses with the new stable hand, collected the parcels together and made his way to the house, the girl following, and equally burdened. She seemed to have bought rather a lot for a small amount of money, and he grinned when he remembered the seven per cent.

The house bustled with activity. Hal came striding out from the kitchen in his shirtsleeves and a dusty apron to cast an eye over the newcomer. 'You must be Miss Pelham.'

She nodded. 'My name is Sarah.'

Ryder told him, 'Show Miss Pelham to the kitchen, Hal, and introduce her to the staff. Perhaps you could find her something to eat and drink while I go and see Mrs Pelham.'

Hal's smile faded. 'Mrs Pelham is asleep. Besides, there's something you should know before you go up there.'

Arms filled with packages, Ryder headed for the stairs, flinging over his shoulder before taking them two at a time, 'I already know, Hal. The town's full of it.'

'Go easy on her. She's very weak.'

'Don't worry, I promise I won't strangle her.'

He nearly tripped over the dog, making it yelp as he entered the room. He stared down at her – his lovely Adele. How vulnerable she was with her pale, fragile face and with the naked column of her throat visible, so he wanted to place a kiss in the shadowed hollow there. The last few years had changed her from a healthy and innocent young girl into a gaunt woman who seemed as delicate as crystal. He would get her well and her beauty would bloom again, was his first thought.

'Adele,' he murmured, and reaching out he touched her mouth with his fingertip.

The room was warm. Perspiration left a damp sheen on her forehead and she began to toss and turn and mutter in her sleep. The sweep of dark lashes guarding her eyes fluttered, then opened. She gazed at him, eyes shiny with fever and whimpering like a puppy. 'Is it you I owe my life to, sir?'

'Indeed, it is, Adele.' Did she not recognize him then . . . the man who'd once loved her more than his own life? The hurt in him was profound . . . nearly unbearable. Then he remembered his beard.

He smiled when she closed her eyes again. An idea shimmered in the dark depths of his mind like a new star being born. He must consider ways and means in which the debt she now owed him could be repaid.

He whispered in her ear, 'You mustn't die, my Del . . . not until you explain your actions that day. I absolutely forbid it, do you hear?'

She sighed and mumbled something unintelligible.

The carriage clock on the mantelpiece chimed, reminding him the house was being brought back to life. Hal would have wound it.

He was reluctant to leave Adele's side, but she was not his responsibility now. The sooner she recovered and left his hearth the better it would be for his own peace of mind. At least he would be able to think straight once she was gone.

He turned, to find the girl standing by the door, watching him. She must have followed him, and was light on her feet. A girl of her age shouldn't wear such a worried expression.

'I told Hal to take you to the kitchen.'

'I wanted to see Adele first . . . to make sure.'

'You thought I'd harm her, didn't you? Come here.'

She stepped forward, her eyes as wary and golden as those of a fox, but she wasn't afraid to have her say. 'Men do hurt women when they're angry. You were angry and I was afraid for her.'

She has courage, he thought as they stood side by side looking down at the women in the bed. 'Does she look as though I've abused her?' He had to admit she looked as though somebody had.

'No . . . I'm sorry.'

'You made me feel like a criminal in my own home, but I can understand your fear.' He supposed the girl had been talking about her father with her reference to anger. He wondered, even knowing he didn't want to pursue that notion.

His thoughts were erratic, full of cracks and threats, at odds with each other. He dragged an ounce of normality to the surface. 'From now on, when I tell you to do something I expect you to obey me. Is that clear?'

'Yes, my lord.'

'Do you think you can manage to look after the invalid single-handed? The doctor will visit and will advise you if necessary.'

'Yes, sir.'

'Good. Will you be comfortable on the truckle bed for now, Miss Pelham? There's a room adjoining, but it's extremely dusty.'

She nodded. 'I'll see to it tomorrow.'

He turned towards the door, saying, 'Inform the housekeeper if there's anything you require. Just remember the servants are all newly appointed, and have a lot of work ahead establishing their routine.'

'Then I'll offer her my help. On behalf of Mrs Pelham and myself please accept my thanks for your hospitality, my lord. I will try not to disrupt your household more than necessary before we move on. That's what Adele would want. She's not going to die, is she?'

'No,' he said curtly, shocked to the core at the thought of such a possibility.

Once outside the door he leaned against the wall. He was trembling, and drew in a deep, steadying breath. He expelled it slowly, allowing the tension to drain from his body. Every emotion he'd experienced all those years ago when Adele had discarded him had returned with a vengeance. He'd survived the meeting, but only just. Awareness had peeled from his hide like a rotten onion, each layer exposing another, deeper bruise. He wasn't even sure if Adele had recognized him, and the thought that she mightn't have rankled.

Would she die? Not if he could help it. He wanted her to live. He needed her to face up to what she'd done to him – needed to know why she'd done it.

Sarah had told him that Adele hadn't mentioned his name very often, unless they were alone and she remembered her childhood. But she'd told the girl to tell him she was sorry. A little blast of happiness centred inside him at the notion that she'd survived.

Then he reached a conclusion that for his own well-being he would avoid her altogether!

Three

Madigan House began to bustle with servants and its character emerged from under the accumulated dirt like the glow of sunshine. Not that there was much sun in evidence. Winter had proved to be cold so far and the snow kept them isolated.

With food and rest Ryder's unwanted invalid began to improve. Her coughing fits were less aggressive and the periods between them longer. Hal visited her every day and brought Ryder frequent reports.

'Mrs Pelham doesn't suffer from such severe exhaustion now.'

Ryder told himself he was indifferent. He poked at a posy vase containing a knot of satiny snowdrops he'd stopped to pick that morning from under a hedge on his ride. 'Is that so?'

'She was hungry today and ate all of her chicken broth.'

There came a vision of Adele's pearly teeth biting into a chicken leg and tearing off the flesh – of her tongue delicately probing the corners of her mouth to capture any broth that might have escaped. Lucky chicken. He sighed as he lied, 'Excellent . . . the sooner she's able to fend for herself the sooner they'll depart.'

He ignored the fact that he could have sent her home for her aunts to nurse or that his feet sometimes carried him unwillingly along the corridor to where she resided. He was unable to stop them.

Once, he'd heard her sing and he'd smiled and pressed his ear against the door panel, but the pesky little terrier seemed to have appointed himself Adele's protector and had thrown himself vigorously at the bottom of the door and yelped.

'Come here, Gypsy, it's nothing but a draught,' she'd called.

Feeling like an intruder in his own home Ryder had made a dash for the main staircase in case she let the beast out and it sank its sharp little teeth into his leg.

Once Adele and her stepdaughter had gone he wouldn't have to creep around his own home. He'd forget her and get on and enjoy his life, like he had before. He stared into space for a moment. There was something wrong with that, but he couldn't think of what it was.

'If you don't pay attention you'll fall off the ladder, Ryder,' Hal said, bringing him back to the present.

They were in the library. Ryder was up a ladder replacing the dusted books while Hal passed them up. It was a tedious job, shelf by shelf, and he had to be vigilant to keep them in proper order.

Hal resumed his musing. 'Mrs Pelham got out of bed and walked around the room this morning. She was wobbly and exhausted afterwards.'

'She should wait until she's stronger,' Ryder said evenly, ignoring a sharp thrust of alarm.

'Perhaps you should advise her to that effect, Ryder. She's eating well now, so will soon gain some strength. She's headstrong though.'

'Mrs Pelham doesn't need advising since she's an adult and is well aware of the benefits of eating well . . . besides, having appointed yourself as her nursemaid, you can advise her.'

Hal pushed back at him. 'What shall I tell her to account for your bad manners, that you are suffering from the megrims because she tweaked your nose half a dozen years previously? It's a long time to hold a grudge.'

'It was more than a tweak, and you can tell her whatever takes your damned fancy.' This advice was followed by a warning frown from Ryder. 'Best you stop playing Cupid, Hal, else I'll be tempted to kick your arse and flatten you.'

Hal grinned. 'You haven't managed it yet, my fine lord, but you can only try. You're so stiff with pride that you'd snap.' He clicked his fingers in the air and smiled.

Ryder threw a book at him and Hal tossed it back so quickly that Ryder nearly fell off the ladder trying to catch it.

There was a timid knock at the door.

'Come in,' he bellowed from his precarious perch.

A maid entered with visiting cards on a silver salver and looked timidly up at him. 'Two gentlemen have called to see you, my lord.'

'Don't look so scared, girl, I wasn't shouting at you.'

Hal took the cards and read them out. 'Stephen Tessler and Luke Ashburn.'

Familiar with the names, Ryder said, 'Stephen Tessler is my financial representative and Ashburn is a young man who was employed to look after the estate in my absence, or so I understand.'

'You were lucky it happened to be a person of integrity. Shall I withdraw? I can always find some silver to polish.'

'No . . . stay, Hal.' He slid down the ladder and nodded to the maid. 'Get rid of that posy; Mrs Pelham might enjoy them. Show the gentlemen in. Bring in some tea, and some cake if we have any. I thought I smelled some apple parkin earlier.'

'That you did, my lord, it's just come out of the oven.' The maid smiled and placed the snowdrops on the tray.

Ryder and Hal hastily shrugged into their coats while the visitors shed their topcoats and hats and handed them to the maid in the hall

Ryder smiled at the older man as he entered. 'Good day, Stephen.' He introduced Hal. 'As you can see we're not sorted out yet, and we're making ourselves useful to the staff by cleaning the bookcases.'

Stephen offered his hand along with a smile. 'I apologize for arriving unannounced, my lord. It's my pleasure to see you again and to introduce Luke Ashburn.'

'Ah yes . . . I've been expecting you, Mr Ashburn, but I would have appreciated you making an appointment, since we are still understaffed and you now find me at a disadvantage. I believe you've been managing my estate.'

Ashburn smiled widely as his approving gaze roved around a library that was now redolent of beeswax and oiled leather. 'The staff you have are serving you well, and you could hardly call it management. I've spared some of my time to keep a good eye on the place since your appointed caretakers departed – for which I was paid.'

'So I understand.' Crossing to the fire Ryder placed another log in the grate and pushed it to the back of the fire with his foot. 'And you made good use of the kitchen garden and the smokehouse . . . something we were pleased to take advantage of when we arrived.'

'I believe it was custom that a portion of the food produced on the Madigan estate was for the poor. I couldn't spare the time to grow corn crops, especially since we had no licence to work your land, but a few vegetables and a couple of pigs and sheep go a long way when one is hungry. The Reverend Bryson told me your great-grandfather had started the practice, and he suggested I continue it − rather, keep it up on your behalf.'

Ryder turned, pleased that the man held tradition close, despite his other shortcomings. 'The poor need to be cared for, so thank you. One for one, my father termed it . . . one for us and one to cater for the needy.'

One kiss for Adele and one for himself in return.

Ryder dragged his mind away from the sweeter memories. 'It was a pity you turned my manservant out. He would have saved you the time to spend on your own pursuits.'

'I noticed from the estate books that your personal servant had retired with a generous bonus, and someone told me you'd furnished him with his own cottage. I thought he might be taking advantage of the fact that you were away.'

'That same someone forgot to inform you that John Moore was tricked out of his money and ended up in the poorhouse.'

Ryder was the recipient of a direct and challenging look. 'Are you seeking to place the blame on me for his plight, my lord? May I say that I was looking out for *your* interest, not the interests of former estate workers.'

Life in the army had made Ryder impatient with people who minced words. This man was the opposite, straightforward enough to be thought of as offensive if Ryder had been in a different frame of mind. He allowed him to have his say.

'The hiring of caretakers seemed an unwarranted expense, as did cleaning the place, since you had no permanent staff left. I came on a weekly basis with one of my field workers to make sure all was well. We tended the kitchen garden at the same time. Mr Tessler and my uncle advised me over certain matters, such as the repair of tiles loosened in a storm and a broken window. A ledger was kept on all expenditure. It's in the clerk's office.'

'The interior of the house was neglected, even the essential rooms.'

'They are only essential if people use them, my lord. It seemed a waste of time as well as money to employ a new housekeeper to clean so many empty spaces, when there was nobody in residence to fill them. So I had the furniture covered with dust sheets and ignored the rest. Had you let us know of your intention to return . . .?'

Ashburn had a lot to say for himself and Ryder raised an eyebrow as he gently pushed him to see how far he'd go. 'May I just say I'm not accountable to you, or anyone else.'

'An enviable position, my lord.'

'You think so? Actually it's a more responsible position than I'd prefer.'

Ryder eyed him. He was a handsome young man of medium height, slim and well muscled. His grip had been firm, his voice confident although slightly aggrieved.

'My lord, I understand your displeasure at having the privacy of your home invaded by a stranger. If you will allow me I will present you with my final account and will depart. It's itemized, so judge for yourself if my efforts on your behalf for these past years were wasted, and pay me accordingly – or pay me not at all if that is your will.'

Ashburn was easily offended.

'Don't be so hasty, Mr Ashburn. I'm not criticizing you, and since you arrived unbidden, you will do me the courtesy of staying until you are dismissed. I'm well aware that when I left I abandoned my responsibilities towards the estate to the hands of others. You know as well as I that the accounts are presented to Mr Tessler, a man who acts in my absence, and I won't deviate from the custom. But your uncle spoke well of you and I'm prepared to believe him. I'm rather surprised you haven't been mentioned in the past to me.'

The man shrugged. 'My position on the family tree is

precarious to say the least. Perhaps he didn't see the need. The reverend paid for my education and helped raise me in recent years, so alas, any compliment he might affix to me is double-edged. However, I stop short at following in the good reverend's footsteps.'

Good was not a label Ryder would have hung on Oliver Bryson. 'Not up to the preaching?'

'I'm up to it, but I haven't got the inclination to sort out the saints from the sinners, and I find the latter infinitely more amusing.'

Hal's huff of laughter brought an appreciative smile from Luke Ashburn and Ryder grinned at his friend. 'May I present Halifax Stover. We soldiered together for many years and he's my guest whilst he sorts out the path his future will take. He practised law before he took up soldiering, but he can turn a hand to anything.'

Hal offered a short bow. 'Ashburn . . . Mr Tessler, my pleasure.' Hal removed himself to the window seat where he could observe rather than take part in a conversation that didn't really concern him. The two visitors seated themselves in the chairs by the fire.

The refreshment was brought in and served, the maids departed.

Ryder gazed at Stephen. 'I take it you're here on business.'

'Yes . . . but not your business. Despite your long absence the balance of your estate is enviable.'

'I've already been taken to task by that young man over there, Stephen. Must I suffer a second lecture on my shortcomings?'

Stephen didn't hedge. 'I'd heard that Miss Lawrence had returned to the district and was your guest.'

Ryder tried not to sigh. Everyone in the district would know by now. 'You are referring to Mrs Pelham, I believe. What of her?'

Stephen Tessler said awkwardly. 'She wed the man, then?'

'Mrs Pelham is now widowed. She and the young woman who's looking after her intend to move into the property Mrs Pelham owns in Brackenhurst when she's recovered.'

Luke bristled as he interjected. 'It's that property I wish to see her about. I understand she has a claim to the cottage. The ownership of it is actually in dispute because I bought it as part of her father's estate. I'm willing to offer her a settlement.'

'I don't think Mrs Pelham is well enough to receive visitors or to make that sort of decision yet. If she accepts a settlement, then she and her aunts will have nowhere else to live.'

Ryder wasn't surprised when Luke Ashburn said, 'I bought the property that had once belonged to Mrs Pelham's father from the legatee with a loan from my . . . the reverend. It included several cottages that formed the boundary of Brackenhurst village. It was my understanding that Duck Pond Cottage was part of the smallholding I bought, but we couldn't find the deeds. It was certainly the largest building in the village, apart from the church and the vicarage . . . a small manor that the landowner would normally have resided in. If it's not part of the parcel of my land then it will appear as if a large bite has been taken from the estate – a bite I've paid for. I'd intended to move into Duck Pond Cottage and make it my home.'

'One would hardly notice the bite, unless we could fly. Were you not made aware of the circumstances surrounding Duck Pond Cottage before you purchased the smallholding?'

'I'd heard rumours.'

'That you chose not to investigate properly. *Caveat emptor*, my friend. Let the buyer beware. Didn't Mr Tessler advise you?'

'I was in London at the time and Luke acted in haste.'

Ryder knew the property well, since he'd spent much time there, making polite conversation with Adele's relatives while his eyes had feasted upon the vision of loveliness she presented.

She'd been chaperoned all the time so how the hell had she met Edgar Pelham? His jaw tightened. The cottage had been left to Adele by her maternal grandmother, with the provision that her two unmarried daughters could make their home there while they lived. It would have been part of Adele's dowry, and Ryder's by default if they'd wed.

'Is Duck Pond Cottage on your estate plan, then?' Ryder asked.

'It's on the plan but I was told Mrs Pelham now owns it. I visited the Manning sisters to enquire about the whereabouts of their niece. As soon as I started asking questions the two women chased me off with a broom.'

Hal suggested with a grin, 'Perhaps they were the wrong questions.'

The man offered Ryder an ironic look. 'They were very protective of their niece, though one wonders why after—'

When Tessler cleared his throat there was a sudden silence.

Ryder stared at the man. 'After what?'

Luke's eyes shifted sideways. 'Your pardon, my lord . . . I spoke out of turn.'

'You most certainly did. Let me make one thing clear. Mrs Pelham is my guest and is to be referred to with the respect afforded to all widowed ladies. I will not have her subjected to gossip and innuendo, especially while she's recovering from an illness. As for selling you her birthright, where else would she go?'

Alarm stabbed at Ryder. Surely she wasn't going to leave the district when she'd just returned. Adele had grown up here. But then, she had left once before. Ryder gazed from one to the other. 'As your business is not with me I would suggest we postpone further discussion until Mrs Pelham is able to attend and I can arrange for somebody to act as her adviser. Good day, Mr Ashburn. Hal, if you wouldn't mind.'

When the door closed behind the two men, Ryder said, 'A moment in private if you would, Stephen; I won't keep you long.'

'My lord, if this is about Luke, I can only endorse his character. He is hard working, but sometimes he is too honest for his own good.'

'It's not about him, though he needs to learn some manners. He's young and brash, that's all. I want to know if the trust Adele's grandmother left is still intact?'

'The capital is, but most of the interest has gone in repairs to Duck Pond Cottage. Two years ago the stream became bogged and flooded the ground floor, causing considerable damage. Part of the brickwork collapsed and the front of the house needed new mortar. It was discovered that some of the floorboards had damp rot, and had to be replaced. Luke does what he can. He doesn't want the place to fall into disrepair in case it proves to be his property. On the other hand, if he spends too much it could be wasted, since he may never be reimbursed. The cottage is beginning to look a little shabby.'

'I understand. You said my own estate is sound.'

'Extremely. You have a solid building on equally solid ground that stands firm against anything the weather can throw at it. It has needed very little maintenance. Financially you're in an enviable position. If you never lift a finger to earn another penny you'll die wealthy, and that thought brings me to this, my lord. Prior to your intended marriage you made a will . . . and considering the present circumstances it needs to be updated.'

'The will can stand for now. The time to change it will be when I have an heir.'

'You have no wife.'

He smiled. 'Thank you for pointing it out, Stephen, but I'm not over the hill yet. It shouldn't be too hard to find a suitable woman to bear me a son or two.'

'No . . . I suppose not.'

'Now that's settled there's something I want you to do. And as with everything that's been said in this room, in complete confidence.'

'I'm at your service, my lord.'

'Transfer one thousand guineas into Mrs Pelham's account, and pay the young man with you what he's owed for this past quarter.'

As Ryder knew he would, Stephen Tessler protested. 'But my lord, surely you're not going to repeat past mistakes now you are older and more sensible. Mrs Pelham has proved unreliable in the past and has a stain on her character. You should entertain a little, acquaint yourself with young ladies who've emerged from childhood during your absence.'

'Enough, Stephen! I'm old enough to run my own life. Besides, Hal and I have made the acquaintance of several young ladies in London before we came here, and I'm ready to settle down.'

Ryder wasn't convinced that being in love with Adele had

all been a mistake. Playing the gentleman when he should have reined her in had been. Now he was several years older and wiser and Stephen was suggesting he throw himself on the marriage market.

He didn't want to go through the rituals of courtship again, but he would have to . . . the balls, the pretty manners, the flirting eyes, inviting smiles and the moment when a woman gave in to his advances. He'd already been through all that with Adele, but they still had some business left between them, for she'd never said goodbye.

He smiled. She'd been such an innocent that he hadn't seen it coming until it was too late. Now he realized he was paddling in dangerous waters thinking of her at all. 'I gave no indication that I intended to marry the woman.'

Tessler looked relieved. 'But one thousand guineas! It's an outrageous sum and one that won't be easy to disguise in the books.' Tessler was practically wringing his hands at parting with such an amount, even though it wasn't his money.

'It's a pittance when weighed against my stated worth. I'm sure my purse will stand the onslaught. Just do it, Stephen. As it is, Luke Ashburn will have to bear the loss of his hasty purchase by himself. If the deeds of the cottage are found and the acreage of land it stands on is challenged I will testify on Mrs Pelham's behalf, since I know the cottage was a legacy from her grandmother, and part of her dowry settlement.'

'Am I to take it that—'

'Take nothing for granted, Stephen. For the books you need only record the truth. The one thousand guineas is the reimbursement of the part of Mrs Pelham's dowry that had already been settled on me by her father two days before we were due to wed. It will be returned to her, along with her allowance.'

The sigh that left Stephen was slightly deflating. 'Ah yes, the dowry. You're aware it would be quite in order for you to retain it.'

'Then Mrs Pelham would be without funds to fall back on. Do I strike you as a man who would leave a lady of my acquaintance in financial distress?'

Stephen looked suitably chastened.

'In the meantime, I'll ask Hal to take a look at the cottage with me. He has studied law, but his father was an engineer and he grew up with a practical education in the home. Have the sisters been informed of their niece's return?'

'I expect so . . . people gossip.'

'As I've noticed. I just hope they don't take a broom to me, like they did to your protégé.'

The accountant's mouth pursed a little. 'About Luke.'

'What about him?'

'If you need someone to manage the Madigan estate I'd be obliged if you'd consider him.'

'He hasn't displayed himself to any good so far.'

'You couldn't get a more honest man and he's hard-working and clever. He doesn't like being tied to a desk.'

'He's certainly his own man, but can he take instruction, I wonder?' Ryder frowned. He didn't like being pressured over this, since he was hoping that Hal would take the position, despite his intention to leave and follow his fortune in the spring. 'I'll consider him, Stephen . . . I promise. Ask him to attend me here in one week with a plan for working the estate. If he'd like to dine with me in the early afternoon I can promise him the best pork pie in the district from my new cook – especially since it was part of Ashburn's pig that was hanging in the smokehouse.

'There is one thing you might like to consider. It might cause a conflict of interests for you to have too many fingers in the pie, and I shall have to take that into account when I hire management staff.'

They set off for Brackenhurst at a leisurely pace early in the afternoon and reached Duck Pond Cottage half an hour later. It was a large cottage, solidly constructed of brick, a double-storey building with a maid's room and an attic under the tiled roof. Smoke trickled from the chimney. To one side stood a brick stable and a small barn. The door hung from its hinges and chickens pecked and clucked around the entrance.

The garden was overgrown with untidy clumps of grass and the pond was spilling over a low stone retaining wall to lap at the gate. Apart from the water it was exactly as Ryder remembered it.

Hal frowned. 'If that wall is indicative of the pond's usual depth then the stream must be blocked lower down. Even after the thaw this should have receded quicker.'

'There's a sluice gate, I recall.'

'Then I'll wander off downstream and try and find it while you chat to the ladies. It's probably clogged with rubbish. I'll see if there's a hayfork in the shed.'

As they pushed the creaking gate open the chickens scattered. A couple of clacking ducks rushed at them in a fast waddle from the back garden, their chests puffed out with importance and threat.

Hal grinned. 'Here comes the navy . . . one each. I wager I can throw mine further.'

They scooped the ducks up and tossed them in the air. Ryder's landed in the pond in a heap of ruffled feathers and squawks, while Hal's gracefully circumnavigated the water before doing a final skim and landing next to its partner. Both quacked in consternation and fluffed their feathers at being routed so easily. They headed off downstream.

Two women rushed from the house yielding brooms. 'Shoo! Out . . . out, you men! This is private property.'

The second one grabbed the other woman by the elbow, bringing her to a breathless halt. 'Stop at once, Prudence, it's Lord Madigan!'

Prudence peered at him, and then smiled. 'Bless my soul, so it is. It's been a long time since we set eyes on you, my lord. Have you brought news of our Adele? The rector's wife said she has been found and she has a lung infection. She said Adele was at death's door and she'd tell us when we'd be allowed to visit. That was a while ago and we've been so worried.'

He put a hand under her elbow when she bobbed a curtsey. 'Mrs Bryson has no authority, since Adele is being cared for at Madigan House. She has indeed been ill, but she's recovering her strength. Hal has a note for you from her and as soon as my carriage is ready for the road I'll send it to collect you and bring you for a visit.

'There, I told you Mary Bryson was a busybody as well as a sticky beak,' Patience scoffed, and taking the folded letter from Hal's hand she tucked it in her sleeve. 'We will read it later, Prudence. My lord, you have forgotten your manners, who's the handsome young man with you?'

'So I have. I'm so used to him that sometimes I forget he's there. Miss Manning, Miss Prudence, this gentleman is Sergeant Halifax Stover, my friend and companion over the past few years.'

Hal kissed their hands. 'My pleasure, ladies.'

'You don't look a day older than when I left,' Ryder said.

The two women exchanged a glance and a smile. 'You were ever the flatterer, my lord.'

When Hal offered them a smile and bowed, Prudence elbowed Patience in the ribs. 'We'll be the talk of the village tomorrow for entertaining two young men . . . what fun.'

'Hal is going to help me investigate the sluice, so he'll need the help of a hayfork if you have one. After that we'll inspect the house and see if it needs any repairs.'

'The pond water rises and creeps under the flagstones in the kitchen when we sleep sometimes – such a nuisance. We fear we might drown in our beds. I told that to the young man who bought the estate, Ashburn his name is. The cheek of him, he just laughed and said the worst that will happen is that our petticoats will get damp. If he'd ever worn a petticoat he'd know how uncomfortable that would be!'

'I'm sure he would.'

'He offered to rent us a dry cottage if it got too deep . . . said he'd move in here instead. We don't trust him, do we, Prudence? He's Mary Bryson's nephew, and she knocked at the door as brazen as you like one day and told us this cottage belongs to her nephew, not to Adele, so we'd better look after it. And that, after we grew up here.'

Prudence snorted. 'Mary always made mischief with that wicked tongue of hers, and her man has never been able to cure her of it. Not that he wants to. He likes to know everybody's business. Our mother left the cottage to Adele because she knew we'd always have a home here. We'll be all right now she's come home. We knew she'd come one day. It was good of you to take her back.' Her voice trailed off when his smile faded and she kissed his cheek. 'I beg your pardon, my lord, for a moment I'd forgotten the hurt she caused. Forgive me, but I can't condemn her for it since she's my beloved niece.'

He kept his voice gentle. 'Of course, but you must understand, Miss Prudence, that Adele paid me the ultimate insult. She is my guest due to necessity and I see her as little as possible. When she's recovered she'll be restored to your care along with the young woman with her, and that will be the end of it. We will speak of it no more. Now . . . we must start our inspection.'

'Will you stay to take some refreshment afterwards, my lord?' Patience asked a little tentatively.

'Thank you but no, I have work to do restoring Madigan House into a workable dwelling.'

They left the women looking disappointed and located the sluice, which was set in a low wall across the stream and had a metal gate that slid up and down to regulate the water flow. There was a small but tightly packed wedge of debris built up, but it didn't entirely block the sluice. A couple of good pokes with the handle of the hayfork dispersed it.

Hal said, 'It's simple enough to fix. It's been deliberately closed, but only enough to cause a nuisance rather than real damage. Who's responsible for its maintenance?'

'Whoever owns the Lawrence property. Luke Ashburn I suppose. He wants that cottage and is playing games. Under old common law, possession is nine-tenths.'

'But it's a rule of force, not a law.'

'Exactly. If Ashburn can get the Manning sisters out and he moves into the cottage himself, he can then apply to a magistrate for a new set of deeds, citing possession. He already has a strong case without the deeds, and it would be much stronger if he had possession.'

The water was running clear now. It was one of the chalk streams that filtered through the downs. It serviced many village ponds before it disappeared into the Purbeck Hills, then travelled on to the sea.

One bright summer's day Adele had made a paper boat and

written a message on it for him before launching it. She'd been
fifteen, and wouldn't tell him what the message said. She'd
blushed and he'd kissed her. Her first kiss, she'd said later, and
that on a mouth so soft he'd wanted to eat it.

He could almost hear her voice, creamy with a mixture of
amusement and laughter. 'If you can catch the boat you can
read the message.' He'd waded into the stream after it, slipped
and fell, and her laughter had been free and uninhibited when
his hat went sailing off. 'Catch me a trout for my dinner,' she
said and he'd floundered about groping in the dappled shadows
under the bank.

Smiling a little Ryder dragged his mind back to the present.
'Any luck, Hal?'

Hal squatted on the bank and peered into the shadowy
depths of the stream. 'There's a stone blocking the hole so the
gate cannot be fully extended nor completely close. I might
have to wade in and retrieve it.' He poked at the sluice gate
with the handle of the hayfork. 'That stone is too big to have
washed there by itself.

'Be careful. The water will be cold, and it's deeper than it
looks there. Use the horse. There a rope in my saddlebag that
we might be able to loop over the stone and drag it to shallow
water.'

The exercise was accomplished without too much trouble.
A small current of water ran freely through the gate as the
excess from the pond began to drain.

Lifting the stone between them they heaved it aside and
inch-by-inch they cranked the handle of the sluice to halfway.
They managed to achieve an even flow over a short space of
time. The ducks kept a vigilant eye on them and quacked their
approval now and again.

The two men emerged wet, cold and uncomfortable, to
discover they were being watched by a rustic geriatric who
was sucking on an empty pipe. An equally ancient dog nudged
against his leg and offered his master an expression of adoration
through clouded eyes.

'He won't like you doing that,' the man offered.

'Who won't?'

'Mr Ashburn.'

'Refer Mr Ashburn to me if he complains and give him this message. Tell him we've repaired the sluice and expect it to be properly maintained from now on.'

'And who might you be, sir?'

'Lord Madigan.'

The man grinned and touched his hat. 'Reckon you are at that since he wasn't one to avoid getting his hands dirty when there was real work to be done. Welcome home, my lord.'

New year came and they celebrated, the church bell making a clamour. Adele was too weak to really enjoy it. Her aunt Patience had knitted her some pink woolly bed socks and Prudence had made her a knee rug from brightly coloured squares.

Ryder carried her down the stairs in company of a maid. The intimacy of his warm body reminded her of times past, of childhood, and the happiness of being with him, so she felt all weepy. His chin, closely shaved and a mere inch or so from her mouth, tantalized. 'Ryder . . . my lord . . . thank you.'

'There's no need to thank me. I thought your aunts would like to visit for a short time, though the doctor thought it might exhaust you. I've told them they may take afternoon tea with you, and must stay no longer than an hour.'

His clipped tone said he was still vexed with her. She wanted to kiss the little dimple at the side of his mouth, make him as aware of her as she was of him, but the maid was there, effectively blocking any intimacies.

The doctor had been right. Adele was soon exhausted by her aunts' chatter as they fussed about her, but she clung on to the precious hour.

Ryder personally escorted the two women home in the carriage.

Four

Adele was grateful for Ryder's hospitality, though he rarely sought her company unless it was with Hal in tow, and he didn't invite her to join him at table.

His polite indifference to her presence in his home was hurtful, but understandable.

Hal collected her aunts for another visit, and they chattered on until she was exhausted and fell asleep. It was almost dark when she woke, to find her visitors gone and Ryder standing by her bedside gazing down at her. He said nothing when she spoke his name, just nodded, and then turned on his heel and left.

People visited and she heard snatches of talk and grumbles of laughter. Ryder raised his voice on one occasion. Hearing her home mentioned she had eavesdropped on the conversation by standing at the top of the stairs. The voices were coming from the study and the door was ajar.

'I can understand your frustration over the matter, but I don't care whose land you think Duck Pond Cottage is on. Until your claim is proven and the law decides I will not have the lives of the Manning sisters disrupted. Duck Pond Cottage has been their home since they were born. Their mother brought it into the marriage. If the water in the stream is allowed to back up and the chalk under it becomes waterlogged, the foundations will be weakened and then the place will be of no use to anyone. Do you understand me, Mr Ashburn?'

'Yes, my lord.'

'Good. Then let's put that behind us and get on with looking at your plan for the estate.'

The door had been closed before she'd heard an answer but it was clear that there was a dispute over the ownership of the cottage. She had the deeds and she had her grandmother's will, so her claim was safe if it came to anything.

On the first day of March she'd recovered enough to leave

Madigan House. Ryder had not once been desirous of her company. Whilst he'd avoided her she'd done the same to him. Two months earlier a posy of satiny snowdrops on her tray had given her hope that he might forgive her, but it had come to nothing.

She'd heard the distant rumble of his voice now and again, and had watched him come and go from her window. Sometimes she'd sensed him near, as though he stood at the other side of the door, hand raised to knock, but too hesitant. Now and again the dog had sniffed the gap under the door and kicked up a fuss, but it had probably caught the scent of a mouse.

Mostly, Sarah stayed with her so she had a companion. Sometimes the girl took Gypsy for a walk and returned with her face glowing. Though she was free to come and go as she pleased, Sarah took responsibility for Adele and shouldered most of the work. She kept their room clean, washed and ironed their garments and fetched their meals from the kitchen.

Hal spent an hour in their company during the afternoons. He told tales about his life as a soldier embroidered by caustic little comments that made her laugh, and he kept her up to date about what was going on in the house.

The doctor's twice-weekly visits became one. On his final visit he pronounced her free from infection.

Only rarely had Hal mentioned Ryder, but she'd caught glimpses of him from the window. Six years had skimmed the downy softness of youth from his cheeks and his face had become angular. He was still handsome. More so in fact for his face was now tempered by the maturity he'd grown into and the presence that had come with it. He was a lean, taut man with a graceful walk.

One day a carriage with the Madigan crest pulled by a handsome pair of dark bays appeared in the drive. Hal had promised to escort them to Brackenhurst when they were ready.

That time had come. She was loath to go, but had no reason to stay. Neither was there any encouragement. She finished packing the trunk Hal had brought them and rang for Mrs Betts. 'Would you tell Mr Stover we're ready to depart?'

Hal and Sarah took the luggage down followed by Gypsy,

who displayed no intention of being left behind. Adele had already written a note to Ryder, thanking him for his hospitality. She took a final look around their chamber doubting if she'd ever come here again, for he was unlikely to invite her. If things hadn't gone horribly wrong all those years ago she would have been the mistress of this house and might have had a child or two to share with him.

She sighed, propping the note for Ryder against the inkwell. She should express her thanks in person, but she doubted if he'd want her to seek him out.

'I'm coming, Sarah,' she said, hearing a footstep behind her.

'It's not Sarah . . . it's me.'

She spun round, shocked, and then took a hasty step backwards and brushed against the desk. The hessian bags fell to the floor with a clatter, and the contents slid and spun across the floor, scattering everywhere, until a series of solid clunks brought everything to a halt against the blanket chest. Ryder scooped the spilled contents up and pushed them back into the bags.

Had he materialized from her thoughts? Her guilt enabled her to see the wound she'd scarred him with, reflecting in the depths of his eyes like a turbulent ocean. Her heart thumped erratically before it returned to normal. 'Ryder . . . what are you doing here?'

There was a wry twist to his smile. 'I live here . . . remember. This was my bedchamber before I left.'

She didn't know what to say or what she should do. Apologize perhaps.

'Ryder . . . there's something I need to say.'

'I received your message from Sarah. It doesn't need to be repeated.'

Knowing he would never forgive her she said awkwardly, 'Thank you for your hospitality.'

'Think nothing of it. I'd do the same for anyone in the same situation.'

That hurt, and tears pricked the back of her eyes. 'I won't bother you any more.'

'You don't bother me now, so no . . . I don't suppose you will.'

He was lying, she thought, and she wanted to reach out and touch his cheek but the air of remoteness about him kept them apart. She said, 'Don't, Ryder. You're too fine a man to indulge in spite.'

His glance flitted over her face, touched on her eyes, her nose and then lingered on her mouth for a moment. His expression softened a little. 'You always could disarm me. You haven't changed much, Del.'

Del? Only Ryder had ever called her that and the feeling of loss at hearing it again was nearly her undoing. He was close – too close, so she could smell the soap his servant had shaved him with. He'd left the fine bloom of youth behind and was a man – a man with all the power that came with that state. He knew it and was making her aware of it.

If she took a step forward she could lean into his warmth and feel his arms circle her, like she used to. She closed her eyes against that moment of temptation, remembering the way his chin used to rest on the top of her head and his breath stir through her hair. A little shiver trembled through her and for a moment she felt safe. She took a deep breath, inhaling the essence of him before she said, 'I must go, Sarah will be waiting for me.'

'Yes . . . it wouldn't do to keep anyone waiting.'

She ignored that. 'I'll reimburse you for my wardrobe once I'm settled.'

'There's no need.'

'Yes . . . I must, I don't want to be in your debt.'

Was there a touch of irony to his mouth? 'As you wish. You know, Del, you're the only woman I've ever cried over since my mother died, but at least I've now been given the opportunity to say goodbye. Since we are no longer on familiar terms, from now on it would be best if we addressed each other in the correct manner, don't you think?'

Heat flooded her face and she murmured, 'Familiar strangers, do you mean? I'm sincerely sorry for the wrong I caused you, my lord. May we leave it there for now or do you wish to humble me further?'

'Not as much as I'd like to.' It was Ryder who took that step forward. Taking her chin between thumb and forefinger he tilted her face up to his. His mouth against hers was moist, tender and wounded. She wanted to kiss his hurt away but found herself powerless in the face of the accusation it contained. It had been a long time between caresses but an essential ingredient had been missing from it – love.

'That will be reimbursement enough for now,' he said and ran his finger down her nose. 'Goodbye, Mrs Pelham.'

'My lord,' she whispered, and she turned on her heel and ran from the room before she had time to protest, or worse, weep with self-pity for what she'd lost.

She went down and the doors leading off the hall were closed against her. She could hear Gypsy yapping, sharp and urgent in the house. Somebody had closed him in the library. She remembered he was Ryder's dog, not hers.

It had been a while since she'd been outside. The wind had an exhilarating, buffeting playfulness to it, reminding her it was March. She flattened her palms against her bonnet lest it fly away on its one ostrich feather . . . though she'd heard that the ostrich was too heavy to fly. She enjoyed the sensation of the fresh day and the dapple of sunlight and shadow as the trees did their own joyous dance.

It was if she'd just begun to emerge from a long sleep – a nightmare really. She should have run from Edgar, and kept running, but she'd had no money, and what he earned was gambled away. The times she tried it he'd come after her. She shuddered to think of the consequence that followed.

She had not thought to see Ryder again.

Her mouth was vibrant and alive with his taste and the shadow of his kiss tantalized. She ran the tip of her tongue over its heat and the wind cooled the moisture into another diamond-sharp clarity of memory. She smiled at the pleasure it afforded her, despite the anger it contained.

Hal gave her a searching look as he handed her into the carriage, but said nothing as he climbed in after her and tucked a rug over her knees. The coachman cracked his whip and they were off.

Looking back at the house Adele saw Ryder emerge from the front door, the struggling dog in his arms. He placed him down and Gypsy began to chase them. At her request, Hal called to the coachman to stop and the dog came racing up and flung himself through the opened door into the carriage and into her lap.

Ryder stood in the porch, making no attempt at concealment – but why should he when this was his home?

She flattened her hands and cheek against the window as they took the gentle curve towards the gate, looking back at him. The sun came out and his image twisted through ripples of slightly distorted glass, as if he were dancing. He wore an air of loneliness. A lump came to her throat when they were out of sight.

Hal offered her a smile when she straightened. He was a quiet man with an air of toughness about him – someone you'd want on your side.

'Will you be staying long at Madigan House?' she asked.

'I'll stay long enough to help the earl repair the estate cottages. I would hope to finish the commission by the end of August in time for the harvest. Someone took advantage of the earl's absence to practically demolish the workers' cottages. Ryder is of a mind to marry and settle down. He wants the estate to be in good working order in case he fathers an heir.'

Jealousy grated shreds from her heart. 'And then what will you do?'

He shrugged. 'I'll probably move back to Hampshire. I don't know anybody there but an aunt left me some property. I could go back to my profession, though I prefer working in the open air to legal. Or I might go back into the army.'

'You're not married, then?'

'My wife and unborn infant died from scarlet fever.'

'That must have been hard to cope with. You should marry again and produce a family. It would give you a purpose in life and you'd make a wonderful father.' She placed a hand on his sleeve. 'I'm sorry you're going, Hal, but Hampshire isn't too far away. I hope you'll visit us, since it feels as though you belong to my family.'

To which he laughed. 'Are you proposing to me?'

'Oh my goodness, is that what is sounded like? I'm afraid not, Hal, and you know why. It would be doing you a disservice since I see you as more of a brother.'

'Then I'll be contented to remain in that role. You should take your own advice perhaps.'

'I'm not looking for a husband.'

'Perhaps one is looking for you. He might tap you on the shoulder one day.'

She imagined Hal was referring to Ryder and shook her head. It would never happen now. All the same, it would be sad if she never saw Hal again. He was a decent man with an air of toughness about him, and she liked and trusted him. 'Perhaps you should open your office in Dorset, then we can see you often.'

'Now that's an idea worth thinking about,' he said.

When the carriage drew up at the gate of Duck Pond Cottage, Adele's aunts came rushing out. Words and exclamations tumbled out of them and she was kissed soundly from all directions, as was Sarah.

'You look so thin, my dear . . . don't you think so, Patience?'

Tears filled Patience's eyes. 'Just a little, but we'll soon fatten her up, like the goose at Christmas.'

Not quite as plump as that, Adele thought.

Hal was kissed on both cheeks by the aunts and the chatter began. 'Such a sweet man, the cottage is drying out nicely now you've repaired the sluice gate.'

'Did the earl come with you? No? Oh dear, such a pity, and we've knitted you a muffler apiece.'

'It's a reward for looking after our niece so well. But never mind; first served is best served, or so they say, and you shall have the first pick, Sergeant. One is blue and the other red.'

'You must be feeling the cold after spending all that time meditating in a hermit's cave in India, don't you think so, Prudence?'

Prudence shivered. 'And fancy the earl surviving the bite of a deadly giant cobra too. Goodness . . . how heroic and exciting a time you must have had. Who would have thought it.'

Hal raised an eyebrow and grinned. 'Fancy, indeed? The snake takes on more proportion with each telling. The earl charmed the snake right out of the basket with a song, and then he bit the snake in retribution. It died on the spot.'

Sarah giggled, Prudence snorted and Patience chuckled. 'That's a tall tale if I've ever heard one. We were not born yesterday, young man. The sergeant can wear his muffler and carry the other one back to the earl,' she said.

'Of course he can. How clever of you to think of it, Patience.'

Sarah was next for their attention. 'My goodness, what a lovely, quiet girl, and such a tragedy to be left all alone in the world.'

Adele was of the mind that it would have been a bigger tragedy had the girl's father lived, but she mustn't dwell on the manner of his death. 'Sarah is like a sister to me, but I must warn you: when she has something to say she usually speaks her mind.'

'Goodness . . . did you hear that, Patience? We shall have to behave ourselves.'

'Better still, we must teach her to misbehave. It's much more fun.' Prudence patted Sarah's cheek. 'We like women who can voice their opinion, especially when men talk such nonsense. You mustn't believe a word they say, my dear. Snakes . . . hah! I'll give the earl a good old English adder as a cushion to sit on. He can sing to that.'

The gravity in Sarah's expression was replaced by a shy smile, and then she laughed.

'That's better,' Patience said. 'Woe is a young lady who has nothing to smile and be happy about. What say you, Sergeant?'

'That you and your sister can only set her a good example.'

'What a sweet, polite man you are. I do like a man who has provided service to his country, they are so robust, obliging and invigorating. Now I must go and make us some refreshment.'

Sarah said. 'May I help you, Miss Prudence? I can carry the tray through perhaps.'

It was an offer that brought a smile winging between the sisters.

The luggage was deposited upstairs and Hal stayed for some refreshment, allowing the aunts to fuss over him with good grace and seemingly a good-natured enjoyment.

Afterwards Adele walked with him to the carriage. It had attracted a sprinkling of curious villagers, most likely hoping to catch a glimpse of the earl, though she caught their glances on her several times and they were quickly withdrawn if she engaged their eyes.

Hal stood tall and straight, the red scarf a flamboyant loop around his neck. Before boarding the carriage he gazed down at her. 'Take care of yourself, Mrs Pelham.'

'I'll try, Hal, though I'm eager to get started on the garden.'

'Don't tax your strength. I'll come and dig the kitchen garden over for you tomorrow. I'll also trim the grass surrounding the house and clean the windows. You'd better make me a list of tasks that need doing.'

'The earl might not like it.'

He grinned at that. 'Last time I looked his lordship didn't like a whole lot of things, but he's managing to swallow them without choking.'

Within the month Patience and Prudence ran out of gossip and the four women were settled into a routine of living together and sharing the tasks that needed to be done.

The kitchen garden was flourishing, the vegetables poked through the dark crumble of earth and promised a good supply for the house. Daffodils grew everywhere and the rose bushes pushed out buds on their neatly pruned branches as March changed into April. There was a rush of bluebells and the earth was soaked with showers.

Adele liked nothing better than working in the garden. Dressed in her oldest clothes and with a straw hat protecting her face from the sun she relaxed as she settled back into her environment.

The interior of the cottage itself hadn't changed. The tapestries on the wall and chairs had been embroidered by Adele's grandmother, though they were now faded. The rooms seemed smaller than she remembered, probably because of her recent stay at Madigan House where the ceilings were lofty and you could set up home in the fireplace if you had a mind to.

But something was missing from her life, a certain tension. Here, she didn't hold her breath to listen for Ryder's footsteps. She didn't rush to the window to catch a glimpse of him if she heard his horse whinny, and she didn't sniff the air for the elusive scent of the lime soap his valet made to shave him with.

She and Sarah had rooms at the front of the house. The beds had wooden frames and a head canopy of faded blue damask to keep the winter draughts at bay. The floors were decorated with bright hand-woven rugs that her grandfather had brought home from his travels in Persia. Though a little faded and worn now, they still muted the noise of shoes pattering on the floorboards.

Sarah said, 'I like it here. I feel at home. The cats are female.' She lowered her voice a little. 'Gypsy is a male, like the statue with the fig leaf near the door to Madigan House. Do you think the earl and Hal Stover resemble that when they are without clothing?'

Adele gasped, and her threatened blush subsided in the face of Sarah's giggle. She joined in, aware that Sarah was old enough to know of the differences between men and women. She'd learn even more in the country, especially now it was spring. The girl was old enough to marry, as Adele had been at that age . . . though her own marriage to Ryder had never taken place since Edgar Pelham had intervened to prevent it.

Sarah said, 'The cats are watching Gypsy, waiting for the right time to put him in his place. It sounds strange, but houses talk, even though they are the keeper of secrets.'

Duck Pond Cottage certainly talked. The old oak beams endured and the stairs had a familiar creak to them. Doors opened and shut in the draughts, but quietly on the turn of a sigh as if someone invisible had drifted through the panels and closed it behind them.

A pair of territorial tabby cats guarded the dwelling. After much cocky aggravation from Gypsy, they launched a two-pronged attack on the dog that saw him bloodied and yelping and hiding under the bed. It seemed the pecking order had been established to the cats' satisfaction.

'Perhaps that will teach you not to be so bumptious,' Adele said, bathing Gypsy's wounds and spreading salve on them. The dog kept a wary eye on his adversaries from then on. It was an uneasy peace for a while, and then they seemed to accept each other, apart from an occasional swipe of a paw or a passing growl.

Nobody visited unless it was a carter with the milk, or the occasional tradesman. It seemed odd that her aunts had few friends when they'd been such social creatures before she'd left the district.

When Adele queried it, Prudence said, 'It's because of Mr Ashburn. He bought your father's estate from his heir, and he regards this house and the land it stands on as part of it. We've told him it belonged to your grandmother, who left it to you. Everybody knows that. He maintains that it automatically became your father's property when he married your mother.'

Patience cut in. 'The businessmen amongst them don't care about anything that doesn't affect them. As for the others, they're frightened they will lose their tenancies if they take our side in the dispute. But let's not stir up a hornets' nest. The last time I spoke to Mr Tessler he told me he has it all in hand.'

Prudence scoffed. 'You're not called Patience for nothing. That was about six months ago. Now the earl is home things will get done, you mark my words.'

Adele hoped so. She didn't want to go running to Ryder every time she needed a problem solved. 'Mr Tessler has not communicated with me over this. I can clear it up quite easily since I have both the deeds and my grandmother's will. Mother gave them to me and told me they were my claim to the property. She said the cottage was not part of my father's estate and she had no intention of letting it go out of her family.'

'Oh, my dear, how wonderful of your mother to leave the documents in safe hands, and she didn't say a word. We told your father's heir that Duck Pond Cottage and the adjoining meadow didn't belong to the Lawrence estate, but he didn't listen. He was so eager to get rid of it he accepted the first offer, which was far less than its worth. We think he had debts to settle. He wouldn't listen to reason and neither would Mr Ashburn, who bought the land, and thus assumed control over your father's estate.'

'I expect the earl would have bought it, had he known.'

Prudence took over the conversation. 'Not that we blame

Mr Ashburn for that, since he's a young man making his way in life and will snatch an opportunity when it's offered. All the same, the matter was dealt privately and very hurriedly, for nobody, including us, knew of the sale until it was signed, sealed and delivered.'

'And beside that . . . we cannot see how Mr Tessler can act for both parties and still remain impartial.'

Her aunts were getting agitated and Adele changed the subject. 'I'm going to see Mr Tessler because I need to make enquiries about my estate. How do you usually get into Poole . . . walk?'

'We tie a piece of rope to the gate if we need a ride. Usually Mr Ashburn or the reverend takes us. Sometimes they can't spend the time. Otherwise we walk to Blandford. As you know, it's a bit of a traipse, but is closer.'

'What happened to the donkey cart?'

'It's in the stable. The wheel collapsed when we hit a tree root, and we were tipped out. Then the donkey disappeared one night. We must have left the stable door open and she wandered off. It wasn't the first time, but usually she came back. I think gypsies took her the last time.'

'I see.'

Adele wondered if she could afford to buy another donkey and cart. She wouldn't know that until she'd seen Mr Tessler. She hoped the Reverend Bryson would pick her up, not because she liked him, but because it was her first outing alone since her illness and she wasn't confident that her strength would hold up.

She hung the rope on the gate then went back inside, wasting several futile minutes looking for her hessian bag, which, amongst other treasures, she thought contained the deeds to the cottage and her grandmother's will. The packages had been sealed with wax containing the Lawrence signature, but her mother had informed her of the contents, which stated that the ownership of the cottage stayed in the female line. Had she married Ryder it would have been passed to their daughter, if they had one.

There came the sound of a vehicle drawing up outside the cottage.

'I'll search for it while you're gone, it can't be far away,'
Patience said.

Adele rushed downstairs, pulled a blue shawl around her
shoulders and fussed with her bonnet in the hall mirror. She
was wearing a cream gown she'd left behind in the wardrobe
with her other clothes. It had not gone out of fashion. 'I wanted
to get that matter settled with Mr Tessler and now I'll have to
wait until we've found the documentation,' she said to Sarah.

When she stepped outside it was to find the Madigan estate
carriage with its coat of arms waiting for her. It was highly
polished. The dark bay carriage horses were glossy and their
tails tied high. The door swung open, the step unfolded and
Ryder alighted. Dressed all in black, he had a touch of the
sinister about him.

Adele was rooted to the spot as she remembered the last
time they'd met, and his parting kiss. His lack of beard still
took her by surprise, though she had seen him clean-shaven
before. He had an ironic twist to his mouth, and Lord, but he
was handsome, especially with the maturity of several years'
absence etched into his face.

She was too old to blush yet she did when she remembered
in minute detail how close they had been on one occasion.
'Ryder . . . my lord. I didn't expect you.'

'Is that exasperation I hear in your voice?'

'I imagine you'll hear what you want to hear.'

'*Touché*, my dear. I'm at your service, so where are you going
this fair morning?'

'To see Mr Tessler and find out where I stand in regards to
funds, but I cannot find the deeds to the cottage and my
grandmother's will.'

'When did you last have them?'

'I can't remember. I assumed they were in one of the hessian
bags. Sarah said I wouldn't have put anything in the trunks
that we didn't want anyone else to see. She's going to help the
aunts look for them while I'm out.'

'Perhaps they were left behind at Madigan House. I'll ask
the staff to search for them.' He slid his hand under her elbow.
'Don't just stand there, Mrs Pelham. Get in . . . get in.'

Patience came running out waving a piece of paper. 'You

forgot the shopping list.' She bobbed a curtsey when she saw Ryder. 'My lord, how are you this fine day?'

'In splendid form.' Ryder took the paper from her and tucked it in his waistcoat pocket.

When Adele seated herself he took the seat opposite and tapped his cane on the roof for the driver to set the carriage in motion. She dredged up some courage. 'Ryder . . . my lord . . . I need to ask you something.'

'If it's what I think it is, the answer is no . . . I haven't forgiven you, and I doubt if I ever will. But we're older and wiser now and we're bound to run into each other. The best we can do is to pretend to be civilized.'

'Do you hate me so much that you can forget the friends that we once were?'

A smile twisted his lips. 'Hate? That emotion was replaced with indifference years ago, my dear.' He gazed out of the window. 'If I'd realized it was you I found on the heath perhaps I would have left you there.'

It was a cruel thrust and a solitary tear ran down her cheek. It sounded more like the need to hurt than indifference, but he certainly knew how to go about it.

He leaned forward then reached out to scoop the tear from her cheek with his fingertip. 'Don't cry, my Del, I would have gone back for you. One thing hasn't changed.'

'What is it?'

His eyes engaged hers and a shiver ran down her spine when he said softly, 'I still want you.'

Five

Adele folded her hands in her lap and gazed down at them. It was a while before they spoke again, and Ryder who broke the silence.

'Are you comfortable with your back to the horses?'

Her response was a taciturn nod. She made no effort to engage in conversation, polite or otherwise.

'Good.'

The exchange was followed by another awkward silence, in which Ryder examined the woman he'd once loved. Due to his care, for he'd ordered dishes for her that were nourishing as well as pleasing to the palate, the pinched, worried face she'd presented to the world on her arrival had filled out a little. Her hair glowed like horse chestnuts in September and her eyes were a greenish grey like moss growing on a stone. He tried not to smile. In the past Adele would have taken him to task for describing them thus.

She still needed to gain some weight, for her gown hung a little loosely.

He'd meant it when he'd said he still wanted her. She was a thorn in his side . . . an insatiable itch. He wanted to lose himself in her – punish her. He could have kicked himself for thinking that way when he'd prefer to take her in a loving exchange. There was still something vulnerable and innocent about her, and he craved what he'd been promised as a young man and was then denied.

She looked younger now than the half-dead creature he'd plucked from the snow on the heath. No wonder he hadn't recognized her then. He'd worked to keep her awake – to support the dead weight of her body at the same time as managing the horse, while he got them to his home, and to safety.

The carriage hit a deep rut and lurched to one side. Giving a yelp of surprise Adele was pitched from the seat and ended up half on his lap. The feather on her hat tickled his nose, making him want to sneeze. He moved his head to one side, automatically circling her waist with his arm to support her.

Ryder found himself looking into panic-filled eyes. She cringed and struggled to escape, whimpering, 'Let me go . . . please don't hurt me.'

'Sorry, my lord,' the coachman called from above. 'The rut was filled with mud and I didn't see it.'

'Take it easy from now on, Bates, the lady was unseated.'

'That I will, my lord. Sorry, Mrs Pelham.'

Ryder lowered her back into her seat and took her hands in his. 'You're trembling. Why were you afraid I'd hurt you?'

She jerked her hands away. 'I wasn't . . . I was unprepared for the jolt and you misunderstood.'

Her voice contained a tide of tears being held back and he softened the moment with some humour. 'If you don't want to end up on my lap again you'd better hold on to the strap, Del, the road is rougher than I thought along this stretch. I'll make arrangements to get it repaired while we're in town.'

'I'm sorry, Ryder . . . my lord . . . I wasn't referring to you.'

'As a matter of interest, to *whom* were you referring then?'

'Nobody . . . it meant nothing. It was simply a reaction.'

Somebody had ill-treated her and it wasn't hard to guess who; the lout she'd run off with.

Ryder recalled that Edgar Pelham had been handsome in a foppish kind of way. He'd certainly found his manners to be an affectation for the most part. There had also been something spiteful about him. There had been no love lost between them. Ryder had taken him to task over some shoddy work and his insolent reply had grated. Ryder had dismissed him.

He'd then gone whining to the reverend, Oliver Bryson, who had recommended Edgar Pelham in the first place. Ryder had reinstated him but had cause to admonish the man again. When he'd left the district Adele had gone with him.

Oliver Bryson had been overbearing, but then, it was part of his nature. Ryder had grown up with it. But absence had given him a clearer view and he'd changed. He would no longer allow the man to dominate him.

As for Adele . . . Ryder's initial flash of anger disappeared into a burst of moral indignation. It served her right for leaving him at the altar, and served himself right for taking Adele's adoration for granted. The humiliation of that moment burned through him again. He leaned back in his seat gazing steadily at her, wishing she would disappear in a puff of smoke so he could forget her.

He gave a little hiss of derision. Forget her! No matter how hard he'd tried, he hadn't passed one day without thinking of her over the past few years. He'd often wondered where she was, and whether she was happy, and now he was ashamed that he'd allowed anger to guide his thoughts on this occasion.

She'd been gazing through the mud-streaked window, her hand firmly curled around the strap now. Her cream gown was one he remembered from the past. A blue shawl hugged her shoulders for warmth and matched the ribbons on her bonnet.

Warm and serviceable but dull, came into his mind. Were she his wife she would wear the best gowns money could buy.

Her luggage hadn't turned up yet, but he intended to make more enquiries.

He put the thought aside. It was the daffodil time of year and the flowers spread across the landscape in their different shades. Some were robust gold trumpeters, others a delicate, fluttering pastel, like little butterflies dancing over the cabbages. Yet others resembled a pale spread of lemon curd. England's landscape had a calm beauty, compared to the busy plumage of the Indian subcontinent with its brilliantly exotic colours.

'Lovely,' he murmured, and didn't know whether he was referring to her reflection in the window or the flowers dancing on the meadow.

She turned, an enquiry in her eyes. 'Did you say something?'

He shrugged. 'It was nothing of importance. I was admiring the daffodils and thinking how pretty they were and I must have said something out loud. Do you have any plans for the future, Mrs Pelham?'

'My needs are few but it depends on what's left from my mother's legacy. I imagine it will be depleted somewhat now . . . though I have the cottage.'

Only if she could prove it was hers. Ashburn had a strong claim, and a ruthless nature. He wouldn't think twice about turning the Manning sisters out, and Ryder was glad he hadn't managed to do so by now. He grinned. The sisters wielding broomsticks were a force to be reckoned with. 'You will need to set funds aside to maintain it.'

'Yes . . . I've noticed a couple of damp patches on the walls downstairs. I thought it might help if I cut back the ivy.'

'It might, but you've been ill. Overtaxing your strength

could cause a relapse. I doubt if flooding will occur again now we've fixed the sluice gate. It was partially blocked and your aunts told me the cottage garden was inundated with water on several occasions. Hal said it should dry out quickly. The garden is beginning to take shape again. You arrived home at the right time of year to prune the roses back, I see.'

'They should have been pruned at the beginning of winter. Still, they should catch up after this rain we've had.'

'They should make a good display in the summer months, then.'

'Yes. It's been hard work. Hal dug the weeds in and took a scythe to the long grass. My aunts have grown very fond of him and we're grateful for his help. We'll miss him when he's gone, though he's promised to visit us. I've suggested he open his legal office here.'

A smile curved his lips. How banal their conversation had become. What would she do if he kissed the perfect curve of her mouth until she was senseless? He was tempted to. 'Hal leaves for London within the week. He intends to attend cases in the Old Bailey to refresh his knowledge on prosecution techniques, and should be back in the autumn.'

Odd that they could chat about trivial domestic matters when so much that was personal was left unspoken between them.

Ryder needed to know why she'd left him waiting at the altar without a word. He could still taste the humiliation burning inside him – remembered the embarrassed coughs as invited guests took their leave one by one, murmuring . . . what? It had to be condolences for there had no longer been a need to congratulate him. The air had been thick with pity. It had felt as though Adele had died, but it was something deep inside him that had died that day.

Adele's father had rushed into the church . . . breathless and untidy with haste and uttering the unutterable for anyone left in the congregation to hear and digest as he'd condemned his daughter, making it impossible for her to return. 'Adele has eloped with the architect. She's no longer my daughter and I'll never allow her to enter my home again.'

As if Adele was a smear of horse dung to be wiped off one's

boot, and indeed, Ryder would have done the smearing himself had he run into her then.

On investigation the self-proclaimed architect had turned out to be a stonemason's labourer with visions of grandeur, more braggart than skilled. Ryder been tempted to go after the pair, but pride had stopped him.

Then it was back to Madigan House – to the celebratory feast that had never taken place and the nervous bewilderment of his staff as he downed half a bottle of brandy before he'd summoned Stephen Tessler to his side to inform him of his imminent, and very drunken departure.

'Why, Del?' he murmured, and her name sounded like an accusation.

Her eyes came up to his, a turbulent and unguarded blaze of pain. Then a curtain was pulled across them. 'My lord?'

'Oh, for God's sake call me Ryder. I can't stand this formality from you.'

'As you wish, Ryder. What did you intend to say to me?'

Obviously she had her own demons to cope with. 'Nothing . . . it doesn't matter.'

They lapsed into an uneasy silence again and he pondered on several matters . . . Adele's missing deeds for one. He'd never doubted Stephen's honesty before, but now there seemed to be a solid relationship between Reverend Bryson, his nephew, and Tessler. A man could not serve two masters and he wondered . . . where would Stephen's loyalty fall were it put to the test?

Ryder was being pressured from three points and he didn't like it. He was doubtful about hiring the nephew to run his estate despite Ashburn's competence in many areas. He had no reason to dislike or mistrust the young man. Put simply, his arrogance, when coupled with his connections, irritated him. As for the Reverend Bryson, he should caution his wife about the danger of indulging in gossip.

When they came into the outskirts of Poole the traffic became denser and they slowed to a walk until the coachman found a gap to occupy.

'Where are you going first?' Ryder asked.

'To the offices of Mr Tessler. I believe he attends his clients here on Mondays, Wednesdays and Fridays, and the Dorchester office on the alternative two days. I want to find out if I can afford a donkey and cart. It's hard for my aunts to have to walk everywhere.'

He helped her down from the carriage. 'Perhaps you'd allow me to escort you to the sale yard, I might be able to advise you.'

'I expect you know more about donkeys than I do, so thank you.'

He gave a faint grin. 'I know an ass when I see one, and I see one every morning in the mirror.'

She almost smiled, but not quite. 'People will talk if they see us together.'

'They already talk about us, Del. I expected nothing less when I decided to return home, did you?'

'They don't know the truth.'

'Neither do I . . . Would you care to enlighten me?'

She plucked at the seam in her glove and gazed directly at him. He could have drowned in her eyes. 'You do understand it was not my intention to cause you embarrassment by returning, and for that I'm sorry. I'd heard that you'd joined the army and had died of wounds in India.'

'Ah . . . the deadly snake story. Who told you about it?'

She shrugged, saying quietly. 'I can't remember.'

She was lying . . . she did know, she just didn't want to face up to it. 'It wasn't from Edgar Pelham by any chance, was it? Remember him . . . the man you married while I was making a fool of myself waiting at the church? You owe me an explanation. Did you love him?'

If she had, at least he'd be able to console himself with the fact that she'd been happy with someone else. Yet anger roiled in him at the thought that she might have.

'No, I didn't love him . . . How could I when I . . .' She bit down on her lip. 'I cannot trust anyone with the truth.'

'You can trust me, Del. Believe me, I've gone through all the reasons why you might have left me standing at the altar. None of them make sense except that you cared for him more than you cared for me.'

'Have you, Ryder? Are you as sure of that as you sound?'

'Try me.'

She took a deep breath, and then shook her head as though she'd thought better of it.

He placed a hand on her forearm. 'I *will* have the truth of the matter from you eventually. You owe me that, at least.'

'You'd hate me if I told you.'

'It would be impossible to dislike you any more than I already do. To abandon me on our wedding day and marry a man you hardly knew was cruel. If I thought you'd loved him I could have found it in my heart to forgive you, but you never even said goodbye.'

He'd been brutal – too brutal, and he winced at the flare of hurt that exploded in her eyes. Nothing could have prepared him for the shock of her next statement though. He'd forgotten how hard she could respond in retaliation.

'I was never married to Edgar Pelham. The ceremony was irregular.'

He stared after her, his mind grappling with the statement as she turned her back on him and walked off. Was she saying she'd been the man's mistress? The thought soured inside him like poison as he reached a conclusion.

Adele was right – he did hate her more!

Trying hard not to weep, Adele couldn't believe she'd told Ryder she hadn't been married to Edgar. As if that wasn't bad enough, if she told him the whole truth he'd never deign to speak to her again.

To save her reputation she'd married Edgar on board the ship. It wasn't until later that she'd discovered the marriage to be illegal, for the captain wasn't licensed to conduct weddings and a shipboard ceremony wouldn't be sanctioned by the Church. Far from being horrified she'd welcomed the news, for it meant that Edgar would have no right to her property . . . such as it was.

She walked away as fast as she could, and when she looked back there was no sign of Ryder. Mr Tessler's business premises came into sight. Paint the colour of olives supported his name in discreet gold lettering and the glass-panelled door and windows shone in the sunlight.

The clerk showed her into the office. There was another man with Mr Tessler and they both stood when she entered. Of medium height, the younger man was conservatively dressed and wore an air of confidence. A glance from a pair of pale-blue eyes flickered over her.

Mr Tessler smiled. 'I hope you are fully recovered from your recent illness, Mrs Pelham. May I introduce Mr Ashburn?'

'Ah yes . . . I've heard of you.'

From her aunts, who found Ashburn's very existence irksome – but he must know that.

Ashburn's curt nod dismissed her, before he went to stand by the window.

Adele gazed at the lawyer. 'I was under the impression we had an appointment, Mr Tessler. Am I to conduct my private business in front of a stranger?'

Tessler dug his pen into his blotting paper and sighed when the nib bent. 'Mr Ashburn requested a meeting to discuss the ownership of Duck Pond Cottage. He thinks, and I agree with him, that it will save time.'

The assumption annoyed Adele. 'Save whose time? Certainly not mine. Mr Ashburton's business is not my business so perhaps you'd reschedule a meeting for another time.'

'Come now, Mrs Pelham, there is enough time for him to be heard, surely. He has a case.'

She stood. 'I will not be patronized by you, Mr Tessler, and neither will I allow you to intimidate me, Mr Ashburn. The cottage is mine, courtesy of my grandmother, who owned it and left it to me. My father had no right to claim it as part of his estate and I have proof of ownership. This conversation is now at an end, at least until I can get expert advice. If Mr Ashburn refuses to leave, then I must.'

Ashburn spun round. His breath smelled faintly of ale. 'I'll go. Good day, Mrs Pelham . . . or is it still *Miss Lawrence*?'

Mr Tessler came round the desk. 'That's enough, Luke. If the lady wishes to wait until she is properly represented then we must accommodate her.'

'Lady? I don't think—'

The door swung open and Ryder stood there. 'Ashburn. Get out before I throw you out!'

Ashburn shrugged and shame filled his eyes. He mumbled, 'It's nothing that should concern you, my lord. I was just leaving.'

As the man moved to push past Ryder stretched an arm across the doorframe, effectively blocking him. Anger burned in his eyes. 'I know what I heard. I suggest you apologize to Mrs Pelham before you leave.'

Ashburn said without any shred of remorse in his voice, 'I beg your pardon, Mrs Pelham. I lost my temper.'

She had the feeling Ashburn wouldn't beg for anything, or if he did, he wouldn't mean it. When she nodded to Ryder he removed his arm and allowed the man to pass.

But Luke Ashburn couldn't resist having the last word. 'You know we must have this conversation at some time, Mrs Pelham. I suggest we have it sooner rather than later so you can consider your options. I would hate to have to use force to evict you and your aunts, which is what my . . . uncle and aunt have advised.'

Had they then? Ryder closed the door on him.

'Thank goodness you returned,' she said.

'I wanted to apologize to you for my churlish remark.'

The threat withdrawn, Adele began to fall to pieces. Her lips trembled and she whispered as she clutched the corner of the desk for support. 'He gave me a fright and I'll recover in a minute or two.'

Ryder guided her to a chair. 'Sit there. Do you have any brandy, Stephen? A good shot with some water added if you please.'

The lawyer hastened towards the decanter on a low table.

Adele swallowed the brandy with a grimace and a few seconds later the heat rushed to her face and she swooped in a breath. It had been stronger than she expected.

Stephen Tessler was apologetic, but he'd lost his forcefulness in the face of Ryder's annoyance. 'I'm so sorry, Mrs Pelham. I had no idea the young man would act in such a disgraceful manner when I invited him to meet you. Oh dear . . . I feel quite put out.'

Adele nodded, and took a couple of deep breaths to help clear the brandy fumes. They seemed to rush straight from her mouth and into her head, making her feel decidedly woolly.

Ryder said, 'So you should be, Stephen. I'm going to say this but once. I was seriously thinking of offering Ashburn the management of my estate, but after witnessing his behaviour towards Mrs Pelham today I've decided to postpone my decision and cast my net wider. In fact, I'm beginning to question your closeness to various people who have been involved with the Madigan estate in my absence, and their relationship to me. I don't like my business being bandied about.'

A horrified expression appeared on the accountant's face and he spluttered, 'My lord, surely you're not suggesting – I assure you, everything has been strictly above board.'

'Like the sale of Squire Lawrence's estate?'

'I knew nothing of it until the deal had been done and the estate had been acquired by Mr Ashburn. Then I was invited to do the paperwork and I discovered the mistake regarding the purchase of Duck Pond Cottage. I took a stand on that, as you know, the matter is still not resolved.'

'As far as I'm concerned, it has been. I'm surprised that the reverend would sell the roof from over the Manning sisters' heads . . . or that you would sanction it.'

'It was not my place to offer advice, though I did suggest they make a thorough search for proof of ownership.'

'Can I confirm something . . . how did Ashburn pay for the estate?'

'I believe the reverend offered him a loan. It was a bargain even without the cottage. He's a hard-working young man and he intended to farm the land then sell it as a going concern.'

Ryder admired a man who could turn an honest profit from his own effort. 'Did he have a buyer in mind?'

Stephen hesitated and Ryder didn't push it.

'I know you're honest, Stephen, and I would rather have you running my financial affairs than anyone else. I'm not asking you to abandon your friendship with the Bryson family, since you don't need my approval. However, now I've returned, remember that my business is not their business. Neither is Mrs Pelham's business. I was appalled to find him here – doubly so when I saw the contempt with which he treated a woman he'd only just met. She has done nothing to earn such scorn from strangers. We must not let this happen again, do you understand?'

Stephen knew an ultimatum when he heard one. 'You have my assurance, my lord. As for the young man, he's been influenced by his relatives, I fear, and at this moment will probably be regretting his outburst.'

'Good.' Ryder smiled down at Adele, whose cheeks now glowed as red as apples. 'Are you feeling stronger, Mrs Pelham?'

Adele felt extremely strong, if rather lightheaded from the brandy. Feeling an urge to giggle she offered him a small smile in return. After all it wouldn't be wise to allow him to become too familiar. She tripped over her tongue, said, 'Yeth, my lord,' then giggled.

Amusement lightened the dark blue of his eyes. His lashes were dark and thick. He was more handsome than she remembered, more muscular and more commanding – more of everything. In a word . . . Imposing! He'd asked; how could she have left him?

The simple answer was – she'd had no choice. How could she have stayed?

'Did I hear you say *Yeth*? In that case I'll go to the sales yard and inspect the asses while you conduct your business with Stephen.'

Now she did laugh. 'I said yes. I think.'

He smiled. 'Look after her, Stephen. No more brandy. I'll return within an hour.'

The financial adviser saw Ryder out and took his place behind the desk. 'Now, Mrs Pelham . . . how can I be of service to you?'

'I want to know if any of my legacy is still intact, and if I can afford a donkey and a cart.'

'I see . . . Yes to the first. The allowance is worth two hundred pounds a year, which is ample to manage your household with, especially when your aunts' allowances are added to it. That sum has accumulated over the last six years. Then there is your dowry.'

'But that was given to—'

'The earl was generous enough to return it. Because you're still of marriageable age he feels you might yet need it to attract a suitor of substance.'

The thought rankled. How dare Ryder suggest such a thing? She was beginning to appreciate her freedom. Her life was her own to live as she wished. Her aunts had welcomed her home without discrimination. Edgar no longer had any hold on her and neither did Ryder. She still loved Ryder, but with an aching heart, and knew she would do so for ever, as she'd once promised him.

The hour flew by quickly and by the time Ryder returned Adele had a good grasp of what she could spend and what she couldn't. She wasn't wealthy, but was comfortably off thanks to her mother and grandmother. She could get by well if she exercised a little discipline over her spending.

Ryder knocked at the door and entered just as Mr Tessler was saying, 'I advise you not to spend too much on the upkeep of Duck Pond Cottage in case the matter goes to court and the case is ruled against you. Mr Ashburn has kept the repairs up to date so far, since your aunts have a limited income.'

'Then he must be remunerated. Perhaps you would see to it,' she said.

'For him to accept money from you would be to admit that his claim to the cottage is invalid, and that that Duck Pond Cottage is yours.'

'It is mine and I don't care what Ashburn thinks. Return his money, and make sure he provides a receipt. I can prove the cottage is mine.'

Tessler sighed. 'Do you have the deeds and your grand-mother's will with you? I could keep them safely in my strong box.'

She gave Ryder a quick glance and because she didn't want to lie to Mr Tessler she offered him a half-truth. 'They're in a safe place.'

Tessler nodded. 'I will need to see them the next time you come into Poole.'

Ryder waited until they were outside before he said, 'Why didn't you tell him you've lost the documents?'

'Because they're not lost . . . it's just . . . well, I have simply mislaid them.'

'That's an odd way of putting it.'

'Is it?' She shrugged. 'I don't know whether I can trust Mr Tessler.'

'What is it about him that you don't trust?'

'I don't know. He was on Ashburn's side at first, and when he bullied me a little Tessler protested, but it didn't seem genuine. When you arrived he became much nicer.'

'Being an earl does have its uses at times.' He bore her hand to his lips, leaving tender kisses on her palm and where the warm pulse beat in her wrist.

'Don't do that, Ryder. Someone might see us and read the situation wrongly.'

'They are more likely to read it correctly. They will say the earl is a fool if he still finds the woman who wronged him attractive.'

'You've never been that.'

'They will wonder if we are lovers, and they will talk about it after church. You, my delicious Del, will attract the gazes of men, and they will be bolder than you would like for comfort. The women will turn their backs to you while they simper at me.'

'Stop it, Ryder.'

'Why should you be worried about your reputation? You lost that when you left town with Pelham, and deservedly so.'

Pain ripped through her. 'I know . . . and don't think I haven't suffered for it.'

'What did Ashburn want with you?'

'He wanted to discuss the ownership of the cottage. Mr Tessler is on Ashburn's side. I think.'

'Hmmm . . . is he, by God.' They walked a short way, the air an invisible but living fog of tension around them. The town bustled. Fashionably dressed women paraded. The men wore their tall hats and the wind made a mockery of skirts, bonnet and hats alike. Ryder tucked his hat under his arm allowing his hair to blow where it would. At the end of the High Street the quay was busy with fishing boats that bobbed, pulled and shifted.

The quay was piled high with coiled ropes, barrels of salted fish and boxes of candles as the tall ships provisioned for long journeys ahead. Men swung from the rigging like monkeys, whistling and singing. It was a fair and busy day. Across the rippled water Brownsea Island divided the entrance to the harbour. Beyond, a pile of clouds was in the process of being whipped into shreds by the wind.

She remembered a game they'd played. They would whisper something into the wind and see if the other one guessed what it was.

Unable to bear the silence between them she looked up, catching him at the moment when he was gazing down at her. 'Don't be angry with me, Ryder,' she said in a voice that was surely too low to be heard.

'Whispers,' he answered. 'I wasn't angry with you, I was enjoying a moment of being home.'

They gazed at each other and smiled, spat forgotten.

Adele said, 'You returned my dowry. You didn't have to.'

'I didn't feel entitled to keep it.'

'You were.'

He afforded her a glance, deep and blue. 'Are you suggesting I should have kept your dowry in lieu of the wifely services you promised me? As I recall, you performed those without a ring on your finger and with no shame at all. Some would call you a forward hussy . . . though others probably have.'

She gasped at his bluntness and struggled to find an answer. 'What is obvious to me is you're no longer the gentleman I once knew.'

He drew her out of the wind and into the protection of an empty wagon. 'You only knew the youth. You're right, though . . . I lost my pride that day, as well as you.'

'For about a year I kept hoping you'd rescue me.' She gave a faint smile. 'I imagined you fighting a duel over me . . . then reality set in, and I knew you'd forgotten me.'

'I was ashamed to show my face and went to London. You could have left him and come after me. You knew where my London rooms were situated. I waited, and drank myself silly. It took a while to reconcile myself with your betrayal of me.'

There was a catch in her throat when she said, 'Pride would have prevented you from taking me back.'

A wry smile flirted around his mouth. 'Probably, though I might have done, or I might have strangled you and since I was royally inebriated for a month or two we will never know now. Hal lifted me from the gutter, but for my own peace of mind I should have left you on the heath.'

'Then you never would have known peace of mind again.'

'How well you know me.'

'I was surprised to discover you'd joined the army, you were never aggressive.'

'Yet you imagined me fighting a duel, the quintessential romantic hero. You could not have been as surprised as I was.' Laughter huffed from him. 'Hal said I had a death wish, and a bullet was quicker than the contents of a brandy bottle.'

She reached out to touch his cheek and he took her hand in his. 'Someone should have given me a tin medal for surviving your treachery. I could have worn a heroic, broken heart on my sleeve.'

She jerked her hand away. 'Stop wallowing in self-pity, Ryder, I didn't ask you to rescue me from the heath. Anyone else would have done.'

'Nobody else would take on the task and I felt obligated, even though I thought you to be a stranger. What would you have done if the aunts had turned their backs on you?'

'Sarah and I would have found employment somewhere, I expect.'

A little savagely, he said, 'But first you would have prevailed upon me for help with the consequence of your tale of woe, exactly as you have done. I would have helped you, like the fool I always was. You were almost dead when I found you. You had no strength left for employment. May I remind you, my delicious little betrayer, you were entirely at my mercy.'

'And may I remind you that you could have taken advantage of that, but you didn't. I thought you'd died in India. I mourned you then, my dearest friend. I know how wronged you would have felt, and would rather have died a thousand times on the heath than experience again the grief I felt then.'

He laughed, a husky little chuckle, and planted his hands

on the splintery grey planks that formed the wagon's side. 'Now who's indulging in self-pity . . . not to mention a little melodrama? Sentimental issues such as love didn't really come into it. We were children, doing what was expected of us because our fathers said it would be thus. You had fair looks and intelligence. I considered that you'd breed well and would provide the Madigan estate with heirs, but then, so would have fifty other women.'

Adele winced. How cold-blooded Ryder made it sound. 'So you didn't love me at all, you just pretended to.'

'Is that how it seemed to you? So why were you broken-hearted?'

She'd never been able to out-argue Ryder. 'It was you who suggested that I might have been, but then, you always had a vivid imagination. Your pride was dented because you couldn't have your own damned way, and real feelings like love didn't come into it.'

'Wrong, Del, I did love you . . . in a brotherly fashion, then later in my early manhood in a more carnal manner, and that brought a result of sorts, but even so, don't think you were the only woman in my life. I'm no longer the naive youth who imagined himself in love.'

He leaned closer and she caught a sniff of some exotic, but manly aroma. Limes. It took her back to when they'd been youthful sweethearts and she had a sudden urge to press her nose against his smoothly shaven chin and inhale him into her body. His boots bore a flawless shine and his clothes were immaculate. He'd rehired his former valet, or so her aunt Prudence had told her. In the short time he'd been home he'd been transformed from a rather shabby soldier into the elegant and imposing image of her beloved Lord Madigan again.

The depths of his eyes took on a smoky hue. 'Attraction is a perplexing thing, isn't it? I've learned that when I see something I want, if I pursue it I usually end up getting it. I want you, Del. I want you to love me again, and despite what happened between us I want you in my bed.'

'And then?'

'Perhaps I'll abandon you in the same callous way you abandoned me, and when you least expect it.'

She knew Ryder. He didn't have it in him to be so calculating. Or did he! 'You're lying, Ryder, you'd never be deliberately spiteful.'

He stroked his finger softly down her cheek and across her mouth, producing a shivery feeling. 'We'll see, Del. We'll see.'

'You seduced me in the first place and now you seek to ruin my reputation again by placing the blame on me. What sort of man are you? Why is the blame always put on the woman when it's men who do the seducing.'

'I'm a man like any other. As for your reputation, unjust as it may seem, and I agree that it is, it's already tarnished.' He gave a lazy laugh and his eyes hooded slightly. 'I could argue that you seduced me. I remember every moment. You were delicious, and shy, my Del. Your skin shone and it felt like silk under my fingertips. You were all breathless and blushing . . . and so willing to be loved.'

Her mind went into turmoil when she sensed the response in her body. There had been times when they discovered each other under the midsummer moonlight – when they'd become lovers in the flesh. She'd lain in his arms, loving him as he'd loved her, as though there was no tomorrow . . . or so she'd thought.

She fought it now, that physical attraction. Was that all it had been? What a price she'd paid for giving in to that all-consuming moment – when she couldn't say no to nature's urging. She remembered the prickle of hay against her buttocks, the heat of her core as they joined in a loving fever, her shyness afterward. Then he'd touched her tender breasts with his probing tongue and they'd loved each other all over again.

He didn't know about the son conceived from that coupling, born too soon and without the strength to take a first breath . . . his death the result of a beating when Edgar had heard of the child's existence. Her little lost infant hadn't been much longer than her forearm. He'd been fully formed but not ready for the world, and although his eyes were closed he'd had tiny toes and fingers, and a wisp or two of dark hair. She touched a fingertip against the locket she wore, a small dark curl of hair enclosed inside for her to mourn. He'd had the look of Ryder about him, and how she'd loved that helpless little soul, even though he had never taken a breath.'

She cherished the pain inside her and closed her eyes so he couldn't see the anguish in them. 'Is that how you see me now, as *something* you want in your bed? Would you bring me down so completely?'

'We're not completely unfamiliar with the rite of coupling, as I recall. I can no longer marry you of course, since you're no longer tidy. I would be willing to keep you as my mistress, though.'

'It was you who ruined me. There has never been any other—' She shrugged. 'I wouldn't countenance either.'

His eyes sharpened and she said wearily, since she was tired of justifying her existence and all she wanted to do was rest her head against his shoulder and tell him all, 'How many mistresses have you enjoyed, and do you treat them with equal contempt?'

'The least I can do is allow them the dignity of remaining anonymous.' He pulled her close and caught her by the arms. 'Allow this to be a small token, so you know what your dowry would have bought you, had you decided to honour our contract.'

His mouth closed over hers, tender and warm. For a moment Adele gave in to it and died a thousand loving deaths. At that moment she would have willingly become his mistress. But hadn't he just offered her that elevated position?

Panic closed in on her. She couldn't breathe and blindly struck out.

'Easy, Del,' he soothed, as if he were gentling a horse, and when he kissed her fingers she remembered that this was Ryder Madigan, not Edgar Pelham.

Ryder would never hurt her physically. Never! As for Edgar Pelham, he couldn't hurt her ever again.

He was dead.

She knew that for certain. She'd killed him!

Six

There had been a moment just before the fright surfaced in Adele's forest-green eyes and she'd thrust him aside. There had been a moment when . . . when what? Something eluded Ryder. Then he remembered and he snatched it from the air before it disappeared. That moment was the fear in the eyes of men a heartbeat before the fatal thrust of the bayonet.

Though far from being a coward, apart from the companionship of his comrades in arms, Ryder had not enjoyed the battles or the killing that was part of army life. Wherever possible he had taken a life only out of necessity, in defence of himself, his fellow soldiers or civilians.

In Adele he had recognized the same pain and the fear. Adele was afraid of him . . . of *him*, a man who had loved her all of his life? Had he changed that much?

He couldn't let her hurry off; she would head for the road out of town. One of her aunts had told him that Adele wasn't as strong as she imagined herself to be − that she needed to rest during the day. Brackenhurst was too far for her to walk after her illness, especially at the pace she often adopted. She would tire and dusk would overtake her.

He'd been cruel. He'd make it up to her.

How?

He didn't know.

He took her gently by the arm. 'Del . . . I didn't mean it.'

'I know.'

'Let's start again . . . forget the past.'

She turned, the helplessness in her eyes all too apparent. 'We can't, Ryder. We're different people now. You've been a soldier and I've . . .'

'And you have disappointed me.' He waited, watching the struggle going on inside her. Didn't she know by now that she could trust him with anything?

'There's that, but I've also changed. Things have happened that shouldn't have, and we can't go back and pretend they didn't.'

'Perhaps we could go forward and forget that they did. I don't want to spend the rest of my life hating you.'

'Do you hate me?'

'Sometimes I do, and it's justified. Did you mean it when you told me you didn't wed Edgar Pelham?'

Her alarm intensified and she began to resemble a trapped

mouse. He took the basket from her arm. 'Why are you trembling?'

'Because . . . I don't know. It's because I've been ill and I'm tired.'

'Not too tired to try and walk home, I noticed. You're frightened of me, and I don't like it. What did you mean when you indicated there had never been another man?'

She fussed with her gloves and said nothing.

'Edgar Pelham hurt you, didn't he?'

Her eyes came up to his, large and anxious. Still she said nothing.

'He's dead, and he can't do you any harm now. It's not as if he's going to come up out of the sea and strangle you.'

'Sometimes I dream that he does, and I wake and I can't get back to sleep in case the dream comes back. I don't want to talk about him.'

He gave her a considered glance. 'You do look tired. Let's go and get your livestock shopping done. I've found you a pretty little jenny with nice manners. It will be my homecoming gift if you like her. She answers to the name of Daisy.'

Her lips pursed a little, as if she were trying not to laugh. 'What does Daisy say when she answers?'

He wanted to say that he loved her . . . that he forgave her, but every time he thought of it his pain came rushing back. He could no longer expose his heart to her gaze or trust her with his soul in case she crushed them, as she had before.

When he didn't answer she put some distance between them. 'We're being watched.'

'By the whole town, I would imagine.'

'Almost correct since it's Mrs Bryson.'

'She wouldn't have seen us through the wagon, besides the distance is too far for her to see clearly. I've heard her described as the unofficial town tattler.'

The little ripple of laughter she gave told him their spat was over, at least, for the present. 'She must have caught a glimpse because she's watching us out of the dressmaker's window.'

He decided to entertain her. 'Ah . . . a den of iniquity, indeed. I spent an unfortunate half hour there with your young companion. Miss Pelham displayed admirable fortitude to walk into that lair of cats and emerge intact. We both did.'

'Sarah is a sensible girl. She rarely loses her temper and is clever in many ways.'

'She stamps a fine foot when she needs to. I like her.'

'Sarah likes to have her own way at times, but she usually sees the sense in things.'

He placed his hands one either side of her on the warm, splintered wood of the wagon. 'What will you do with her?'

'Do with her? I don't understand.'

'I thought she might be looking for a position?'

'I haven't given it much thought. Yes . . . I suppose Sarah will want to earn a wage, but there's no hurry since I seem to have the means to keep her with me and she's wonderfully helpful with my aunts. We were going to try and discover if she had any relatives. Her mother's family perhaps.'

'With your permission I was thinking I might employ her for the occasional task, like addressing invitations.' A task usually carried out by the lady of the house, he recalled. Had everything gone as planned between them Adele would have been doing it. 'Does the girl have any practical skills besides the domestic talents usually enjoyed by females?'

'First, Sarah doesn't need my permission. Second, carrying out domestic duties is not an entirely enjoyable occupation.'

'Sewing?'

She made a face. 'That's a necessity if one wants clothing to wear and cannot afford a dressmaker, but to sit over a frame of embroidery for hours on end and plying the needle is achingly boring. Sarah writes with a fine hand so she'd easily manage invitations. She reads well and is clever with numbers too.'

He smiled, half his mind still contemplating the delight to be found at the notion of Adele without clothing. Not yet perhaps, since she was still thin to the point of frailty.

There was a disturbance across the way. A shop door opened, the sunshine momentarily flashed from a small pane of glass.

'Mrs Bryson has left the shop and has her back towards us. Shall we make a dash for the horse sales?' he said.

Adele's closeness was disturbing. He was so totally aware of her that his throat felt a little husky. He wanted to place his mouth against the soft little hollow under her jaw and kiss it, as he'd dared to once when they'd been young and in the shy trembling throes of first love. The taste of lime became less of a smell and more of a sensation, so sharp and clean that the moisture in his mouth gave a little spurt.

Eyes widening she took a quick intake of breath and the pink tip of her tongue touched against her top lip.

Their eyes met and she murmured something under her breath. It was too soft to hear clearly but it sounded like his name, or the unconscious entreaty a woman made when she was aroused enough for a man to take advantage of it – or both.

Adele wasn't as immune to him as she pretended, Ryder thought, and then offered himself a personal revelation. What was worse, neither was he immune to her.

He reminded himself he must try harder to maintain his anger. She had proved herself false, after all.

'Ready?' he asked, and she nodded as they emerged from behind the wagon and headed swiftly towards the horse-sales yard.

Mary Bryson's head jerked up as though it was on a string and her eyes narrowed in on them as she launched herself in their direction.

'Quick . . . down this lane.'

And then the next lane, and then another; by the time they emerged into the market place again they were on the other side of the horse pen and Mary Bryson was nowhere to be seen.

Panting for breath they gazed at each other and began to laugh when she said, 'Do you suppose she might have been kidnapped by pirates?'

He laughed. 'I didn't intend to run you out of wind. You should have stopped me.'

She reprimanded him between taking gasps of air. 'Growing a pair of wings and flying would have been an easier option. You should have remembered my . . . legs aren't as long as yours.'

'I stand corrected, but your legs are more shapely than mine so you can't have everything.'

Ryder pulled her to a halt at a stall and purchased a ginger ale apiece. The liquid was poured into glass tumblers from a brown salt-glazed jug that kept it cool.

'I have some scrumpy cider if you prefer, my lord,' the stall owner said and gave a little bob.

Ryder laughed. 'The last time I drank your scrumpy I tried to swim to the island.'

The woman chuckled. 'Aye well, you were just a lad then and it was mid-winter. You had a fire in your belly, no doubt. It were my husband who fetched you out.'

He'd been about eight. The lads working on the quay had fed him the scrumpy and had challenged him to swim to Brownsea Island in the harbour. He'd become disorientated and had panicked and floundered about. Rescued by a stranger he was carried ashore to discover the tide had receded and he was only waist deep in water.

His father, the earl, had been tight-lipped when he'd been returned to him covered in stinking harbour mud.

'You've made a fool of us, Ryder. Please remember you have the family name and the title of viscount to uphold. I will not thrash you on this occasion – but I will most certainly punish you. You will not accompany me to London; you will stay here in the charge of your governess. From now on you will not play with or approach those rough boys. Do you understand?'

'Yes, Papa.'

He'd never seen his father again – and had been placed in the charge of Adele's father, who had immediately packed him off to the school his father had stipulated in his will.

It wasn't until he'd grown up a little that Ryder had discovered that being sent away hadn't been part of his punishment. His father had never reached London on that day, but had been killed for his purse by a murdering felon on the highway. There had been a service at the church for him, where Ryder had been required to stand still for a long time, and the reverend's eyes had been fierce and the sermon full of fire and brimstone, his governess had said.

After the church he'd heard the reverend and Adele's father shouting at each other . . . but the reverend had left when

Ryder had sought the comforting company of Squire Lawrence, banging the door behind him.

The squire had been a close friend of Ryder's family since childhood and had taken over his upbringing when he wasn't at school. The squire had been rather straight-laced, but Ryder had liked and respected the man.

He recalled Adele as being a toddler when he first set eyes on her – a diminutive creature with bobbing ringlets and a smile brimming with mischief. She was learning to walk, prompted by her nurse, and launching herself from chair to chair with an air of determination.

He'd fallen instantly in love. Even in the face of her betrayal, a warm affection for her crept through his body. Their love had changed shape over the years – as they had, progressing from the innocence of children playing together into youth and then the awareness of the difference between them, and finally the ultimate expression of love. How could he have been so wrong? He'd never loved anyone else and had been sure Adele had returned his love.

Even now he felt responsible for her welfare.

He set the thought aside and said to the woman, 'So it was your husband who rescued me from drowning, and I never thanked him.'

'Your father did that. He gave him a shilling and, joking like, said it would have been a florin if he'd left you there.'

Ryder laughed. 'How is your husband?'

'Gone some two years since. I still miss him, though our two sons run the inn now.'

'You're lucky to have them. I'm sorry to hear about your husband.'

'Don't be. I had the best years of my man and we were happy together.' Her eyes flickered to Adele. 'Love can make a fool out of any man, but that doesn't mean it should be dismissed. Even a small piece of happiness is as precious as a jewel.'

'It certainly is.'

'If you want to know what's bin going on in these parts in your absence you just have to ask me. It's given some folks a real shock, the pair of you turning up together. It's fate, I reckon. Any time you want to have your fortune told you come and see me . . . and you as well, young lady.'

Ryder wasn't about to embark on a philosophical conversation about love with the innkeepers' mother, or the merits of a gem. He'd learned the hard way that seemingly perfect diamonds were quite often flawed. He handed over a coin. 'The ginger ale will suffice.'

'I've seen to the other little matter you asked my son about, my lord . . . and may I say it's nice to see you again, back where you belong.'

'Thank you.'

Adele's smile grew even broader a few minutes later when she saw the docile little donkey called Daisy. She had a pretty coat of dark brown with a pale underbelly, and soft brown eyes with sweeping eyelashes set in fawn patches that resembled a mask. She was between the shafts of a maroon cart.

Adele made a fuss of her and exclaimed, 'She's so pretty. What's in that basket?'

'A picnic . . . we'll go out of town where there are fewer people and you can see if she'll suit you. I've been assured that her nature is docile. But if you don't want her I'll find a use for her.'

'I have shopping to do, and what about your coachman?'

'I hope you won't mind, since I wanted to spend the day with you, but my coachman has your shopping list and instructions to buy everything on it. He'll deliver it to Duck Pond Cottage and wait for me there. Will you take the reins or shall I?'

She laughed. 'You're impossible, Ryder. I haven't driven a cart since . . . well, for several years.'

'Then you'll have to learn all over again.'

He helped her into the cart, joined her there and picked up the reins. He was aware of her thigh, soft and warm against his and enjoyed the tension that transferred from her to him. There was no room to move anywhere else.

'Hold on to the rail, Del. I don't want you to fall off.'

Soon they'd left Poole behind and were in the countryside. Bringing the cart to a halt he placed the reins in Adele's hands then knelt in the body of the cart behind her. His arms came round her from behind and his hands covered hers.

They were small and soft and he leaned over her shoulder and lifted one to his mouth. He kissed her palm, then the other.

She pulled away, resisting his advances. A shiver racked through her and he kissed the back of her neck, where a silky chestnut ringlet sprang against her skin, so delicate and pale. Circling it around his finger he straightened it and then let go, so it bounced back against her neck.

Again she shivered. She must be totally aware of him now . . . yet she offered him only a mild resistance. 'Stop playing games, Ryder.'

'You think this is a game?'

'What else can it be?'

He told himself that were it really love he'd declare himself now, and to hell with her past indiscretion – something he must take the blame for, because Adele had been so young and innocent at the time and he'd robbed her of that. Guilt repeatedly stung him, like an angry wasp.

He waited for enlightenment but all he could think of was the soft curve of her mouth, the length of her eyelashes and the way she glanced at him from under them. Her breasts were filling out a little, which was a further distraction, and the soft nubs were enticing. He wanted her, but why, when she'd treated him with such contempt?

He sighed. Suitable women were everywhere, and finding one when he was a man of breeding, considerable wealth and passable looks should be easy. It was easy . . . except the woman he'd chosen wouldn't cooperate. He should move on, but he couldn't tear his attention from a minx who'd already proved herself unfaithful.

His emotions fluctuated between loving her and loathing her.

He told her, 'I haven't decided yet. What I do know is there's a little curl at the back of your neck and I couldn't resist it. It's totally distracting.'

She flung his arms away and rounded on him, her eyes sparking with anger. 'Don't touch me again, I'm not some trollop you've paid to be familiar with.'

Taken aback by her ferocity he fell backwards, bumping around in the cart like a sack of turnips as she set the donkey in motion at a fast clip.

He managed to get a grip on the side before he bounced out into the road, in the meantime, shouting, 'For pity's sake stop punishing the beast. She'll break a leg if she steps into a pothole, or worse – I will. Calm down.'

She slowed Daisy down and he scrambled to his knees, controlling his anger at her unexpected outburst.

When they reached a bend in the road, he said, 'I know a nice little picnic spot not far from here, so stop the cart just round the bend. We need to have a serious talk.'

When she brought the cart to a halt he held out his arms to help her down.

She folded her arms over her chest. 'I can get down by myself.'

Lifting the picnic basket out he growled, 'You're acting like a child, Del. Follow me if you want to eat.'

'It would choke me to eat with you at the moment.'

'So choke, and if you can't manage to do the deed without me, just say. I'll gladly offer my assistance.'

'Hah!' she flung at him as he walked off, his back stiff.

After a while he began to realize that the nice little picnic spot he'd remembered, having now been left to its own devices for several years, had become a rambling wilderness of bramble bushes.

A few minutes later she called out, 'Enjoy your picnic, Ryder.'

He swore, and headed back to the lane at a run, stumbling over roots and leaving crushed wildflowers and toadstools in his wake. He swore again when a bramble snatched at his sleeve.

Too late to catch her up, Daisy had been put to the trot. After all he'd done for her the wretched woman had thrown it back into his face.

'You come back here, Del,' he called after the disappearing vehicle.

Laughter floated back to him on the breeze and she kept going.

Be damned if he was going to lose the remaining shreds of his dignity by running after her like some besotted schoolboy.

He was through with chasing after her!

He mocked himself with a short, sharp laugh. Like hell he was. If she wanted to play games he'd oblige her, and he knew exactly where she'd wait for him to catch her up.

Seven

Adele had barely gone half a mile when the humour of the situation hit her. She couldn't remember Ryder ever holding a grudge for long and was tempted to go back for him. It was the height of bad manners to make him walk home when she'd already taken advantage of his time and generosity.

All the same, he'd brought it on himself. How dare he assume he could start again where he'd finished off? He'd already warned her that he wanted her in his bed. She supposed it would be a reasonable assumption, considering she'd already demonstrated to him how lacking in morals she was – though that particular bed had been a haystack in a thunderstorm! It seemed that Ryder had been discreet enough to keep her fall from grace to himself, while remaining in ignorance of the sad result of their careless behaviour.

The consequence of that encounter was the anguish and the caution it had taught her, but Ryder had the air of a tomcat on the prowl about him, as if he expected to take up some intimacy from where they left off.

She must not let it happen again, though it somehow seemed inevitable. Perhaps it would be a good idea to sell the cottage and move away from the district. No . . . she couldn't do that to her aunts unless it was a last resort. They had given up any notion of marriage and were resigned to spinsterhood. They didn't have the dispositions to transplant easily and would be mortified if her past caught up with her.

She brought the cart to a halt in the cool overhang of a willow tree, where the stream trickled across the road and widened into a small pool. It was on Ryder's land and used to be one of her favourite places to sit and dream.

The willow tree was much larger now. A grassy bank with a weathered seat kept her partially concealed from the road. She waited for Ryder, her stomach giving an undignified, hungry rumble as she contemplated her own foibles. She began to compose a suitable apology.

After a while she heard a crunch of footsteps. They stopped suddenly and she laughed. 'Ryder? I'm here, under the willow.'

The only answer she got was a chuckle. Her throat dried and the air around her seemed to quiver. She'd never heard Ryder laugh like that, so high-pitched.

'Who is it . . . who's there?'

The reply was unexpected, unbelievable, a quietly whispered, 'Edgar Pelham.'

Had he come back to haunt her? Panic sliced through her veins like iced lightning. It rooted her to the spot and turned her throat to dust. A scream gathered force inside her. When she found the courage to move she cautiously drew the curtain of weeping branches aside.

There was nobody in sight, apart from Ryder who was rounding the bend, unconcernedly munching on a pie and with the picnic basket balanced on his shoulder with the other hand.

It reminded her stomach that he carried their food supply, and he was obviously making the most of it. She supposed it served her right.

Though reassured by the sight of him, Adele was far from convinced that she'd imagined the voice and footsteps.

A rustle in the bushes on the other side of the road attracted her attention and the uneasy feeling came back.

She picked up a stout stick lying on the bank of the stream. 'Whoever you are, show yourself,' she said, her voice husky with fright, though she was feeling a little safer now Ryder was in sight.

A gunshot was the cue for an explosion of sound and movement. Everything happened at once. A handful of birds took to the air with a whirring of wings. A deer crossed the road and she could almost hear its heart pump with the panic it was in. Its soft eyes looked into hers and they were filled with pain as it lurched across the stream, blood oozing from one of its rear legs, its hoof held at an awkward position. The bone was splintered and clearly beyond repair. The animal disappeared into the bushes giving panicky coughs. The cart jolted and then rocked on its springs.

Adele cried out and Daisy brayed loudly a couple of times. Adele grabbed at the bridle so she could steady her. Her own heart was thumping so rapidly she could barely find a breath with which to soothe the animal, but luckily the donkey settled easily.

Ryder had dropped the picnic basket and began to run. Adele nearly collapsed from relief when he reached her and said, 'I heard a shot.'

'Yes . . . the ball hit the cart, I think.'

'Thank God it didn't hit you. You're trembling.'

He walked round the cart, found a hole and stuck his finger in it. 'The ball's still in it and I can smell the spent powder. At a guess I'd say this was a rifle shot, and fired from a fairly close range.'

She wasn't interested in the logistics, she was thinking of the pain in the animal's eyes . . . the accusation. She remembered the voice. 'I thought I heard someone speak.'

'Saying?'

Adele couldn't bring herself to tell him she'd killed a man. Such an event would invite notoriety, the scandal would ruin them all – herself, her aunts, Sarah and even Ryder, by association.

'I didn't quite catch the words, it was more like a noise and it may have been my imagination. At the same time the deer crossed the road. Something startled it and it was injured, I think, for it was limping badly and there was blood on its leg.'

The voice had been human, filled with malice. She shivered. She had told nobody about the nature of Edgar Pelham's death. She'd been interviewed by the ship's agent for an hour in a gruelling manner and kept waiting while he wrote a report for her to sign. It was during that time that their luggage had disappeared.

Ryder took a pistol from under his coat and primed it. 'Stay here behind the cart and keep your head down . . . I'll go and look.'

She laid her hand on his arm. 'Be careful, Ryder.'

His free hand covered hers and his blue eyes turned her way. 'You almost sound as if you care.' He smiled to take the sting from his words and disappeared into the undergrowth on silent feet.

Apart from an occasional rustle of leaves, the trickling run of the water in the stream and some birdsong, all was quiet.

Adele's back ached from her crouched position and she couldn't help but gradually straighten up to ease it.

Immediately another shot clipped a branch above her and she was showered in leaves and twigs. She ducked as a pigeon flew off on a whirring pair of wings, leaving a feather floating in its wake.

There were several curses then a violent rustle of foliage, as though a small gale was passing through it. Adele jumped when a man almost fell out of the bushes. He was kept upright by a strong hand fisted at the neck of his coat that jerked him forward.

Almost petrified she gave a scratchy little scream. It was Luke Ashburn, and he had a rifle over his arm with a wisp of blue smoke twisting from the barrel.

More telling was the pistol held against his head, as steady as a rock and twice as deadly. Softly, Ryder said, 'Drop your weapon, and any other weapon you may have about you.'

After a moment's hesitation the man complied and a pistol and hunting knife followed the rifle into the dust. Ryder stepped in front of her, shielding her with his body while still keeping the pistol trained on the intruder. 'What the devil are you up to, Ashburn? You could have killed us.'

'If I had it would have been unintentional. I'm sorry, my lord . . . I was after a deer. Somebody had set a trap on my land and the deer was caught in it. I should have killed the creature before freeing it, since it was more active than I expected.'

'You're on my land.'

'Unfortunately, deer travel and are no respecters of boundaries.'

'Why should I believe you are doing anything other than poaching?'

Ashburn's voice took on some heat. 'You may believe what you wish, but I'd prefer not to be called a liar without good cause.'

'There was more than one shot.'

'Actually, my lord, that second shot was meant for a pigeon. As far as I'm aware you don't own those. It will not happen again.'

Ashburn was being argumentative, and Ryder was curt as he glanced at something metallic in his hand before slipping it into his waistcoat pocket.

'You only just missed Mrs Pelham.'

An exasperated sigh left Ashburn's mouth. 'Would you kindly point that damned pistol somewhere else. It's making me nervous, and I doubt if you'd kill me over a pigeon.'

'There's always a first time. I'm considering whether to have you charged with trespass and poaching.'

When Ryder disabled his weapon Ashburn nodded her way. 'Please accept my sincere apology, Mrs Pelham. I do hope I didn't give you too much of a fright. Perhaps you should hang a bell on your cart to warn people of your presence.'

'And perhaps you should hang one on your tongue for the same purpose, Mr Ashburn, for it strikes me you have too much to say for yourself.' Her glance went to Ryder. 'As the only witness to this affair, may I speak in Mr Ashburn's defence, my lord?'

Ashburn's eyes widened and Ryder looked pained. 'If you must.'

'Believe me, it's reluctantly. Notwithstanding that Mr Ashburn is on your land, both deer and bird have escaped from the fate he had in store for them, so they can no longer act as witnesses. I can state with some certainty that an injured deer did cross my path and a bird flew off in a flurry of feathers. Wouldn't it be a good idea to hunt down the wounded deer and put it out of its misery? It couldn't have gone very far since one of its back legs was badly injured.'

'Exactly what I was about to suggest,' Ryder said smoothly. 'Due to Mrs Pelham's intervention, and I will confess that she is more tender-hearted than I am, Mr Ashburn, I will allow you to finish your hunt on my land for humane purposes . . . and a hindquarter of venison for my smokehouse, of course.'

A grin stretched about Ashburn's mouth and for a moment there was something about him that was elusively familiar – though it was not related to Mary Bryson. 'Of course, my lord, the remainder will go to the workhouse. Thank you, Mrs Pelham, for your wise counsel on my behalf and for pointing out the obvious.'

'You should learn to shoot more accurately.'

'I will keep that in mind.'

She hurled at him, 'Oh for goodness' sake, having a conversation with you is like conversing with a jar of pickled hedgehogs. You've got more answers than there are questions. Believe me, I am grateful. Now . . . please be quiet and allow me the last word.'

He opened his mouth, then closed it again and inclined his head, to say a few moments later, and with some surprise in his voice, 'The last word is yours then, Mrs Pelham . . . good day to you both.'

A huff of laughter came from Ryder as Ashburn picked up his weapons and turned to walk away. He stopped Ashburn in his tracks with, 'You might have finished but I haven't. Stay a moment. You have a large sense of self-esteem for a man with only five acres to his name.'

'More if you include the Duck Pond Cottage acreage,' Ashburn said.

'I don't, but the matter is under scrutiny, I believe. Join me for breakfast in the morning. Ten o'clock sharp. We will discuss your terms of employment if you are still in a mind to manage my estate and we will inspect your fields. If you're to work for me you must learn some respect so I'll expect to see a marked improvement in both your attitude and manners.'

Ashburn turned, his eyes sharpening. 'Am I to understand you're offering me the position I applied for?'

'That's right.'

'I'd heard that the soldier had been engaged, my lord.'

'From whom did you hear that?'

Ashburn shrugged. 'My aunt.'

'Ah . . . that accounts for it, then. Mrs Bryson seems to have her ear held against every keyhole in the district.

Adele wanted to cringe when the glance Ashburn gave her became speculative. She turned towards Ryder, who winked, so she wanted to kick him. He was giving the wrong impression to the man, and doing it deliberately.

'There's always some tittle-tattle going on, and like most gossips, my aunt repeats only what she hears from others and sees with her own eyes.'

'There is no need to make excuses for her. On this occasion she is right. Out of friendship I did feel obliged to offer the position to Mr Stover. He's thought it over and has declined. He suggested you were better qualified for the position.'

'I should thank him for the endorsement.'

'Except he's left the district for a while . . . I'm surprised your aunt didn't notice.'

Ashburn grinned. 'She did . . . she said he was laid low with the gripe.'

Ryder managed to keep a grave expression on his face. 'Hal would thank you for relieving him of the obligation to accept the position. As he pointed out, friendship doesn't transfer easily into paid duty, where loyalty comes with natural barriers of respect towards the employer already set in place. Besides, the sergeant is a lawyer by trade. He doesn't know one end of a sheep from another. However, he came with the certainty of trust and loyalty attached, and that counts for a lot with me.'

Ashburn nodded. 'I hear you, my lord.'

Adele made an effort to stifle her laughter. Goodness, Ryder was certainly putting this man in his place. She felt sorry for Ashburn, until she recalled that the shots that could so easily have killed her. And against her will she remembered the whispered name.

'*Edgar Pelham.*'

It seemed so long ago that her life had been sent off course, when a housemaid had handed her a slip of paper delivered by a child. Adele shuddered. The note had supposedly been from Ryder that night of their parting. The writing had been faint, and hard to read, even in the moonlight.

Meet me on the bridge at midnight, Adele, my love.

She should have known it wasn't from him, for he'd called her Del since childhood.

Thinking it was an adventure, for Ryder had often planned little amusements and escapades and the moon had been full and romantic that night, she'd thrown caution to the winds. After all, they had been intimate before, so what was the harm when they were to be married the next day?

Edgar Pelham had been there alone and he was drunk. He'd told her that Ryder was entertaining himself with his mistress, a woman skilled in the ways of love. Edgar had laid hands on her that were much too intimate, and then . . . when there was no more strength left in her to fight him off, he'd attempted the worst violation. But he'd failed and had fouled the air with a curse before he'd hit her.

To make matters worse her father had seen her slip from the house and had followed her, but it was too late. He hadn't believed her faltering explanation, and in her innocence and embarrassment she hadn't the experience to communicate. She'd been allowed to pack a bag and he'd cast her out.

'If it's her legacy you're after you can wait until she's of age,' he'd said to Edgar, which now reinforced the notion that Duck Pond Cottage, and the land it stood on, was indeed her legacy. She hadn't heard news of her father since, until death had claimed him.

Now she had come of age, but no debutantes' ball for her. Edgar – cold-blooded, calculating Edgar who never forgot anything that would bring him monetary advantage – had decided to bring her home so she could collect it. And her life had changed course, once again.

She was jerked into the present by Ryder's voice.

'You may go now, Mr Ashburn. Be more careful from now on.'

'Yes, my lord, I'll bring you your portion of venison tomorrow. Good day, Mrs Pelham.' He touched his hat and strode off with a spring to his step and whistling a tune.

They looked at each other and smiled, then Ryder said, 'I'd better go and rescue our picnic basket from the ants.'

Now the drama was over Adele felt her energy drain from

her and her hands began to shake. 'I'm not hungry. Perhaps you could take me home.'

Two strides brought him within arm's length. Drawing a small flask from his hip pocket he tipped a little into the lid and handed it to her. 'Drink.'

'What is it?'

'Medicinal brandy; toss it down.'

'You've got a remedy for everything, and it's the same one.' She drank it down anyway.

The liquor was strong and she swooped in a breath as it hit her insides like a hot coal. 'Come here,' he said, and he drew her against him. Tightening his arms when she struggled he pulled her head to rest gently on his shoulder. 'Stop treating me like a criminal and relax for a minute or two until you stop shaking. You'll soon feel better.'

And that was a problem. Here in his arms, his breath a warm caress against her forehead, she felt safe . . . but she knew the feeling wouldn't last. How could it?

'What do you make of Luke Ashburn, Del?' Ryder said after a while, and he twisted a ringlet round his finger and watched it spring back to its place. He seemed preoccupied by the action.

'He's self-opinionated.'

There was a moment or two of reflective silence. 'It seems to me that Ashburn has the need to prove himself, if not to others, then to himself. I can handle that. Anything else?'

'No, except . . .' She hesitated and looked up at him. 'Something is odd. We grew up here but I can't remember him and I've never heard his name mentioned before. Have you?'

'There's a lot I don't remember from childhood and Luke Ashburn intrigues me. I feel as if I should know him.' He dropped a kiss on her mouth, casual yet possessive in its claim, dismissing Ashburn with, 'Perhaps he attended the same university.'

'Curious then, that he suddenly appeared when we were absent from the district.'

'Yes . . . Did you miss me when we were apart, Del?'

He'd changed tack swiftly and his voice was so sympathetic

she was caught unaware. 'Every minute of every day, and when I read that you'd died I wanted to do the same. He . . . Edgar Pelham taunted me about it. If it hadn't been for Sarah—'

She clapped a hand across her mouth. She'd nearly told him about the beating – the one that had killed Ryder's child. Edgar had been drunk and in a foul mood. He'd set about her in such a cold-blooded fashion. Sarah had been a child then and when Sarah had intervened Edgar had thrown her against a wall. The pair of them had fled from the house and had crept into the bushes to lick their wounds. There, sheltered by a bush on some waste ground, Ryder's child, a casualty of the violence, had slipped from her. He'd resembled a little wax doll, and she and Sarah had buried his tiny body and said a prayer over him.

Losing Ryder's child, especially in such a cruel, deliberate manner, had almost broken Adele's spirit. As for Sarah, she'd respected her father until then, but his cruelty had changed that relationship into a fearful one on her part, though it had served to bring Adele and Sarah closer together.

Adele gazed at him, annoyed that she'd allowed him to coax her into talking about her time with Edgar . . . something she didn't want to remember. 'Damn you, Ryder.'

'I was damned the moment you left me at the altar. You ruined my present, and trampled on my plans for my future, as though I had no feelings and they meant nothing.'

'You should despise me.'

He turned, his smile slow and twisted, so it didn't quite reach his blue eyes, which observed her as though she was something that crawled in the mud. 'What makes you think I don't?'

Her heart sank. 'So why . . .?'

Picking up her hand he kissed her palm. 'I want revenge. I want things to be as they were between us and for you to love me all over again, my Del, but I will never get that . . . and then . . .'

'Then?' she said with some sort of dread.

'I'll deal with you as you dealt with me . . . as though I was nothing to you.'

'You were never that.'

'I felt as though I was.' His conversation changed direction. 'But let's not argue, when we were getting on so well. I'll race you to the picnic basket, the winner gets a kiss.'

'What does the loser get?'

He grinned. 'I'll give you one guess.'

She didn't feel like playing games. 'I'm not hungry and I want to go home.'

'You're just jittery, but I'll take you home if that's what you want.'

She nodded. He helped her into the cart and turned them round, stopping to pick up the basket when they reached the bend in the road.

He placed it in the cart, and then climbed up to sit next to her. Taking her face in his hands he kissed her tenderly and thoroughly, and she didn't protest.

'I thought you'd played enough games.'

'The kiss wasn't a game. It was the start of your punishment.'

Her thigh pressed intimately against his as they moved on and the air seemed to whisper and weave around them like thousands of threads being drawn into a cocoon of silk.

Sweet punishment indeed! She placed her head against his shoulder and sighed. 'You've never been vindictive, Ryder.'

His smile spread like butter and he leaned in to nip the lobe of her ear. 'There's always a first time.'

Eight

When they arrived back at Duck Pond Cottage, Adele's aunts came out to admire the new rig and make a fuss of Daisy.

'What a dear creature,' Patience said to Prudence.

'The ass or the earl?'

The sisters exchanged a laugh.

Ryder managed to smile, though he didn't feel much like smiling and his reply was almost automatic. 'Whichever beast you favour, you flatter me, ladies.'

He was thinking that his copse had been a busy place today. Walking on his land and taking a couple of rabbits, or even a trout from his stream, he could tolerate. But when those same people stole commercial quantities or took pot shots that placed the lives of others at risk he must put a stop to it.

To give Ashburn his due, the shot had been accidental. But someone had fired the first shot, and for whom had it been meant? Adele seemed the most obvious target from the position of the shot – but why?

Ryder realized it was his own fault for neglecting his responsibilities. Instead of running away from home like a whimpering puppy to join the army, he should have killed Edgar Pelham and taken Adele back. Nobody would have blamed him . . . except Adele, perhaps.

The back of his neck prickled. He turned his head slightly and Adele's gaze captured his, like a fly being pulled into a spider's web. For several moments they were joined by a quivering thread of the past, when the perspective of everything they'd ever felt towards each other was recognized with a startling clarity.

One for one . . . They'd been made for one another.

She gave a tiny gasp, as if she'd taken his heart into her hands and experienced the beating core of him. The clatter of voices around them faded and he smiled. Could they start all over again . . . forget her past? He had a strong urge to kiss her, to take her home and make love to her over and over again.

She must have read his mind, for the heat in her smoky eyes cooled and she turned them away from him. Since when had she learned to reject his approaches with such disdain? He'd played the gentleman today and had attempted to seduce her gently. He'd learned that she responded well to reminders of the past, when they had laughed at the slightest thing together. His plans for seduction had come to nothing . . . all due to the intervention of some poacher with a gun.

Why was he bothering with her when she'd proved her lack of loyalty? He had no answer and was simply following his instinct with some vague feeling that he'd find a way to take his revenge uninterrupted – though what form revenge would consist of he had no idea.

Perhaps he should forget taking revenge, just marry her and make an honest woman out of her.

He grinned when his stomach rumbled and Patience said, 'I know a hungry man when I hear him. I've just made some broth and dumplings, would you like some, my lord?'

He kissed her hand, and, ignoring the fact that he'd recently consumed a pie, said, 'You are the answer to a gentleman's prayer. I'll probably devour the bowl as well.'

The first shot had been fired by someone else, since he'd already had Ashburn in his line of sight. Somebody else had slipped away, and he'd heard a horse. Whose horse?

Oliver Bryson was a good shot, he recalled. If it had been him in the woods, and if he'd been aiming at Adele – he would have killed her!

But why would he want to?

His blood ran cold when he realized how close she'd come. Surely Oliver Bryson didn't hate her to the extent that he'd kill her to be rid of her. Why should he when she'd never done him any harm?

The Manning sisters were bustling about with bowls of broth and dumplings and they were served informally, seated round the scrubbed pine table in the kitchen, like they had when they'd been children.

He was so hungry he could eat several pork pies complete with a crusting of red ants for spice! Adele swallowed only a small portion of the broth. No wonder she was so slender, but attractive all the same. He mused that he was a hungry man in two ways, lacking in sustenance, and without a woman to bed. He didn't know which he needed more.

He must go and see Oliver Bryson, get to the bottom of this affair.

After they'd eaten, he left the coachman at the cottage with instructions to unhitch Daisy's cart, spread the straw and introduce her to her new quarters.

'I'm going to have a look around and will be back before too long,' he said, and left swiftly.

Ryder took the carriage at a fast clip, but to no avail. There was no sign of anything or anyone sinister between Brackenhurst and Poole. There was a man and woman on a cart, a child sleeping against the woman's breast. They stopped to pick up an old man in a faded brown robe with a cowl concealing his face. His ageing back was bent over a stick.

The day had a slow pace to it despite his personal haste. It filled him with the need to idle along and enjoy the feel of the sun on his back. There was a hum of bees in the air, and he'd been looking forward to his sojourn with Adele at the pool.

He passed the rectory and a little further on found Oliver Bryson's horse munching on the long grass amongst the grave-stones in the churchyard. It whickered a greeting when Ryder ran his hand over him. The beast's hide was warm enough to alert Ryder to the fact it had been ridden recently. Its hooves were muddy, which meant nothing in the country since the ground was often muddy.

Oliver Bryson's rifle leaned against a sunny corner. It was empty and the barrel retained warmth.

Shading his eyes from the sun with his hand, Oliver Bryson advanced from the gloomy interior of the church. 'My lord, this is an unexpected surprise.'

'Is it? I rather thought you might be expecting me.'

'I can't think why. You haven't seen my wife anywhere, have you? Mary said she'd organize some of the village women into doing some tasks in the church.'

'I saw Mrs Bryson about two hours ago in the market place.'

'I see . . . I do hope she isn't indulging in mischief.'

'As to that I wouldn't know, Reverend. Your wife was in the dressmaker's establishment when I saw her . . . do women indulge in mischief there?'

Oliver gave a great booming laugh. 'I should imagine they plot mischief for someone from time to time. Will you come in and take a glass of wine with me?'

The cart rumbled by and the reverend called out a greeting to the occupants. The old man was no longer with them. It struck Ryder as odd that a monk would be in the district when there was no monastery to house him – at least, not one that he'd heard of.

'I'd prefer not to. Shall we be straight with each other, Reverend?' Ryder gazed at the man's coat. 'You have a button missing.'

Oliver gazed down at the front of his coat. 'So I do.'

Taking the button from his waistcoat pocket, Ryder held it out to him. 'I found it in my copse.'

'Thank you . . . they were a gift from my wife. I lost it some time ago when I was tracking a fox that had raided the chicken coop. Is there anything else, my Lord?'

'I was taking Mrs Pelham home from the market earlier and we were shot at. The ball missed her by a fraction and lodged in the donkey cart.'

He raised an eyebrow, but looked not in the least bit worried. 'Oh . . . was the woman injured?'

'She was not.' After the space of a heartbeat Ryder added, 'Neither was I.'

'It sounds as if you suspect me, my lord?'

'Your horse is muddy and your gun barrel is warm,' he pointed out.

'My rifle is in the sun. Besides . . . I shot a couple of rabbits earlier.'

'May I see them?'

'You may not. A lad came begging. He was hungry and said his mother was sick. I gave the rabbits to him.'

'Does the lad have a name?'

'I should imagine so . . . let me think a while.'

Mary Bryson sauntered from the church. Her cheeks were pink and she was breathing heavily as she took her husband's arm. 'I'm sorry I'm late.'

Ryder afforded the woman a nod. 'Mrs Bryson.'

It was obvious to Ryder that he wasn't going to get a truthful answer from the reverend. Still he pushed on. 'Can you think a little faster?'

'Ben . . . I think he was called Ben.'

'There would be several lads called Ben in the district.'

'So I imagine.'

Ryder gave him a blunt, 'And I imagine you know them all.'

Bryson's glance came up to his. 'Of course I don't. Have you finished your interrogation of me?'

'I'm here to advise you to keep your nose out of my affairs. You have neither the authority or the right to condemn Mrs Pelham.'

'You know the reason . . . the Pelham name was an embarrassment to both the Lawrence and the Madigan families. The incident will never be forgotten, you know.'

He was probably right, but Ryder wasn't going to allow him the satisfaction of knowing that. 'It might be if you allow it to rest.'

'You never seem to learn from your mistakes. Damn it man, I *am* your heir and have your welfare at heart. You'd gone off to fight without a word. That was totally irresponsible. You could have died at any time.'

'I had no intention of dying and I did leave a will.'

'Giving your private fortune to the Lawrence woman.'

When Mary opened her mouth and snorted, Bryson gave her a warning look. She shut it again.

'The house, land and title would have gone to you automatically. You may not have a fortune, Reverend, but you are not impoverished by any means and you have a high standing in the district. Eventually you'll become a bishop. Also, we do not share a family name so why would you have felt shame?'

Bryson exploded. 'That is what caused most of the trouble. I was quite willing to leave my calling as a missionary and adopt the family name of Madigan, so it would have been clear who was the legatee. By the time I got here the magistrate had ruled in the squire's favour. It was an insult. I'm your heir, your family. I was trying to protect and nurture you until you became a man.'

'You seem to bear a lot of resentment towards me, considering I had no say in who brought me up. And that was nothing to do with Adele. Considering your dislike of her, surely you must think Mrs Pelham did me a favour by jilting me.'

'A pity you went haring off like a dog with its tail on fire, instead of facing up to your loss like a man. That Lawrence girl proved to be as shallow as I told you she'd be.'

'I'm beginning to believe you wished I had died in India, so the estate would be yours. Surely you have enough money of your own without adding mine to it. I've inspected the books. It appears that you took it upon yourself to increase the rents until the less affluent tenants could no longer afford them. Repairs were ignored, though charged and paid for. That is an act of fraud, my friend. When Adele's father, Squire Lawrence died you contacted his heir to ensure that Ashburn bought the estate off him cheaply, even while knowing his daughter was still alive and might benefit.'

'She wouldn't have inherited anything. The squire had disowned her, as his will indicated.' The man's cheek mottled. 'I won't be taken to task like this, Ryder. You know damned well I was acting on your behalf, as I have always done in your absence. May I remind you that I'm your only blood relation. Your great-great-grandfather and mine suckled from the same teat.'

'As you constantly remind me.'

There was an aggrieved note in Oliver Bryson's reply. 'However thin that blood is I gave up my living and came running when you were orphaned.'

So this was what the angst was all about. 'I was happy living with the Squire Lawrence's family. Our fathers were friends. Adele's father treated me as a son and raised me to be responsible for Adele. I was her protector and friend, and I still am.'

Bryson stared at him, his eyes reflecting his anger. They bothered Ryder not at all. So the reverend had been thwarted in his bid for control of the Madigan estate. That was no reason to place the blame on Adele. It was due to vanity, nothing else.

Gently, he told him, 'Of late I have reflected how cruel an action it was for Edgar Pelham to remove Adele from the two men who loved her most, and bring about her ruin. The result was that he broke her father's heart, as well as mine. The more I think on it the more unlikely a liaison between them sounds. Adele had only met Edgar Pelham a couple of times. He was another of your wife's relatives, was he not? I gave him employment. He repaid that by taking off with my fiancée, a woman he hardly knew. There's something odd about that, as if it were planned in advance.'

Husband and wife exchanged a glance, and then the reverend

shrugged. 'I thought something about him didn't quite ring true. He had a bullying manner at times, and a way of looking at you that was quite intimidating.'

Mary Bryson sprang to life. 'She flirted with him, and got what she deserved.'

'Do be quiet, Mary. You've caused enough trouble.'

'She was just a girl, Mrs Bryson. Didn't you flirt at that age?'

There came an emphatic no from Mary and her hands went to her hips. 'Adele Lawrence was blatantly immodest. She enticed men with her pretty smiles and manners, and deserved what she got if you ask me.'

'Enough! If you can't talk sensibly I suggest that you go inside.'

But it seemed that Mary wasn't going to miss this showdown, and although her face took on a sulky expression she fell quiet.

Ryder said, 'I can almost guarantee that Adele wouldn't have left me without a word. The sadness in her eyes tells me that is not the truth. Something else happened. She's suffered, and I can't get to the bottom of it.' He asked abruptly, 'Did you have a hand in her downfall?'

An aggrieved sigh erupted from Oliver Bryson. 'Certainly not . . . this is maudlin rubbish! The woman doesn't know what loyalty is. Her father disowned her, and if you respected him as much as you say then you must also respect his judgement. Adele Pelham was an empty-headed young woman who was lacking in morals – and probably still is.'

'Talking about any woman that way does you no credit, Reverend Bryson. She's done you no harm yet you vilify her name.'

'And you are a bigger fool now than you were then. Had I been allowed to raise you instead of Squire Lawrence being appointed, you would now have more backbone.'

That was a punch below the belt, and it hurt, but the army had hardened Ryder to a certain extent, and he wasn't going to back down now. 'It was my father's wish that Squire Lawrence take over my care. Equally, had the reverse applied my father would have taken Adele under his wing. Our parents had been friends since childhood.'

'The pair were two of a kind.'

'In what way?'

Oliver Bryson closed his mouth in a tight line, as if to keep a piece of information from leaking out. 'I have nothing more to say to you at this point and refuse to argue any more over that . . . *woman*. Good day, my lord.'

'It's a pity Edgar Pelham isn't still alive so I could shake the answer out of him. But I'll get to the bottom of it, and if anything happens to Mrs Pelham before I do I'll raise Cain to find out the culprit, for I will not have the Madigan estate embroiled in a vendetta.'

'How dramatic and noble of you,' the churchman sneered. 'Edgar Pelham is now at the bottom of the sea and you offer sustenance to his fancy woman and his daughter under your roof. How very ironic.'

'My protection applies to Miss Pelham, too. The girl was an innocent bystander and I won't have either of them pressured.'

'You're being duped. The woman senses your feelings and is acting on them. She probably staged the whole thing to win your sympathy, but then, you never could see beyond the end of your nose where she's concerned. Perhaps you should ask her what happened to the infant she was carrying when you left here . . . and before you ask me, their former maid, Bridget, told Mary. A little weight on the waist, food fancies, and sickness in the morning, all the signs of impending motherhood, I'm given to understand.'

Not by one flicker of an eyelash did Ryder give away the shock he felt, though his jaw clenched and his fingers curled into fists.

Adele had been carrying an infant? Thoughts buzzed in his head like marauding wasps. His first thought, *who had fathered the child?*

He had!

His second thought arrived – and the one he'd rather believe in since it absolved him of responsibility. *Perhaps it was just gossip.*

He shrugged. 'Such symptoms could be caused by gripe, surely.'

'Oh, there was another sign . . . the absence of womanly inconveniences.'

Womanly inconveniences! He drew on his limited knowledge of the monthly event, gleaned mostly from talk around the campfires. When they weren't discussing strategy or gambling, the soldiers usually discussed the whys and wherefores of women, from mothers to lovers. He remembered someone giving a chuckle and saying, 'My wife gets it the wrong way round when I'm home. It's a convenient excuse for the woman and a damned inconvenient one for the man.'

'That Pelham girl is a sly little puss. Engage someone to interrogate her. The retired magistrate, Henry Flemming, will soon get down to the truth of it.'

'There seems to be a shortage of truth hereabouts.'

'Not if another man had fathered it.'

The possessiveness Ryder had felt towards the child vanished, replaced by caution. He wanted to hit Oliver Bryson for besmirching Adele's name on the say so of a maid. He had a good mind to hunt down the maid called Bridget, who he remembered as being tall, thin and pious, and interview her himself. But perhaps not, because Adele would tell him when the time was right. He was sure of it.

A baby! Was it his infant?

'There is altogether too much tale-tattling. My own death was wrongly reported.'

'Ah yes . . . the snake and the hermit's cave in India. It may interest you to know I held a memorial service to speed your soul on its journey. Come, come, my lord, most likely the event was a fabricated tale. Maidservants, especially unmarried Irish ones, have overactive imaginations and loose tongues.'

'On the contrary. My own demise was reported in an army journal. They apologized . . . just a couple of lines in an obscure corner. How did you discover the manner in which I *expired*?'

'Stephen Tessler told me.'

'Was that when you decided to take over my affairs and have me declared dead?'

'We put the wheels in motion then, yes. Stephen wanted

to wait, though personally I wanted to get the legalities over and done with. He was uncomfortable with the notion that he was solely responsible for your fortune and decisions regarding it. I was able to get myself appointed as a joint trustee. I understand from Stephen that you'd prefer not to share a financial adviser.'

'I hope he has recommended another as able as he.'

'He has.' Bryson sounded sullen.

'It's nothing personal, Reverend, unless you wish to make it so. My estate requires a competent financial adviser, which it has in Stephen, and it needs a good manager. Both need to be efficient and loyal. By the way I've just hired your wife's nephew, Luke Ashburn, for the manager's position.'

Colour came and went in Oliver's face and he looked shocked. 'But . . . why hasn't he informed me?'

'He hasn't had the time, and perhaps he doesn't feel inclined. As you once told me, Luke Ashburn has a mind of his own. He's also ambitious. For his own sake, right now I imagine he'll be contemplating where his loyalties must lie. Being a charity case doesn't always sit well on some men's shoulders, especially when they're reminded of it.'

'I will warn you, my lord. If you decide to wed that woman then it won't be in *my* church.'

Had Oliver Bryson always been so overbearing? Yes . . . but Ryder had matured over the past few years. Did Bryson think he'd wed Adele, after what had happened? Obviously. Ryder himself wouldn't rule it out. But would Adele accept him for a husband, when she offered only reluctance to any personal advance he made?

Was it entirely possible that somebody had prevented her from getting to the church that day?

An infant . . . a careless seed sown in a moment of passion! Judge not that ye be judged. One for one.

He should have considered a consequence such as an infant before. Adele had been an innocent, and so young. He'd taken advantage of that.

He wished Hal were still there to talk to as he dragged his thoughts back into line. 'Need I remind you that, as the earl of the Madigan estate I have the right to appoint the church living to whomsoever I believe deserves it? You are bound by its dictates while it provides you with a generous income.'

'You wouldn't put me out to grass . . . I'm your heir.'

Gently, Ryder administered the coup de grâce. 'What my estate does not need is a clergyman or his wife interfering in Madigan affairs, whether it be for public or personal reason. Madigan House is my home. I was born there. A little humility on your part wouldn't go astray, Reverend, I would suggest that from now on you confine yourself to weddings, funerals and christenings, and you keep your sermonizing for those in need of moral support.'

Oliver's mouth opened, then shut again, as though he'd thought better of what he'd been about to say.

Ryder pushed further. 'You are here to serve the parishioners, not to judge whether they are deserving of your administration. Word of mouth can work two ways. It would be a shame if it got back to your bishop.'

Alarm filled Oliver's eyes. 'You wouldn't go that far, surely. It would ruin me.'

'I'm aware of the ramifications and I know you have ambitions regarding the diocese . . . and the Madigan estate itself. Don't pin your hopes on the Madigan inheritance. My intention is to wed and produce a family. I will add that if anything untoward happens to Adele or her family I will run you out of town, and will probably run you through as well. And if anything happens to me, Hal Stover will pursue the matter to the utmost end, and with the power of the law behind him. Now, sir . . . do you still consider me lacking in backbone?'

'It was simply a hasty and unfortunate choice of words, for which I offer an apology.'

'As for that, Reverend, you have always been silver-tongued. I don't trust you enough to accept that apology. Best then that you get to your knees and allow your conscience to consult with its maker. You would benefit from having a little humility. Pride goes before a fall, sir, does it not.'

Looking anything but humble, Oliver Bryson said, 'As you say, my lord.'

As Ryder's adversary and his nagging wife stalked back into

the church and closed the door firmly behind them, Ryder was reassured to know that he'd live, even if with regrets.

A baby, he thought, trying to get a grasp on the notion again. A moment later he quietly asked himself, 'so what happened to the infant?'

Nine

Events of the day had shaken Adele.

Ryder's manner towards her on parting had been remote, as though he had something else occupying his mind.

He nodded briefly to her, using the formal address as he inclined his head. 'Mrs Pelham.' Then to her aunts, 'Many thanks for your hospitality.'

Adele gazed at her aunts after he'd gone, her heart filled with warmth for them. 'I'm sorry to be such a nuisance.'

The pair exchanged a smile, then Patience said, 'Any trouble has been cancelled out by the sheer pleasure of having you here and knowing you're still alive. You were away for such a long time, Adele, and we waited and waited for word from you.'

'Yes, I should have let you know I was well. It was unforgivable of me, and I have no excuse since I knew you'd be worried. It was difficult, you see . . . writing letters without him knowing . . . and finding someone to convey them back to England when I was not allowed a penny of my own with which to buy notepaper . . . or even a pencil.' She bit down on her lip, not wanting to reveal too much.

'Oh, we imagined you'd have a plausible excuse. Were you happy with him . . . that awful man who stole you away from us?'

It was obvious they'd been hurt by her lack of communication. She'd never been in a position to discuss the affair with her aunts and this was the first time they'd approached her with a question. She wished she could tell them everything, but she couldn't . . . not after all this time. She also couldn't answer the question with a lie. 'No . . . I was not happy, but I had Sarah to love.'

Prudence looked up from her needlework, her eyes shrewd. 'He treated you badly, didn't he?'

'I'd prefer not to talk about him, Aunt, I'm trying to forget it ever happened. You should know I would never have abandoned Ryder on our wedding day unless there was no other choice.'

'Are you telling us that man forced you?' Patience gazed at her sister with horror in her eyes. 'Our poor, dear niece, I told you so, Prudence. I said she wouldn't have run away without a word. Wait till I tell Mary Bryson. That will show her what comes of spreading all those rumours.'

'No!' Adele almost shouted, horrified. 'This is my private business. If you tell anyone it will shame me.'

'That nice young man who loved you was badly treated and became a laughing stock. Your father couldn't hold his head up.'

'Yes, I know, but Papa wouldn't listen to my explanation. He condemned me without a hearing and threw me out. That hurt me, and it hurt him, but I cannot blame him.'

'And the earl . . . don't you owe the dear man an explanation? He abandoned his duty here and left, his pride in tatters.'

'I cannot face the earl with my problems.'

'Your problems became his by default. If you have any affection left towards him—'

Adele stood, gazing bleakly from one to the other. 'I have loved Ryder Madigan since we were children together. Nothing can change that. Do you think my desertion of him was that simple? Were I to relate the circumstance and the consequence of that act, it would only prove to be as big a burden to him and to you as it is to me. Let sleeping dogs lie, I pray you. I need to retire now . . . I'm weary.'

'Yes . . . you rest, my dear. Everything will seem better in the morning.'

Nothing would ever be better. If they breathed one word . . . if it got out that she'd killed someone, then the authorities would put her in prison. They might even hang her.

Somebody knew . . . they had spoken Edgar's name. A

shudder racked her and she pulled her shawl tighter as she felt
the colour leach from her face. Somebody had been hidden
in the bushes, watching her, waiting for an opportunity to
catch her alone. Had the shooter been on the ship and witnessed
what she'd done?

She must make an effort to find their travelling trunks and
also the missing deeds. 'Believe me, the earl is better off without
me, and so are you,' she said.

Patience patted her arm. 'There, there, my dear, you are
talking utter nonsense. As it upsets you we shall speak of it no
longer, unless it's your wish to do so. We're not going to do
anything that will lose you again, are we, Prudence?'

'Indeed not.'

But Adele wondered how long her loquacious relatives would
be able to hold their tongues against the snide remarks.

That night the dream came.

The water was cold and above it Adele could see an arm holding
a lantern. The light's gleam made her feel safe, but then it began to
grow dim and she was beset by unease.

'Help!' she called, her mouth releasing a stream of bubbles.

There was a reflection of a face in the lamp. Its smile was loath-
some. 'Please save me,' she begged.

The image laughed when her mouth filled with water and she
began to choke. She panicked and tried to thrash her arms, but she
was tightly wrapped in ropes. With a muted whisper in case others
overheard her, she pleaded, 'I don't want to die, Edgar . . . don't
kill me . . .'

'Wake up, Adele!'

Arms came round her, supporting her. 'You're having a bad
dream. It's all right. I'm here.'

Blurry-eyed with sleep Adele clung tightly to the girl. 'I
thought that dream had faded over the past two months. Thank
goodness it's you . . . don't let Edgar kill me.'

She was rocked back and forth. 'My father can't hurt us any
more.'

So why was she still frightened when Sarah seemed to have
no fear left in her?

Gently pushing Sarah's arms aside she swung her legs out

of bed and donned a faded blue velvet robe, hugging it to her. It was a relic of her past when life had been happier. She'd been the same age as Sarah was now, full of the joys of living and innocently looking forward to her future as Ryder's wife.

The future she'd envisaged had never eventuated. In a short time, and because she'd been given no choice, she'd become a slave to a man with an unpredictable and vicious temper, and an elder sister to a small, sad girl, who'd clung to her. On the spur of the moment she'd taken a life . . . but Edgar refused to die. He was punishing her through her dreams.

She sighed and put him aside. She must go through her clothing, for the aunts had kept the garments clean and undamaged, in good faith that she'd return to wear them. Some of them would be perfect for the blossoming Sarah. 'I'm sorry I woke you so early, Sarah. I'll make us some tea, then we'll sit and talk like we used to.'

She shook off the clinging vestiges of the nightmare. It seemed there was no end to the horror story that was Edgar Pelham.

Sarah smoothed a stray lock of hair back from her forehead. 'You rest and I'll make the tea. I put the kettle on the stove earlier when I let Gypsy and the cats out. They'll be sitting on the windowsill looking aggrieved and wanting to come in again. They're frightened they'll miss something.'

Beyond the window the sky was on the turn with pale brushstrokes of pink and gold. It promised to be a fine day. The high-sailing moon was not quite a ghost. The birds were up already, singing a joyous song. On the pond the ducks sedately circled and Adele looked forward to the appearance of some ducklings. She experienced a sense of calm, of contentment tinted with some regret. Life would have been so different if her wedding to Ryder had gone ahead.

From her window she could see the grey stones of the church tower above the distant trees. Her parents and grandparents were buried there, and there she'd been christened. Adele Jessica Lawrence. There, she and Ryder would have become man and wife.

She must visit her father's grave someday soon, make her

peace with him. If she ever wed it would not be in the Brackenhurst church. Her memories were too poignant.

A cart filled with gravel and sand trundled past, led by a man with a shovel over his shoulders. His donkey nodded with each plodding step, his eyes half closed and sleepy. Ryder had made good his promise to have the holes in the road repaired.

He'd be lonely in his big empty house, for he'd always liked company. He would miss Hal and he would be planning his future without her in it.

Sarah returned, accompanied by the retinue of dog and cats, who arranged themselves comfortably on the bed. She had used the pretty china tea service that had been a favourite of Adele's mother, with its pattern of yellow roses. She placed it carefully on the table and poured out the tea. There were oat biscuits on a plate.

'What plans do you have for today, Sarah?'

'Lord Madigan wants me to start making out the invitations for the harvest ball. Even though he hasn't got a harvest this year he said the ball was a tradition in his father's time.'

'Yes, it was. Ryder and I used to sit on the upper stair and watch the dancers below in the hall. The orchestra was seated on the landing, and the morning room became the supper room for the night. Sometimes we used to copy the dancers.'

'I was hoping to help arrange it, but Mrs Betts has done it before, and said she can manage. I was just to do the invitations, since the earl had specially asked for me. There's a long list to be addressed, over a hundred people . . . imagine that. I shall have to use my very best handwriting.'

Picking up the sides of her robe Sarah twirled around, her honey eyes alight with excitement and the matching ripples of her hair flying. She flopped into the chair opposite Adele, out of breath and laughing.

Had she ever been that young herself – that happy?

'The staff are going to the spring fair tomorrow and I've been invited to go with them. The earl has some business to do in Poole and will join us there later. Are you going?'

She shook her head. 'No, I intend to sort out the clothing I left behind. Besides, my aunts will take the donkey cart and there's not enough room for three of us.'

'You could come with me and the house staff in the Madigan coach.'

'It will be crowded as it is. No, I would rather stay at home . . . I have the beginnings of a headache.'

Sarah poured the tea then gazed at her from under her eyelids, her mouth slightly pursed. 'How convenient. You can't hide yourself away from the earl for ever.'

Astonished, for Sarah didn't usually try to advise her, Adele protested, 'I'm doing no such thing. You have to realize that my childhood attachment to the earl is no longer valid. I have my life to live and the earl has his. We have outgrown each other.'

'Not while we daren't mention your names to the other without a reaction.' Sarah's eyes began to shine and she sighed. 'It's so romantic.'

Adele laughed. 'Either you've been listening to gossip, or a hive of bees has taken up residence in your head.'

'Everyone is talking about you and the earl.'

Her smile faded, like a cloud over the sun. 'Then you must be made aware that not all gossip is based on fact.'

Sarah kissed her cheek. 'I know more than you think, since I was there and witness to my father's cruelty. Now he's dead I have a sense of freedom. One thing I can't understand is why you married him in the first place.' She lowered her voice then shocked Adele by saying, 'He killed my mother when I was little. He pushed her down some stairs and there was a cracking noise. She went all floppy.'

Feeling as if the world had stood still, and all the moisture had been sucked from her body, Adele's voice was barely distinguishable when she said, 'You were small. You must have misunderstood. Memories can play tricks, and I expect she lost her footing and slipped.'

Sarah shook her head. 'I remember it as clear as day. My father said he'd kill me too if I told anyone. Now he can't. I'm telling you now because I know you'll understand. I often remember him hurting you. That time when you lost the baby . . . we were in Boston trying to find some relatives. He punched you and said nobody would employ a woman who was with child, and he knew it wasn't his. There was blood . . . lots of it and I was fearful you might die.'

Of course it wasn't Edgar's infant. He was the type of man who found women unattractive. She'd been thankful for that small mercy.

'The baby was as small as a doll. You cried and said his name was Ryder. We dug a hole with our hands and you tore a strip from your chemise to wrap him in and pulled a little wisp of his hair out to remember him by.'

Sarah's recall was almost perfect, but Adele didn't want to reprise her past. 'Oh . . . my dear, I'm sorry you remember such a dreadful time. We must keep these things to ourselves because people can't understand the circumstances unless they were there.' Adele drew Sarah into her arms and hugged her tight. 'You mustn't blame yourself over your mother's death. You were too young to do anything to help her, and it wasn't your fault. It's all in the past and nothing good can come of it now. Your father has been punished.' And by her own hand. She experienced an unseemly twinge of satisfaction.

'I just wanted you to know you can confide in me, since I was there, and I'll never do or say anything that will harm you.'

And since they were exchanging confidences, Adele said, 'And I want you to know that I do love Ryder, and I always will. Something happened to prevent our union and now it can never be.'

'It was because of my father, wasn't it? But he's dead now, so you could still marry the earl.'

'It's not possible, Sarah. Gentlemen of Lord Madigan's rank apply high standards to the choice of a wife, and I no longer meet them because I've attracted scandal.'

'Now I'm growing up, I can see how events happened more clearly. My father was a violent man, and you took the punishment for both of us, even though you were as scared as I was by his rage.'

'He was violent, but he's dead now. I got something rather lovely and lasting from it, and that's you, my love. Now . . . I don't want to talk about him any more.'

Sarah kissed her cheek. 'When he brought you home to be a mother to me it was the best thing he'd ever done. I love you.'

For Adele, with this one exception named Sarah, it had been the worst thing. 'I know you do . . . and I love you too. Now, let's put that aside else you'll have me in tears. I have a surprise for you. See that trunk in the corner, there is one or two gowns on the top that I thought might suit you. They're a bit too young for me now. Try them on; one of them will be just the thing to wear at the fair.'

Within a few moments Sarah was dressed in a gown of soft cream with a smattering of dark pink rosebuds. Cream lace decorated the hem and there was a velvet bodice in the same colour as the rosebuds, in case the wind grew chill.

The girl gazed at herself in the long mirror, smiling. 'It's so pretty.'

'You look lovely, Sarah. You might find a little straw bonnet with pink ribbon trim in that box on the shelf on the shelf.'

The gowns had been carefully wrapped in tissue paper. It was her aunts' work. They would have washed and repaired each gown before storing them.

Sarah pulled out the next gown and shook it out. It was silk and the colour of bluebells − or of Ryder's eyes! The overskirt was a drift of delicate lace and it had little puff sleeves. There was a fragrance of lavender lingering about it.

Adele stared at the gown. She'd forgotten how beautiful it was. Ryder had sent her a string of pearls to wear with it. Pearls were the gemstones for June and signified modesty, chastity and purity.

The gown had never been worn. It was virginal. It confronted her . . . mocked her. Perhaps it had not found her worthy of the role she'd expected to take on as Ryder's wife after they'd become lovers − perhaps it had been right.

'That's beautiful,' Sarah said in awe.

Adele's voice was husky with the emotion she felt. 'Not that one.'

Sarah said with some alarm, 'Is your throat sore?'

'No . . . it's the dust.' She took the gown, and carefully folded it back into its bed of tissue, saying briefly, 'That's not a day gown.'

'Is it for a ball? I'm longing to go to one. Do tell me about it.'

Adele unfolded the next package, revealing a white gown with a muslin overskirt, and with just the right amount of frills and flounces to satisfy the taste of a young woman of Sarah's age.

'This one should suit you.'

Sarah fell on the gown with delight, holding it against her as she twirled around the room.

Adele sat at the window and sipped her tea while Sarah went through the trunk, picking out this and that and asking her opinion.

One of the cats snuggled into her lap and purred, the dog snored at her feet and the ducks on the pond quacked and squabbled. The sun erupted into the morning in a fiery ball of orange glory that turned the landscape into gold. She felt oddly contented. It wouldn't be unpleasant if she didn't marry, and spent the rest of her life here.

When Sarah went off with her pile of garments and accessories, and with a big smile on her face, Adele took out the lacy blue gown again. Pulling it on she gazed at herself in the mirror. The bride it had been made for had been a little bit bigger then, for it now hung loosely. She slid a hand into the pocket and her fingers closed around a small package. Inside, a lace-edged handkerchief lovingly hugged a string of pearls.

The pearls had once belonged to Ryder's mother. He'd given them to her to wear on their wedding day. It was said that pearls were the tears of the moon. Their glow was a little tarnished now, as though keeping them in darkness had dimmed their light. She must clean them.

There was a note.

For my love on our wedding day.

Dearest Ryder, she thought, she must give them back to him. Taking the gown off, she carefully packed it away again.

Ten

Adele said, 'The day promises to be fair. Why are you going to Madigan House so early, Sarah?

'They might forget me if they leave early.' A trifle self-conscious in her pretty gown, Sarah asked, 'Do I look all right?'

'Perfectly lovely, dear,' Patience said. 'Don't you think so, Prudence?'

'If we had a Queen of the May, Sarah would be the one chosen. Keep your bonnet on so the sun doesn't ruin your beautiful skin. Are you ready now, dear?'

'Yes, Aunt Prudence.'

'Off you go, then . . . scat!'

Adele's aunts were still flitting around and fussing after Sarah had gone.

'Are you sure you don't want to go to the fair? We can squeeze you into the cart,' Patience said.

Adele laughed. She was looking forward to spending a quiet day in her own company. 'Spare a thought for Daisy.'

More seriously Prudence remarked, 'We don't like to leave you here by yourself. You will be careful, won't you?'

'Of course I will. I like being by myself sometimes, and I'll be well guarded. You know how noisy Gypsy becomes if there are strangers about. Then there are the ducks; they see threat in everything that moves. I intend to transplant some cabbage and prepare the ground for the turnips in the kitchen garden. Then I'll make a thorough search for those documents I've mislaid. They can't have just disappeared.'

'You're becoming a hermit, Adele. You're still young, you can't hide yourself away indefinitely, you know.'

Adele smiled, making light of it. 'One day is hardly indefinitely. I'm not hiding . . . I promise. And I need to get the ownership of this cottage established.'

Nevertheless she felt less confident when her aunts had gone.

After she'd picked a few vegetables to last them a few days she picked a bunch of sweet peas to enhance the table. The crumbly dark brown earth accepted her fingers into its warm skin without resistance. The plants would rest there, taking nourishment from the earth until they were strong enough to push through and climb high towards the sky.

Sitting back on her heels, her tears ran unheeded as she thought of her own baby, planted in Boston soil. He'd been undeveloped, his skin as fragile and as translucent as wet tissue paper. He'd hardly been recognizable as an infant, but she'd known him and loved him. Had he felt pain when the blow of a fist had crushed the tiny beat of his heart and his bid for life?

She planted a row of seedlings that she'd bought the week before at the market, thinking that babies needed love. Sarah had needed love. That need had reached into their souls and brought them together. It was still bringing them together, she thought as she made her way back to the house, followed by the dog. All this time had passed and Sarah had only just felt comfortable enough to tell her about the death of her mother.

Poor Sarah. She must have been shocked beyond measure. But her father was dead now and that had freed her – but while it had freed his daughter Edgar's death had trapped Adele in a cage of her own making, for she could not bring herself to admit such an awful deed. Indeed, sometimes she couldn't remember the crime clearly, as though she'd buried it deep in her memory.

And Ryder was still suffering. Because they'd grown up together their relationship had always been based on love and trust. The adult expression of love had come later. Her rejection of him must have been doubly hurtful.

The cats rubbed against her legs and purred as she inspected a savoury pastry her aunts had left for her in the larder. She would eat it later. She cast a dubious eye over the glass of milk – to help build her strength up, the aunts would have said if they'd been here. She decided she had enough strength for the day.

She poured half into Gypsy's bowl while the other half went into the cats' saucers. They began to lap it up, ears flattened and eyes half closed with the pleasure of it as their tongues raced towards the last drops.

Now, where should she start her search?

It occurred to her suddenly. When she'd left Madigan House she'd knocked the hessian bag onto the floor and the contents had gone everywhere. Ryder had helped to pick them up, but the packages with the documents might have easily slid further under the bed than they'd cared to look.

And Ryder and his staff were at the fair!

Her conscience warned: it's not right to enter into someone's house without permission.

She wouldn't be breaking in. She still had a key in her dressing-table drawer, which had been as she'd left it.

Times have changed.

She sighed, exasperated. 'For goodness' sake, don't be so prissy. It's not as if you intend to steal anything, you're just looking for some property you left behind. You'll be back within an hour or so, and Ryder will be none the wiser.'

Snatching up a carrot she slid through the door before she could change her mind and, with Gypsy at her heels, she crunched her teeth into it and savoured the fresh taste of a couple of bites.

A little while later she pushed open the door to Madigan House and stood in a shaft of sunlight illuminating the hall.

To satisfy her conscience she called out a couple of times. Nobody appeared.

She breathed the house in, listening to the silence buzz around her, until the house relaxed and recognized her as a friend. Gypsy sat patiently at her ankle, gazing up at her. Several clocks passed the time of day in different tones of ticks and tocks. Small cracks and snicks made themselves known. The opened door allowed a stream of air inside and dust motes flurried and whirled about in a beam of light. When they were children Ryder had told her they were sun angels dancing just for her.

She closed the door behind her, left her carrot head on the tray in the hallstand and headed for the staircase. Decades of ups and downs had left their mark on the banister rail that now resembled a roll of toffee. It had been shaped by the dozens of hands and aristocratic behinds that had polished it to a high gloss.

Ryder had taught her to slide safely down the final length when they were children, for they'd made this empty house with its many treasures their playground. He'd stand at the bottom and catch her, or sometimes pretend not to so she giggled and screamed until she was safely in his arms.

Her feet sank into a lush red-and-blue-patterned carpet that took her silently up the risers.

She hesitated at the door of Ryder's room, and then knocked.

Gypsy whined, then nudged at the door. It opened on oiled hinges and he trotted inside and curled up on the rug in front of the fireplace. Not that there was a fire in the grate.

'Ryder, are you in there?' she said, her voice wavering a little with a sudden attack of nerves.

Of course not, otherwise Gypsy would have greeted him. Get on with it. Do!

'It doesn't seem right.'

Oh, for goodness' sake, go home then.

'I might just have a quick look.' Kneeling, she turned her head sideways and flattened her cheek against the floor. The sun didn't penetrate under the bed and she allowed her eyes to adjust to the dim light. There was a piece of folded paper in the corner, where the angle of the leg was, and just out of arm's length. She wriggled further in and took a hold of it.

Downstairs, Ryder entered his home, frowning. The door should have been locked. As he placed his hat on the hallstand he noticed the carrot head. It hadn't had time to dry out.

Gypsy came down the stairs and rolled on his back. The dog had grown used to him now, even though he was very much Adele's dog.

He stroked the animal and smiled. 'So . . . your mistress has summoned up the courage to pay me a visit at long last. Take me to her, then.'

He silently followed the dog up to his room, somewhat surprised that she'd be there. He was confronted by an unexpected vision.

The rounded shape of Adele's delectable derrière!

He took a chair, prepared to enjoy the exhibit, which was draped in a triple tease of jaconet, frothy muslin, and lace with ribbons threaded through.

Getting in was one thing, getting out was another thing altogether, Adele thought. She disturbed a mouse and jumped as it made a run for safety. Gypsy chased after it, yapping noisily. Adele lost her nerve and in her rush to get out from under the bed, where worse creatures might lurk, the back of her gown caught fast on something.

The door picked up a stray draught and quietly closed, the furtive sound raising the hairs on her arm.

Effectively hooked, she muttered, 'A thousand fine curses.'

She wriggled further in, trying to free herself. Her stocking worked its way down her leg.

Something stroked the same leg and she gave a little yelp. *Ghosts?*

'A spider,' she muttered as the creature took a tickling course down the length of her calf – or worse. As she took a swipe at it she wished she'd stayed home.

'Not any old spider, it's me . . . Ryder the spider.'

When he gave a low chuckle she jerked, and the back of her head collided with the wooden slats of the bed above her.

'Ouch!'

He tickled her calf with the feather he held. 'Stop wriggling, then.'

The relief she experienced was enormous. 'Thank goodness it's you.'

His return was as smooth as a cat's purr. 'Yes, my love, thank goodness.'

'Help me out of here please. My gown is caught on a splinter, I think.'

'But you present such a pretty rear end?'

She didn't know whether to laugh, or to snap at him. She did know that she felt extremely foolish and Ryder wouldn't forgo the opportunity to tease her. She appealed to his gentlemanly side. 'Please, Ryder, don't do this to me, I'm embarrassed as it is. And be careful you don't get stuck as well.'

'I could think of worst fates for the two of us.'

So could she.

He folded back the feather bed and light flooded over her through the wooden slats. Why hadn't she thought of something simple like that in the first place?

'It's caught on the waist on my skirt.'

'I see it. It's a bent nail.' She was freed and then her skirt was eased down. He gently pulled on a combination of her skirt and ankles, sliding her out from under the bed with regard to her modesty. He gazed at her after he'd lifted her up, saying nothing, but brushing a dusty cobweb from her hair with his forefinger.

'Before you ask why I was under your bed, I thought my lost papers might have been there,' she said, and she giggled, though a trifle nervously.

'Is that your excuse?'

'Why else would I be here?'

'There used to be two reasons why a woman would be in a man's bedroom uninvited. She might be a servant cleaning it . . . obviously not in this case. Or it could be a large hint to the owner of the room that she finds him fascinating and is trying to attract his interest.'

She snorted, 'If her hint is that obvious his interest isn't worth the effort of gaining. This conversation is ludicrous, don't you think?'

'Absolutely. It seems now that there's a third reason. The lady is looking for the deeds to her house . . . such an unlikely place to look, though, wouldn't you agree?'

'I thought it more than likely at the time of thinking.'

He sighed. 'So did I, and believe me the room has been thoroughly searched. I don't know what the village folk will make of this, though . . . a lady hiding under the earl's bed? She could have done him all sorts of damage.'

'I'm working up to it,' she warned.

He laughed, and his glance darted from her dishevelled hair to her eyes before settling on her mouth like a blue velvet butterfly. 'But I've been remiss. Did you hurt yourself? Is there anything I can kiss better? That little pout perhaps.'

Her little pout let it be known it would enjoy such attention and began to tingle. She ran her tongue over it. 'I'm not playing games, Ryder.'

'Neither am I, but should the opportunity present itself I might be persuaded.' He ran his hands down the contours of her face, a light caress.

She closed her eyes, and, reaching up, took his wrists in her hands to stop his onslaught in her senses. They were firm, well shaped and strongly muscled without being bony. His fingers were long, and sensitive in their touch – gentle. His palms smelled of leather.

Aware of the danger he offered her she opened her eyes. 'We can't do this. I won't allow it.'

'But we're not doing anything yet.'

'Do you intend to try?'

'Of course I do, and may I remind you that I'm stronger than you.' He placed a foot behind her ankle and gently hooked it. She fell backwards onto the tossed feather bed and sank into it, unable to gain any traction to free herself. He joined her there, straddling her body, trapping her with his hands either side.

After a few seconds the warmth of his body spread along the length of hers and her mouth sought his. He was right. He was the stronger, and she had no resistance she cared to offer him. She accepted without protest when his body snuggled against her thighs through her clothes, and when the man in him gave cause to harden and edge into her soft warmth.

He gazed into her eyes, watching her reaction to the inroads he was making. Her thighs couldn't hold fast against the steady pressure of his as little by little he gained ground, until finally they relaxed. She closed her eyes, feeling as weak as a kitten.

He walked his fingers up her thigh, taking her skirt with them, and then moved up under it. It seemed as though a fire had been lit under her, and when he gently touched the very core of her she gave a little sob. She didn't want this – not this, with every thread of her loving him and knowing he could never give her what she desired most, except she would be at his beck and call to use.

Any children she bore him would be bastards! Born of love on her part, but bastards all the same . . . like the tiny infant she'd left behind in Boston. How could he deliberately do that to his own offspring?

Opening her eyes, she looked steadily into his, saying nothing.

After a while his expression became one of shame and he rolled to one side. 'I'm sorry, I shouldn't have treated you like that, but couldn't you have flattered me a little by showing some response?'

'Since when have you needed flattery? Now, help me up, please.'

He took her extended arms and pulled her upright. 'You have a barbed tongue, my lady.'

'And you know how to provoke me. Does the sight of a lady's stocking always turn a man's mind to . . . to . . .'

'Loving?' he suggested. 'Quite often.'

Not bothering whether her actions might provoke or not, she pulled up her wrinkled stockings and retied the ribbons. 'You should have turned your face in the other direction, then. I'm going home.'

He blocked the door with his body, his eyes contemplating her through narrowed eyes. The tension in him was palpable. 'Not until I allow you to. There's something you haven't told me, Adele, and I've been putting it off this last few weeks.'

Her blood ran cold for a moment. Had he found out what she'd done? Was that why she hadn't seen him for a while? 'What is it?' she said, half choking on her dread.

'I was told we created an infant between us. Is it true?'

The relief was enormous. *This* she could handle. 'Who told you?'

He didn't answer her question. 'It's true, then?'

She nodded, the anguish of that moment thickening in her throat. She had to tell him about their infant, he deserved that, at least.

'Where is the child? Did you leave him with someone to raise?'

'Would that I could have . . . He arrived much too soon when he had not the strength to take a breath.'

'I did father the child, didn't I . . . you're certain?'

'Who else would have fathered . . .' Her eyes widened. 'No . . . no! Edgar Pelham might have been a cheat, a liar, and a bully, but he was not a man . . . at least, not in that sense of the word.'

She lifted the locket from under her bodice and placed it in his hands. 'Open it.'

Looking mystified, he did as she asked. Facing the miniature of Ryder and kept in place by a smooth oval of glass, a thin swirl of fine, dark hair told its own story.

Ryder inspected it for a short time, and then he gently pressed the locket back in her palm again, his eyes slightly moist. 'Am I to take it that you kept me close to your heart for all this time? I'm flattered. Did our son have a name?'

Bless him for believing her. 'I called him after you. We . . . that is, with Sarah's help I buried him in the place where his little life ended . . . under a tree in Boston. It was a pretty spot but I hated leaving him there by himself.'

'May he rest there in peace, then.' Ryder gave a faint smile. 'Thank you for telling me, I'm sorry, it must have been hard to cope with,' and he drew her into his arms. For a short time she clung to him, the feeling of grief shared uppermost. His breath brushed gently against the top of her head, their hearts beat as one as they shared a moment of sorrow for the infant they'd never known.

Adele drew comfort from being in Ryder's arms, but as well as the comfort there was danger in such sneaking tender awareness. It would encourage her to drop her guard. Ryder would forgive her many things, she knew, but she doubted if he'd want to be associated with a woman who'd committed a horrific crime such as murder.

'I must go home now,' she said.

'I'll take you.'

She didn't argue, and soon, Henry was picking his way through the copse, giving little whickers and grumbles. Ryder's body was warm as she clung to him. The air was humid and the land basked in a haze of its own making. The horse picked up speed when they reached the road that took them to Brackenhurst.

The village was deserted, except for the ducks, seated in the shade of the long grass at the edge of the pond. Somewhere a dog gave a muffled bark as it guarded its master's home. Gypsy answered.

A cloud of midges danced in a frenzy over the pond, which had a timelessness to it, so it seemed to her that time had gone backwards and everything was as it had always been.

Ryder swung his leg over Henry's neck and leaped to the ground, then took her by the waist to bring her down.

She remembered the crumpled scrap of paper she'd found under his bed and took it from her pocket. 'I found this.'

He smoothed it out, smiled, and then kissed her – just a

small one on her forehead. 'Thank you . . . I thought it was safe in my bedside drawer.'

'Is it precious then?'

He mounted, and gazed down at her, his nimble fingers busy folding the paper back into its creases without him looking at it, as though he'd done the same thing many times before.

Her mouth dried when the paper took shape as a boat.

'Yes, it's precious. It's a note from a lady telling me she would love me for ever. I received it the day before we were due to wed.' He kissed the paper boat before sliding it into his waistcoat pocket. 'Odd how you can look for something and when you think you've found it, it still manages to elude you. Love sailed off in a paper boat. The thing is, Del, despite what's happened I think . . . *know* I still love you, and that's causing me problems.'

She hadn't wanted to become a problem to him. If she'd known he was still alive she'd . . .

You would what?

Damn Ryder! And damn that Indian snake for not doing its job properly. She cancelled that thought immediately. How did she know what she'd have done? Mourned for him for ever, she supposed. All the same, she'd never have come back here had she known Ryder was still alive. Why hadn't he just left her to die in the snow?

Adele had no choice but to harden her heart. 'It will do you no good, Ryder. You must forget about me and find someone else.'

'How can I forget you when you walk the same lanes, breathe the same air and live in the beat of my heart? I found you under my bed this day. Tell me it wasn't my imagination, that I'm not going mad.'

'It wasn't and you are not.'

'Tell me you don't love me.'

'I don't love you.'

He tossed that remark aside with a grin. 'You're lying. I know you do.'

'I love you as a sister would. That's the way it must be between us.' She couldn't tell him she adored every beautiful hair on his head. She turned and fled into the cottage, grateful for its safety.

'You don't have to lock me out. If I wanted to gain entry I'd tear the door from its hinges,' he murmured against the panel. 'Once day I might do that. I'll carry you off to my lair and eat you.'

She stifled a giggle, knowing he was capable of doing exactly what he'd said he'd do if she provoked him enough.

She was relieved when she heard Henry clop off. Ryder had left her feeling warm and relaxed.

That's what being in love feels like.

Hugging the thought to herself she curled up on the old couch, dog and cats making themselves comfortable against her. There was something comforting about stroking a cat and feeling its throaty purr vibrating against her fingertips. She gazed drowsily at the light coming through the window and began to drift. Lord, but what a mess her life had become.

She hadn't asked to fall in love, especially not twice as hard and twice as strongly as she had before. There was only one thing she could think of that might eventually resolve matters between them. Hal had said that Ryder wanted a wife and a family. She should leave the district and allow him to fulfil his plans.

Nearly asleep, she thought she heard the sound of a cart, an everyday sound that was somehow reassuring. The gate creaked. Her aunts were home early.

The cats stopped purring, raised their heads and stared at the door. A growl rattled in Gypsy's throat.

There was a knock and Gypsy threw himself from the couch and became a quivering frenzy of barks and snarls that would have done credit to the fiercest of guard dogs. The cats fled to the top of the stairs, where they arched their bodies and tails and watched, poised for further flight should the need arise.

Blood pounding against her eardrums Adele followed after the cats and cautiously positioned herself behind the shadow of a curtain on the landing window.

The ducks quacked and then fell quiet, as though the threat

didn't concern them. The porch roof effectively blocked her vision. The world fell quiet again and waited.

There was a grunt and a scraping noise, as if somebody had tried the door. Thank goodness she'd locked it. All the same she felt uneasy, and her mind jumped from windows to doors in case she'd left any open when she'd gone tearing off to Madigan House.

The gate creaked again, and again came the cacophony of animal warning sounds. This time a Hawthorn tree in full bloom blocked her vision and the smell attracted the bees so the air was filled with a low humming sound. Beyond the lower branches a barely discernible figure in black clicked its fingers. She ducked her head to get a better look, but could only see the man's back.

The cart moved off.

Gypsy stopped his noise and thrust his snout into her hand, cocky that his effort to rout the marauders had succeeded and seeking his reward, the contentment of having his ear fondled.

'I wish I were as brave,' she told him. 'As it is I'm becoming frightened of my own shadow. I can't suspect villainy from every stranger who knocks at the door, can I? Let's go down. I'll share my pasty with you, and then we'll go to the meadow and pick some strawberries so I can make some jam. It would be a shame to waste them.'

She fetched her pasty from the larder. It was made from leftover pastry, meat and vegetables. There was a pie with vegetables for supper. It sat on the marble shelf waiting to be warmed through, and it looked delicious. She'd made an almond tart and a jug of custard for a pudding.

She left a note on the kitchen table so her aunts wouldn't worry about her absence from the cottage if they returned early, and then made sure the larder door was firmly closed against the cats. She locked the back door behind her.

Outside, the air was full of thistle seed, as if thousands of tiny angels had been released to test their wings. Goldfinches darted amongst them, flashes of orange, yellow and brown.

Gypsy yapped somewhere, warning finches and field mice alike of his imminent arrival as well as his whereabouts. The gate was padlocked and she climbed nimbly over its bars and down the other side.

It was a little early for berry picking, but there were enough ripe ones to make a pie with. As Adele worked, her fingers and mouth stained red. The sun ate two hours from the horizon, polishing the sky to bronze. Her back began to ache but she kept working until the small basket was filled to the brim. Slowly she straightened and stretched her back against her hands.

It was late afternoon and the shadows lengthened stealthily along the ground. Gypsy came when she called his name, leaping out of the tall meadow grass and disappearing under it again, as though he was on a spring.

Another movement caught her attention, more subtle. Ryder was leaning on the gate watching them. He blew her a kiss. 'I've come to save you from the curse of the strawberry field.'

'I haven't eaten enough to bring me out in red lumps. What are you doing here?'

'Your aunts have invited me to stay and eat supper with you and they're eager to tell you about the fair.'

She became suddenly aware of herself – aware of her untidy state, of the bonnet with its ribbons undone and her hair, a tangle of curls. When she tried to scrub the berry stains from her mouth with her handkerchief he laughed. 'You'll have to wash your face in the stream. Here . . . pass over your basket while you climb over the gate. You picked quite a few considering it's so early in the year.'

'It's been warm. As for climbing over the gate, I'm a woman. I no longer climb over gates. It's undignified.'

'Then how did you get in when the gate has a padlock, fly?' The corner of his mouth dimpled. 'You won't climb a gate but you hide under the beds of gentlemen instead. A much more dignified pursuit.'

'Oh, you . . . you are aware of the perfectly innocent circumstances of that event.'

'Ah yes . . . but you should have considered the consequences.'

She passed the basket of strawberries through the bars. 'I

gave you no reason to provide me with a consequence. Pray tell me what it is, when it would be your word against mine.'

He ate a handful of fruit before answering, and then set the basket down. He gave her a teasing look. 'Come on . . . climb to the top and give me your hands. In return I won't tell Luke Ashburn that you've stolen the berries from his meadow.'

'But this is my father's—' She shrugged. 'We always used to pick strawberries here, remember?'

'Yes . . . I remember, and blackberries in the autumn. We always used to eat more than we saved.'

'I will send Mr Ashburn a pot of strawberry conserve for his breakfast toast, if there is any berries left by the time we get home.'

She gained the topmost of the five wooden bars without mishap, and he reached out for her. Hands spanning her waist he lifted her down, setting her gently on her feet.

They headed for Duck Pond Cottage. After a while he bore her hand to his mouth and left a kiss in the palm before entwining his fingers through hers.

The dusk closed around them, a soft, clinging hug of indigo silk. One by one the stars came out and the new moon offered them a slice of a smile. They were at one with the world, she and Ryder – at one with each other, as they had been as children.

It was a moment of perfect happiness.

Eleven

'Somebody left our trunks on the doorstep, so they weren't lost after all,' Sarah said when Ryder followed Adele into the cottage. 'I've forgotten what was in them after all this time, haven't you, Adele? We've dragged them into the morning room. Aunt Prudence said they would be out of the way there.' Sarah took her by the hand. 'Come and look.'

'I'll take the strawberries to the kitchen and see if your aunts need a hand,' Ryder said, and headed off.

Adele thought, so that was what the visitor had been about. He'd been a messenger and had simply delivered the trunks. If she'd left by the front door instead of the back, she would have seen them earlier. Reluctantly, she allowed herself to be towed towards the morning room, where she stared down at two familiar and scruffy wooden trunks.

A smell of mould rose from them and she felt sick when she saw the name stencilled on the lid. Edgar Pelham – architect. Southampton. The lock had been forced. Not that the trunk had contained much of value, she recalled, unless one counted the remains of a man's life.

Adele hated the fact that Edgar Pelham had intruded into her life again. Would she never be free of his shackles? She had a strong urge to drag the trunks into the garden and set fire to them. What if he had lived . . . what if he'd clawed his way on board the ship in the dead of night and crawled into one of the trunks? What if he'd died there . . . or worse, was still in there, alive, coiled up like a hibernating snake waiting to strike?

She shook herself for being silly and fanciful. 'I don't think there will be much of value in the trunks. We only had an extra skirt and bodice apiece to our name.' How glorious it was to have a full wardrobe of pretty garments, even if they were a little out of date. Nobody worried much about such things in the country, unless it was for a special occasion.

Sarah said. 'He . . . my father . . . may have put his trade journal in it.'

'Yes . . . he may have. It wasn't in his cabin, but then, neither was my journal.' Unease dug its fist into her stomach. *What if he'd read it?* Then she thought, *does it matter, if he is dead? After all, he couldn't tell anyone what was in it.*

She must stop thinking about herself and remember that Sarah was Edgar's child, even though he'd denied it to the girl on several occasions. Surely Sarah was too similar in looks for Edgar not to have fathered her, and she was bound to be curious about her kin.

'Is there anything in the trunk you wish to keep?'

Sarah gave her a hug. 'I know you're reluctant to deal with this. Even the sight of his name makes you withdraw into yourself. We'll go through it in the morning when we're stronger and see if there's anything of interest.'

'Good. Now, let's go and light the candles, and provide some company for Lord Madigan.'

Sarah pulled a twig from Adele's hair with several leaves attached. 'Aren't you going to tidy yourself up first?'

'Lor . . . Why did he have to stay for dinner when I'm not dressed suitably to entertain an earl.' She gazed in the mirror, and then placed her hands over her eyes so she didn't have to look at her windblown hair. 'Do I look untidy?'

Sarah grinned. 'Disgustingly so . . . but then, so does he.'

Dropping her hands Adele yelped, 'I look a fright,' and she took the stairs two at a time and quickly changed into a gown of amber taffeta with a muslin overskirt – one that had been left behind when she'd fled. It had been one of her favourites. Picking up her brush she attacked her hair, wincing every time she encountered a knot. Finally, she got it under control and secured it at the nape of her neck with an arrangement of two silk roses and bronze ribbons. Taking a deep breath she ventured forth.

Ryder was waiting for her at the bottom of the stairs when she went down. 'You look lovely, my Del.'

She felt lovely. No . . . it wasn't that. She felt loved. In turn that emotion urged her to tell him what he wanted to know. That niggling urge to confess was rapidly becoming a need, and therein laid the danger. Ryder had studied some law and in time could serve as a lay magistrate. No matter that she'd been defending herself, she should have said so in her statement. Should her deed come to light there would be consequences.

As usual she brushed it to the back of her mind, like dust under a carpet. There it diffused into a murky black stain. Sometimes she buried the terrible deed so deeply that her memory of it changed shape, and she nearly forgot the details altogether – until Edgar Pelham's name was raised.

But she would not spoil this day by being melancholy at the end of it.

Over dinner, Ryder kept them all laughing with greatly exaggerated tales of his exploits in India with Hal Stover, and he persuaded Adele to share some of their earlier childhood memories.

Her aunts gave commentary on the fair. Prudence said, 'Mrs Bryson won the women's shooting match, like she always does. She has a sharp eye.'

'And a tongue to match,' Patience said, then added with more satisfaction, 'My cake attracted the best offer for charity.'

Prudence said smartly, 'The earl took pity on you and made the largest bid. Isn't that so, my lord?'

He laughed. 'That question could start a war. Actually, I thought Adele had made the cake. What happened to it?'

'I put it on a bench while I packed the picnic box, and Daisy took a slobbering bite from it. She's partial to sweet things.'

'She isn't the only one,' and his eyes feasted on her and brought a blush seeping to the surface.

Prudence gazed from one to the other, murmuring slyly, 'There . . . see how diplomatic the earl has become.'

The evening was over too soon.

As Ryder was leaving he said casually to Sarah, 'We must send an invitation to Hal. He's staying in my rooms in London. By the way I hired a man who acted as a butler at the fair today. His name is William Swift. Formerly he was an assistant to an estate manager. He will present himself tomorrow afternoon. I'll leave you to show him round the house and introduce him to the rest of the staff.'

'Yes, my lord.' Sarah appeared pleased by the extra responsibility.

Ryder's glance came Adele's way and he smiled. 'I've enjoyed your company today, Adele. Will you walk with me to the gate?'

It was only a few steps, and Henry greeted him with a little whicker.

It was a dark night, the new moon now obscured by cloud, and full of rustling noises. An owl hooted . . . another answered. 'Be careful you don't get lost in the dark,' she said.

'Horses have better sight than us in the dark and Henry knows the way. He's good at avoiding obstacles and finding his stable, especially when there's a meal at the end of the journey. I'll see you home first.'

She laughed. They had often played this courting game, and she couldn't resist it. 'Then I will escort you to the gate again and we'll be here all night, coming and going.'

'I can think of a worse way to occupy our time.' The heat from his body reached out to her and she absorbed its sweetness. 'Goodnight, my Del.'

'Goodnight, Ryder.'

She didn't want to part from him.

Neither of them moved for a few seconds, and then they stepped towards each other at the same time.

'Oof!'

'Sorry.' Laughter infused his voice. 'I was going to kiss you goodnight.'

'I know . . . remove yourself from my foot first.'

He obliged, and then he took her face between his hands and tilted her face up to his. His mouth landed on hers as soft and tender as a butterfly seeking nectar.

A disembodied flame of candlelight floated beyond him in the darkness.

'Adele, dear, are you all right,' Aunt Patience called out.

Prudence whispered, 'Come away, I expect he's kissing her goodnight.'

'Good guess and bad timing,' Ryder grumbled.

Patience again. 'He's taking a long time about it. His behaviour is unseemly.'

'Rubbish! Look where being seemly got us . . . nowhere. The earl's behaviour has always been exemplary, and he'd do nothing to hurt our Adele.'

'Nevertheless,' Patience said, and quite firmly, 'it's time for her to come inside.' She raised her voice a little. 'Goodnight, my lord.'

There couldn't have been a larger hint and Ryder huffed out a laugh as they both took a step backwards. 'You have good watchdogs in your aunts.'

'Yes, and I love them dearly.'

'You've given purpose to their lives, I think.'

'I think you're right.' She touched his cheek. 'Go, before they set the ducks on you.'

'God forbid!' Briefly, he lifted her hand to his mouth and gently bit the fleshy pad at the base of her thumb.

He aimed his next remark to the flame floating in the darkness. 'Goodnight, Aunts,' and mounting Henry, he disappeared into the dark night, leaving her kissed but craving more.

As Henry picked his way confidently along the road that led home it started to rain. It didn't bother Ryder, it was soft and light, almost drifting, and he was thinking that Adele was softening a little towards him. She wasn't so reluctant to accept his attention and she flirted, hiding behind humour like she used to. It was as if she felt safe to dwell on childhood matters.

She had told him about the loss of the infant, but reluctantly, only after he'd introduced the subject. She'd trusted him with that most painful of memories, yet still, he suspected there was more to it. Remembering something Adele had said then, his eyes sharpened. She'd blurted out that Edgar Pelham had not been manly, in the sense that he didn't consort with women. It was an indelicate subject, not one he'd care to pursue with her – or *any* woman come to that – but there was a small flare of relief in knowing it.

Then there was the mystery of the trunks. He'd previously contacted every cartage company in the district and all had denied knowledge of them. Yet here they were, delivered to their proper destination. He'd have to cast his net wider.

Edgar Pelham – architect – Southampton had been stencilled on them. He recalled that the lock had been forced to open it. The person who'd done that would know what it contained.

Adele might have mistakenly packed the deeds to the cottage in it. He frowned. She'd displayed very little interest in the trunks or the contents. In fact, she'd avoided it. He understood that she'd be trying to obliterate the folly of her earlier flight from the district, but by burying it inside her she wasn't succeeding. The gossip was rife. People avoided her . . . that must hurt.

There was something else too. He'd more or less accused Oliver Bryson of shooting at Adele in the copse, but today he'd learned that Mary Bryson was a good shot, and suspected she'd been a Pelham before her marriage. And the reverend had expected his wife at the church on the day Ryder confronted him. He'd asked Ryder if he'd seen her. His brain chose that moment to issue an image of an old bent man in a brown robe, his face hidden by a cowl. Shortly after Mary Bryson had conveniently appeared at the church.

And where did Luke Ashburn fit in?

As often happened, Ryder's mind had started stitching things together. Tomorrow, he determined he would go to Southampton and find out who had sent the trunk.

That night Adele was woken by a thump. It came from the room beneath her, where the trunks had been left. Her heart beating rapidly she slipped out of bed and crept down the stair. The door to the morning room creaked when she opened it.

Her eyes were drawn to one of the trunks. It was changing shape, melting, and beginning to resemble a coffin. She watched in horror when the lid started to open.

'Who are you?' she whispered, as if she didn't know whose remains the coffin contained.

'Edgar!'

She found some courage. 'He's dead . . . you're dead. You might give me a fright but you can't hurt me any more because you don't exist. I won't let you.'

'Come here, Adele.'

Fear made a mockery of her previous statement. It thundered through her veins as her feet dragged her reluctantly across the room. The coffin held a body and its eyes gleamed in the darkness. It held out its arms, slimy with seaweed. 'Come.'

'Go away!' She pushed him with all the strength left in her. This wasn't real; it was a bad dream.

He took her by the throat and squeezed. She began to fight for air.

'Breathe!' A puff of wind blew up her nose and she gasped against its force.

Still she couldn't breathe. The constriction in her throat was too tightly knotted.

A sharp smell sliced into her brain and her head jerked backwards. Instantly, the vestiges of sleep fled, leaving her mind clear and acute.

Smelling salts! She sat up, gazing around her. 'I thought I was in the morning room.'

The dog whined and scratched on the door.

'Hush, Gypsy, you'll wake the aunts.'

The voice belonged to Sarah. There came the sound of a door closing and the dog bounded onto the bed to take up position near her feet.

'Has he gone?' Adele asked.

'Has who gone?'

The dream began to fade. 'I don't know . . . someone.'

'You were dreaming.' Sarah was seated on the edge of the bed, a candle held aloft.

Still slightly panicked, Adele gazed past her into the dark recesses of the room. There was no sign of Edgar or the trunks, and the tension left her.

Sarah smiled at her. 'I'm sorry I had to use smelling salts. You were dreaming, gasping for breath and clutching at your throat. I couldn't wake you. It must have been a bad dream because you cried out.'

'Yes it was . . . I can't remember it now. I'm sorry I woke you, Sarah. Go back to bed.'

'You didn't wake me; there was a shower of rain and it was noisy running through the gutters. It's stopped now and I can see dawn on the horizon. I'll stoke up the stove and make some tea. I might even open the trunks.'

Adele shuddered at the thought of being in the same room as the trunks, especially in the dim light of a candle; she couldn't help it. 'You won't be able to see much. Wait until it's light, and then I'll help you.'

An hour later and the trunks were open, the contents spread about the morning room. Their own garments smelled sour, and Adele grimaced. She and Sarah had been allocated the top tray of the trunk. 'I hate the thought of strangers rifling through my clothing, though doesn't it say something when thieves are too fussy to steal it? There's nothing worth keeping so I'm going to burn anything that belongs to me. I thought I might have put my journals in there, but now I think they were packed with the cottage deeds in the hessian bags.'

'Me too.' Sarah sat back on her heels, and then reached for

a package containing papers. There were trade certificates inside, made out in Edgar Pelham's name. 'How odd. My father seemed to be skilled, but people criticized his work. Sometimes he seemed like two people living inside one skin.'

Not wanting to discuss Edgar with her, Adele rose. 'I'm going to start on breakfast. Keep anything you want. We'll burn what's left, including the trunk.'

'There might be something valuable you'd like as a keepsake.'

Adele remembered the forced lock. If Sarah thought she was going to find something valuable in the trunk, she would be disappointed.

'Unless it's the missing papers and my journals, I don't want any reminder. I'll leave it to your good sense.'

Even so there were frequent visits to and fro as Sarah dithered on what should be kept and what shouldn't – a book with architects' drawings of various buildings. It soon became apparent that the tools of Edgar's trade were missing, as was the watch inscribed with his name. There were a couple of notebooks. Sarah threw them on the rubbish pile, and Adele retrieved them. They might contain some useful information.

Sarah sat back on her heels. 'No deeds.'

'I didn't really expect you to find the house deeds in a trunk. The last time I saw them they were in one of the hessian bags.'

'Yes they were. I looked after them, though. The only time they were out of my sight was when I was asleep.'

'Didn't you spend a night in the workhouse?'

Sarah nodded. 'Reverend Bryson took me in for the night, though I got very little sleep because I was so worried about you. Over breakfast his wife was very inquisitive, and rude, and she treated me as though I was a criminal. She kept asking me questions about you. I told her she had no right to ask so many personal questions about things that didn't concern her. She called me ungrateful, and then she slapped my face and took me to the workhouse in Poole. I was only there for an hour or so when Lord Madigan came for me.'

'What did she want to know?'

'Where had we come from, and why hadn't you informed

anyone you were arriving . . . and where was my father? She seemed annoyed when her husband came home and told her that the earl had found you on the heath.

' "Good news," he said, and he was smiling, as though he was happy about it. Mary Bryson soon changed that. She pulled on a sour-plum expression and said the earl had tricked people into believing he was dead, and that bringing you back together was the devil's own work. She said you didn't deserve to survive, and you shouldn't have come back, flaunting yourself and causing everyone trouble. She shouted at me, and then the reverend made her drink some medicine and after a while she calmed down. I was glad to leave her home.'

'No doubt. I haven't done either of those things and certainly don't need her interference in my life.'

'Mrs Bryson thought the earl had died in India, and her husband would inherit the title. She'd convinced herself that she'd become a countess.'

'I don't see what that has to do with me.'

'She was practically deranged by the thought that the earl might forgive you and offer you marriage. I felt pity for her, and sorry for him.'

Anger crawled inside Adele's stomach and she was tempted to confront Mary Bryson. But it would only add fuel to the fire, and do more harm than good after all this time. Besides, anything she said to the woman would be spread over the district like poison the next day.

Once again she wondered if it would be better to move . . . but she'd have to sell the cottage, and she needed to find the deeds and prove ownership before she could dispose of it. Then she must consider her aunts. They wouldn't be uprooted too easily.

But then, why should she be driven from the district she'd grown up in? She had the same right to live here as anyone else – more than most, in fact. Let them move out if they didn't like her as a neighbour.

When the trunk was empty Adele said, 'Did you notice that the objects missing from the trunk were the most valuable? The watch inscribed with your father's name was gone, to start with.'

Sarah shrugged. 'Perhaps he was wearing it when . . . he died.'

'Perhaps, but he only wore it if he wanted to make an impression. He was fearful it might attract felons who recognized its worth. Where are his gold cufflinks . . . the box of matching silver buttons and shoe buckles? Also there was some money. I don't know how much. Those items became your legacy when he died.'

'But you were his wife.'

Adele gazed at the girl. 'You have always been a true and loyal friend, Sarah, and for that reason I would offer you a confidence – however, before you answer I would just like to say it's one you may not welcome, but please don't judge me.'

Sarah kissed her cheek. 'You needn't say anything. I grew up absorbing the gossip and I know the marriage you made with my father wasn't *normal*. Because of that I was scared you'd run away and leave me. I'm grateful you didn't. I don't need to know anything more than what I observed. You were good to me and for that alone I'll love you for ever. As for any legacy, I want nothing that belonged to my father. He was a cruel and evil man, and although children are supposed to love and respect their parents I could only fear him.

'Sarah, dearest, my life wouldn't have been worth living without you.' Tears in her eyes, Adele took the girl in a heartfelt hug.

A short time later they finished their task and between them, carried the trunks and their contents out into the rain-washed air, to where the scorched and ashy patch of the bonfire was situated.

Together they threw them into the grey dust of earlier bonfires, where they landed with a thump and created a large grey puff of dust – soon to be consumed by fire. She felt a small swell of pity for Edgar, who had died, unloved and buried without ceremony or epitaph in the deep.

'Should I say a prayer?'

Adele cast off any shred of duty she felt towards him, though the guilt remained. 'Only if you want to. He was your father, not mine. As far as I'm concerned we're burning old trunks we have no more use for. I have no sentimental attachment to it. I'll go and collect a hot coal from the kitchen.'

'Was he my father? I sometimes wonder.'

'Only you can answer that, my love. If you want to say a prayer you can do so in private, but spare a thought for your mother.'

Adele returned to the house. Her aunts were stirring upstairs as she slid a glowing coal into a small bucket. She clutched it carefully in the jaws of cast-iron fire tongs held at arm's length.

She had just touched the coal to the trunk when Sarah darted forward and plucked up a folded paper. It was singed and curling at the edge where the fire had licked at it. It must have slid from a rip in the lining when the trunk had jolted along the ground.

'It's a note . . . and it's addressed to you, Adele.'

To Mrs Pelham . . . from James Pelham Esquire.

Her heart thumped! It was a trick. Edgar had told her he was alone in the world. Tempted to throw the paper back into the inferno she managed to stop herself. She'd never get to the bottom of this if she didn't face up to it.

Mrs Pelham,

This luggage was delivered to my Southampton address – and in the state you find it. I am Edgar Pelham's father. Enquiries led me to discover that my son had died, having fallen overboard from the Mary Jane, and drowned in the English Channel – a proper service being said for his soul by Captain Joseph Hargreaves.

You might be aware that I had cast my son out, and for good reason; we have been estranged for several years. Recently I was in touch by letter with a cousin in America who gave me news of him – and that led me to you.

I will be blunt. I was not desirous of news of my son, who has been a disappointment, being a thief, a liar and a man given to violence. That aside, I would not wish him dead, but I do have questions regarding the whereabouts of some valuable family items, which it is my intention to pursue.

I shall be in Poole for a few days, where I'll lodge at the Antelope Inn. Should you or your representative not contact

me during that time, please be informed I shall have no other
alternative than place my concerns in the hands of a
magistrate.
    James Pelham

Adele's heart fell into a dark hole, but despite her reaction
she reminded herself that the Edgar Pelham who haunted her
dreams was not this man called James Pelham, but his son.
Edgar was a sickening spectre conjured up by the guilt festering
in her own mind.

The fire caught and the trunks flared up with a hiss. She
had drowned its owner but his malevolent presence hadn't died.
Perhaps she'd succeed in getting rid of it in the flames.

What concerns could James Pelham have about two old
sea-stained trunks containing grubby clothing – clothing
without any great significance or value, but James would not
have bothered sending it on had there not been anything of
value in it. Why should he have bothered, unless – and a cold
sort of dread sent goosebumps skittering up her spine – unless
he suspected the worst?

When Sarah sent her a glance of enquiry, Adele handed her
the letter. She had a right to know. Seconds later the girl said
a little thoughtfully, 'My grandfather didn't mention me.'

'Perhaps he doesn't know about you.' Something that was
hardly likely. Adele only hoped it was only going to be that
simple.

Twelve

Ryder smelled the smoke before he reached the cottage. He
left Henry munching contentedly on the long grass at the edge
of the pond and leaped over the gate, making his way to the
walled kitchen garden. It was early summer and he felt wonderfully alive. For the first time since he'd been home, he truly
appreciated the beauty of his heritage. The clement weather
was lingering, and the farmers of the district were hoping for

a good harvest to celebrate. Ryder had his kitchen garden, the produce of which they would need all of this year for the house. This year the corn crop had failed, due to the seed being of inferior quality. Ashurn had shrugged it off. 'We ordered it too late.'

Next year things would be different, he told himself. He would personally order the seed.

He came across Adele and Sarah, their arms around each other's waists, as women stood when they were close emotionally, and of one mind. They were watching an old travelling trunk go up in flames – one of the pair that had been lost for all that time, he imagined.

They turned when they heard his footfalls. Adele's smile was spontaneous and wide, and the note of welcome in her voice pleased him when she said, 'Ryder . . . what a pleasant surprise. We weren't expecting you.' It was as if she hadn't seen him for a month of Sundays instead of just the day before, when he'd accepted the invite to dine with the aunts and had taken the opportunity to kiss her luscious mouth when he said goodbye.

'You sound as though you missed me. Are those the trunks that went astray?'

It was Sarah who answered. 'One of them . . . it belonged to my father,' and she waved a singed sheet of paper under his nose. 'Look, my lord. The man who delivered it placed this note inside but we can make neither head nor tail of it.'

He took the paper from Sarah, gave it a quick glance and gazed at Adele. 'The note is addressed to you. Do I have your permission?'

She hesitated for a few moments, reluctance in her every movement and expression now, as though he'd spoiled her mood just by asking. Then she shrugged. 'As you already know, the trunks have been missing for several weeks. The lock has been forced and he has indicated that some of the contents are missing. It appears that he intends to accuse me of stealing them.'

Does he by God! His glance absorbed the contents of the note. 'He didn't state what was missing. Very little of value, if the stained clothing was anything to go by.'

'From what I can remember, there were silver buttons and

buckles and a watch with his name on it. But then, as Sarah pointed out, he might have been wearing those items when he . . . drowned.' She drew in a deep breath. 'His body was never found.' She moved on quickly. 'Oh yes, and there was a leather purse with some coins in, and a small satchel containing banknotes.'

He flicked his eyes up to hers. 'A large sum?'

'I don't know. I never saw inside it, and Edgar always kept it with him. Apart from my own, he never discussed finances with me, and he was frugal. But surely the trunk and the contents belong to Sarah now, so how can this man have the authority to question me over the contents?'

Smoothly, he cut in, 'It's a pity you burned the trunks, since it might have been useful evidence. Don't look so worried. With your permission we'll sort this out between us. To start with he won't want the expense of taking you before a magistrate over a couple of mouldy travelling trunks. That was just added to intimidate you. Apart from that, he has no idea of what might have been in the trunks to start with, so how can he prove that something is missing?'

'What will you do?'

'Because of my position, and as is my right, I'll dictate the place of meeting. That will put him at a disadvantage to start with. I'll then demand written statements from any witnesses he might have. Now, I have some news of my own, which no doubt you'll welcome. Hal Stover is returning in a fortnight or so.'

Sarah clapped her hands. 'What fun. May I go and tell the aunts? They will probably invite you for breakfast.'

'I'm sure I can manage to eat a second one.' Would that the sight and mention of his own name evoked such a favourable exchange of cooing noises and smiles, especially from Adele, he thought, as he watched Sarah scurry off.

Immediately, awkwardness descended on them. Odd to think he'd kissed her senseless the evening before. Now she was as shy as the daisies decorating her hat.

He chuckled. So was he.

She gave him a startled glance, and then blushed, as if her mind was running along the same lines. She stared down at her hands, plucking at a seam in her glove. A mustard-hued smock covered the pink gown she wore, which was patched and a trifle worse for wear. A straw hat kept the sun from her face. Every time he set eyes on her she appeared lovelier. Flawless skin. Body nicely rounded, so he wanted to smooth his hands over the warm skin under her apparel. One day soon he'd take the wrappings from her and he'd taste her flesh and bury himself inside her warmth.

'Look at me,' he said and her eyelashes quivered, and he found himself suspended in the cool greenish shade of morning eyes. It was a little game they'd once played to see who could hold the gaze longest. He imagined her head on the pillow, her foxy hair spread in glorious array, her eyes gazing an invitation, and him kissing her like there was no tomorrow . . .

Her laughter dripped into his ears like pearls when he blinked. 'Stop it at once, you look like a trout coming up for air with your mouth all puckered,' she said, and a deliciously soft giggle tore from her mouth, one that said he could kiss her as soon as he'd manoeuvred her into the shadows where they couldn't be seen. He moved a little to the left, and laughed. 'You're flirting with me.'

'And you're being obvious.' She took a step to the right, towards a patch of shade, and dropped her handkerchief. He played the game, and when he stooped to retrieve it she pushed him over and took flight towards the house.

So, his lady was in a playful mood. He caught her by the waist, picked her up and twirled her round in a flurry of laughter.

'Put me down, Ryder. My aunts are watching from the kitchen window and they will not approve of such hoydenish behaviour. It will create a wrong impression.'

'More likely it will create a correct one. They didn't object to me romancing you last night.'

'That's because they didn't see you in the dark . . . they just guessed. Besides, they are hopelessly romantic. They still have their dreams, if not for themselves then for me. Although they will never come to fruition, please have some respect for them. We're no longer children, so put me down.'

The barriers that kept her previous spontaneity under control still existed, but only when she remembered them.

He set her on her feet, put some space between them and nodded. She was out of breath and even more dishevelled. He had no claims to her and the innocence of their childhood should be put behind them. Her father had placed her trust in him and he'd abused it. He'd taken advantage of her innocence and ruined her life . . . his own — all their lives in fact. He was ashamed, yet angry with her for pointing it out. It hurt that she would have preferred the company of Edgar Pelham.

'You're right, it's too early in the morning to romance a lady, unless one happens to wake up by her side or she's rolling in a haystack with him. Perhaps you'd prefer a rougher approach.'

Her smile faded and she walked away from him.

'Del, please wait,' he murmured.

She turned, her body upright, and her voice was thick with tears when she said, 'Why? Do you have another insult to add to the last two then, my fine lord?'

'Please accept my apology . . . forgive me,' he said, all the while knowing he'd never forgive himself.

The eyes that scrutinized him from head to foot were as bleak as stone. Her lip curled. 'You are no longer welcome in my home, my lord.' Turning her back on him she hurried away, leaving him there.

'Del! You don't mean it.'

Not by the twitch of an ear did she indicate that she'd heard him. It was as if he no longer existed for her.

Her footsteps quickened and then she began to run. He couldn't leave the matter like this so he ran after her. 'Del, wait.'

She reached the door first and slipped through. Closing it in his face she turned the key in the lock.

Inside, Sarah and the aunts stood, their mouths open in astonishment. Adele gazed from one to the other. 'That man is not allowed over the threshold again.'

Looking shocked, Patience indicated the plate of food in her hands. 'What shall I do with his breakfast?'

'This is what I think of his breakfast,' and she pushed the

window further ajar, snatched up the plate and its contents and threw it at him. Gypsy caught a straying sausage in mid-air and ran off with it, while Ryder deftly caught the plate and the rest of its contents.

He went to sit on the garden seat, and, using his fingers he began to eat. Gypsy joined him there in begging mode. The dog had no pride.

Patience looked scandalized. 'You can't treat Lord Madigan like that. He's an earl.'

'I just have, and I don't care if he's King George, King Neptune, King Canute and the mutton-headed House of Lords rolled into one.'

A snort came from Ryder, and then he began to laugh.

She burst into tears and stamped her foot – not that it would make much of an impact on the rug. Raising her voice she said, 'Just at this moment I think I hate you, Ryder Madigan.'

Outside, the laughter was replaced by an abrupt silence.

She realized she'd gone too far when the gate creaked.

'Goodness, what have I said? It's not true.' She gazed out of the window. Gypsy was attacking the breakfast plate, his tongue lapping up the remaining eggs and ham, swallowing without chewing so to get every scrap as he licked the plate around the lawn.

Ryder whistled for his horse.

A song thrush answered him, a melody pouring from its throat.

Ryder whistled again, inviting an answering neigh from Henry, to whom he addressed his next remarks. 'First she leaves me at the altar, now she shames me in front of her family. It seems the lady no longer has any respect, or use for her faithful swain.'

'Ryder . . .' she implored.

'Good day, Mrs Pelham.' The creak of leathers was followed by the click of a tongue and the horse carried him away.

Prudence placed an arm around her shoulders but Adele slid from the embrace. She felt detached from the day, which had begun with such promise.

Patience offered her a sharp rejoinder. 'Such a childish tantrum is unbecoming of you, Adele, especially when the earl has been so good to us. He has never been one to hold a grudge and it's time you observed the niceties society expects. You must make your apology to him and he will accept it. Then it will be forgotten.'

A childish tantrum – was that what it had seemed to them? She admitted it. That's exactly what it had been, yet . . . and she shrugged. 'You don't understand.'

Unexpectedly, Sarah challenged that notion. 'How do you expect anyone to understand when you haven't told the truth? Lord Madigan is not the liar, cheat or bully that my father was.'

'Don't go on, Sarah, please,' Adele begged. 'I tried to tell him . . . some of it, anyway.'

The girl sighed. 'My father treated you badly and you've convinced yourself all men are to be avoided.'

It was a simple truth from a girl who'd observed, but had yet to experience the capricious nature of love.

Patience patted her on the shoulder. 'Your mother and father would be ashamed of you, Adele.'

'My father was ashamed. He preferred to listen to gossip and lies. If he'd listened to me – if he'd truly loved me, he would not have thrown me out to fend for myself, but would have defended me. Edgar Pelham tricked me with a note, supposedly from Ryder, and asking me to meet him.'

'Alone, and at night?' Patience said, scandalized.

Adele inclined her head. 'It's not what you think and it was all very innocent.' Perhaps not all, but she'd been in love with Ryder, and he with her, and some things were private and not for her aunts' ears. 'I arrived there to discover Edgar waiting. He told me that Ryder had a mistress and he was with her. He contacted my father, saying we were lovers, and told him if he wanted me back he'd exchange me for a sum of money. My father preferred to keep the money in his pocket, so I had no choice.'

'Oh, my dear, we never knew . . . Did you have a very bad time? Why did you marry the scoundrel? You could have come to us and we could have moved to another town where nobody knew us and nobody was the wiser. I must admit I'm surprised to learn that the earl broke your father's trust.'

'I doubt if he did. I shouldn't have listened to Edgar Pelham. I was given to understand that I was not married legally to him since we were married on board the ship. Then there was Sarah. I'd grown to love her and couldn't bear to leave her. She'd already lost one mother and was such a tiny little thing with nobody to love her.'

Moving to her side, Sarah took her hand.

Adele felt drained as she looked into the shocked eyes of her aunts. 'I'm sorry. It's not something I wanted to become general knowledge.'

'Did that Pelham scoundrel know the marriage wasn't legal?'

'No . . . but neither did I for a long time. I found out quite by accident in conversation with the wife of a ship's captain, and I kept the knowledge to myself in case I could use it when the time arose. I was going to ask the advice of Reverend Bryson. He'd always listened to my problems and advised me.'

'A mistake since it was the reverend's sneaky way of finding out your family business, and that of the earl – and it would be a bigger mistake if that wife of his was lurking nearby, like a malevolent wasp waiting for a spider to come along, so it could paralyse it and lay its eggs inside it. Don't you think so Prudence?'

Prudence nodded. 'They don't lay eggs, but larvae. We went to a talk given by Harold Dutsworth once. It was so exciting!'

'Only because he was showing an interest to you.'

'Nonsense. He had his eye on Annie James, who had just come into a fortune.'

Patience sniffed. 'I thought it was disgusting, The point I was trying to make was that Mary Bryson snoops. I wouldn't be surprised if she was hanging under the eaves this minute, her ears flapping like bat's wings.'

Sarah giggled, then squeezed her hand and hiccupped, 'Sorry, Adele.'

Adele almost giggled herself. 'Let's hope she isn't listening, then.'

'If Mary places a foot on our land I'll pull her tongue out by the roots and feed it to the ducks . . . that I will. Now, stop trying to divert me from the business at hand. I'm determined to hear the truth. How did that horrid Pelham creature manage to fall overboard?'

'Have some thought for Sarah, Aunts. He is her father, after all.'

'The girl is adult enough to be aware of the truth, and she probably noticed more than you think she did.'

'Yes . . . I suppose she did.'

How had he fallen overboard? She couldn't really remember. 'We . . . that is, he and I had an argument . . . on the ship . . . about my legacy and this cottage. He said he'd heard that my father had died and he was going to take control of my trust. I told him then that we were not legally married and he wasn't entitled to claim it. He lost his temper and he punched me and I fell and banged my head. When I recovered consciousness I was soaked through and a seaman was pumping water from me. He saved my life. He told me Edgar had . . . gone.'

There was a sharp intake of breath from Prudence and a soft, 'Oh . . . my goodness, how sad that not even his father could mourn him. Edgar Pelham appeared to be such a gentleman on the occasion I met him . . . on the surface, at least.'

'He didn't take me in,' Patience said fiercely.

'I told him I was leaving him when we reached England.' Her head ached when she tried to remember. 'There was somebody else there . . . standing in the shadows looking on. I thought it was an angel.'

Patience said, 'Perhaps it was your guardian angel; they say we all have one.'

Sarah's grip on her hand tightened a fraction. The girl was trembling as she said, 'We were going to leave together, remember?'

'Of course I remember. I wouldn't have left without you. I thought there were people I trusted here and could have asked for advice. Apart from you, there was Stephen Tessler and the Brysons. But those people I'd once considered to be my friends had become enemies in my absence.'

A snort came from Patience. 'They turned out to be leeches!'

'I thought Ryder had died in India, and the Reverend Bryson would be living in Madigan House. I also thought that the scandal would have died with him. It turned out to be the opposite.'

It was late in the evening, nearly dusk. The air was still, the water calm, but cold. Above them the ship's sails gave an occasional languid flap, as if trying to capture a wind to take them home. She could see Edgar's face under the surface, his mouth open and panic in his eyes as his mouth reached for air.

Kneeling, she held out her shawl for him to take hold of. Instead, his hand closed around her wrist and he pulled. Her mouth filled with a torrent of water.

He scrambled over her body – the body that had never drawn a response from him except cruelty, for women repulsed him. His weight pulled her down. His hands clawed into her stomach like burrowing crabs, dug into her breasts and scratched deep into her thighs as he sank. Hands, feet and teeth, he fought for his life at the expense of hers, fingers hooked painfully into her shoulders.

She was choking . . . choking!

Seaweed in her mouth.

Hands clawing at her skirt.

Rough.

Rope tangled.

The tide put up a fight to release her hair. She emerged, her first breath of air uttering a curse.

'Drown!'

She released her shawl into the currents. Water muted his scream and the light in his eyes dimmed.

'Drown!'

She opened her hand and Edgar was gone, while she was still held fast by her hair. A hand pulled her head back exposing her throat, a knife flashed silver. He was going to cut her throat, but it didn't matter. She was already dead.

'Breathe.'

There was no strength left in her to breathe. She let go . . . perhaps she'd reunite with Ryder and their baby son.

'Dammit, woman, I didn't get my bloody whiskers wet for nothing . . . you take a breath now!'

Her chest exploded.

But it was not Ryder who was looking down at her when she'd coughed out the ocean and opened her eyes. It was a stranger, grizzled by the winds and rain, salt and pepper in his beard, rough-handed – legs rooted to the deck like a tree in a forest.

Behind him the shadow melted into a doorway.

'The sea has taken your man.'

Please God, don't let it be Ryder.

The notion faded when she opened her eyes. Of course it wasn't Ryder. In her mind he'd already been dead. It was Edgar Pelham she'd killed, and she felt surprisingly calm about it, as if she'd merely liberated herself.

But she couldn't tell them that. These three women who loved and cared for her, and whose eyes burned with concern for her didn't deserve to have such a burden placed on their shoulders. It would simply compound her sin.

Adele was tense, her nerves in knots like neglected tapestry silks. It occurred to her that the one hasty word might have killed Ryder's love for her. His love had been constant, even when he believed she'd betrayed him. He'd said so. Ryder wasn't shallow and she'd answered his declaration with words of hate. She hadn't meant it.

'You're right, Aunt Patience, I must apologize to the earl. Sarah, perhaps you'd deliver a note to him at Madigan House.' She sighed, and said, more to herself than anyone else. 'I should never have returned.'

But she had returned . . . she'd had no choice but to return. Now she had, so should she stay or should she go?

It would all depend on Ryder.

Thirteen

Ryder's ears burned as he headed home. His heart was squeezed as tight as a sea sponge – one that had dried to the consistency of stone and been tossed onto the flotsam line above the high-tide mark. He was trying hard to believe Adele hadn't meant what she'd said.

He felt trapped, and he needed to get away from this closed-in village environment with its expectations and its hypocrisy. He'd planned for his life to be much simpler. He should be able to go about his business, manage his estate, marry well, entertain his friends and in time, teach his sons enough respect to grow into fine young men. All without comment, malicious or otherwise. He might have a daughter as well, a pretty little thing who could twist him and her brothers around her fingers. She would be like her mother.

He allowed Adele back into his imaginings, thinking she'd be upset if he married another woman and carried out the plans he'd once shared with her. Of course she would. They had loved each other once. Still did, as he'd learned to his cost. People would pity her and she would hate that.

He sighed. When had he stopped being the victim and become the hunter? He couldn't do it to her. A little time apart and he would renew his pursuit. A week or so in London with its theatres and other pleasures should set him up nicely. It would be time enough to hibernate when he returned.

'Back already, my Lord?' John said, looking surprised when he walked into the house.

'I've decided to go to London for a few days and I have some business to attend to here before I do.'

'I'll air your travelling clothes and pack your greatcoat in case you need it.'

'You needn't pack a bag; I've got plenty of extra clothing in my London rooms. I'll be leaving early tomorrow and will be away for a week or so. I'll take the post from Poole, it's quicker than the stagecoach.'

'But not as comfortable.'

'That's the price one has to pay for a faster journey.'

'You've not forgotten the social evening, have you, sir?'

'I certainly have not. Mrs Betts has everything in hand and the staff are experienced in such matters. She has her duties for the next fortnight, and William Swift will be in overall charge, so you can put your feet up and take a few days off. You might like to call in on the Manning sisters from time to time and see if they, or Mrs Pelham, need any help.'

John made a humming sound in his throat.

'I'll bring Sergeant Stover back with me, and with plenty of time to spare before the social event. The household should run smoothly until I get back.'

'As long as nobody else intervenes, my lord . . . everyone is so looking forward to the social gathering.'

'Good. Perhaps I shall find myself a wife.'

'But I thought . . . we all thought . . .'

'That I might marry Mrs Pelham?'

'Yes, my lord, you are so well suited. She's a delightful young woman and well . . . you do seem to have forgiven her.'

'As you say, John. I thought I'd forgiven her too, but I learned just a short time ago that some cuts run too deep to heal quickly, and mine are still raw. I'm sorry to disappoint you, but it appears that the lady doesn't want me now.'

'I heard differently, so don't do anything hasty,' his manservant advised.

Everybody in the district seemed to have an opinion on his feelings towards Adele – whether for or against. Ryder's eyelids flickered as a small flare of hope shafted through him. His voice took on a half-hearted edge as he remembered how pretty and delicate she'd looked that morning with her hair loose and her green eyes shining. 'Good Lord, man, for how much longer is my relationship with Mrs Pelham going to be fodder for gossips. I don't want to hear it.'

'As you say, my lord, but I imagine you only hear the half of it.' John's lips pursed and there was a slightly affronted familiarity about him.

After a while, Ryder sighed, 'Go on, then. Tell me, John.'

'It's said Mrs Pelham was tricked, that Edgar Pelham sent her a note to say you were engaged with another lady on the eve of your wedding. It's said that Mrs Pelham whispers your name in her sleep.'

That was a good tale, almost believable. He didn't bother asking who'd filled his personal manservant's head with such a romantic notion. The wide-eyed Sarah Pelham was the chief suspect. She was the only one who had access to Del's bedchamber at night. But she'd also had access to her father's actions in the past.

Sarah had become a favourite with his staff. She was part

of his household for half the day, and his pert little lady clerk was often seen poised busily over an account book or a sheet of paper, relieving him of the tedious job of making copies of letters, documents and accounts that he needed to keep for his files. He didn't know how he'd manage the estate without her, and supposed a Prince Charming would one day come along and run off with her, for she'd make some man a fine wife.

Ryder laughed. 'Do I respond?'

'Now and again, my lord, I can vouch for that.'

Something said with too much relish for Ryder's liking, so he snorted. 'If I were you I'd put that notion from your mind.'

'Mrs Pelham is a lovely woman who is bound to attract the attention and the praise of men. Forgive me for being familiar, sir, but I've always thought you were well suited.'

But the women would be wary of her, he thought. Even if she married him she would not become respectable overnight and they would guard their husbands, lest she ran off with them. Ah yes . . . Adele would always have a hint of scandal about her now, and she deserved it. But then, so would he. Their lives would be carried out in the public gaze and commented on accordingly.

Ryder was attacked by a vision of them calling to each other across the woodland separating Madigan House from the village, like a duet in an opera. It was an amusing notion. 'Stuff and nonsense, John. You'll have me singing a romantic ditty under her window next.'

John grinned. 'I'm sure she'd enjoy it. The pair of you were always good friends in childhood I understand, and later, in the years when you were growing into a man . . . you couldn't tear your eyes away from each other when you were together. You spoke of her often when you were apart. It was quite touching.'

Ryder caught the grin and chuckled. 'I do believe you're pulling my strings. If you dare tell anyone of anything you've just said to me, I'll cut your wagging tongue off.' He turned when he reached the door. 'If you hear anything else of interest you must let me know.'

'Of course, my lord.'

'I'm off to Poole, where I've got business to conduct. Tell the coachman he's not needed, it will keep you out of mischief.' That reminded him to visit the Reverend Bryson on the way, and make his peace with him. After that he'd go and see this James Pelham, who had delivered the missing trunks.

He summoned Luke Ashburn into the library. 'I'll be absent for a week or so. William Swift will be in charge of the household.'

'Yes, my lord.'

The man had a face as long as a wet weekend. 'Is something bothering you, Mr Ashburn?'

'The reverend asked me to talk to you, but it goes against the grain now I've grown to know you better.'

'Tell me what it's about?'

'He wishes to retain his position in the parish.'

'Oh, is that all. I was about to pay him a visit.'

'Were it me I'd have him dismissed.'

Ashburn's cold-blooded remark astounded him. 'You seem to have very little compassion towards others.'

'It depends on the circumstances. His troubles are of his own making.'

Curiosity filled him. 'Where did you grow up? Certainly not in the immediate vicinity, since I'd never heard Mary Bryson mention you.'

'I was raised in a charity school in London. Run by priests, it taught orphaned boys of the clergy. They were strict, and the students were destined to serve the Church. I ran away several times, received a severe birching and then ran away again. I was brought back with the same result, and the addition of a bread and water diet for a week. I must say they were diligent in their duty for I finally learned some sense.'

So that's where Ashburn had gained his air of defiant independence. 'Before that?'

Ashburn gave a twisted grin. 'I can't remember before that, my lord, and neither do I want to. Can you?'

The log on the fire exploded, sending out a shower of sparks.

Ryder gave a short laugh. 'I suppose not. Is that a polite way of telling me to mind my own business?'

'No, my lord . . . it's just a fact. I saw the value of having an education all around me. I also observed the plight of the poor and the comparative comfort of the wealthy.'

'And the Church?'

'The Church does its best but I proved to be an unsuitable candidate for the priesthood. When the reverend turned up claiming me as his wife's nephew it was a relief at first. It gave me a chance to get something back for the years of misery I endured.'

'And then?'

'He was overbearing rather than welcoming. Mary kept reminding me I was a charity case.'

'Notwithstanding that the reverend paid for your education and board, are you Mary's long-lost nephew? I fancy there is a familiarity in your features and those of the reverend.'

Ashburn's eyes narrowed. 'You're astute, I'll give you that. For a long time I kept asking myself the same question.'

'What was the answer to it?'

'I'm more likely to be his son.'

Astounded by the thought Ryder said, 'You're claiming to be Oliver Bryson's bastard?'

This time Ashburn's grin widened. 'Nothing so base. He fell in love with a young woman barely out of the nursery. They ran away to Scotland together and were wed by the anvil priest Robert Elliot.'

'Witnesses?'

'Two, as required.'

'And you were the result of the marriage?'

'Rather, I was the cause. To fend off the scandal, the reverend and his new wife were packed off to do missionary work abroad. My mother, Jane Ashburn, died birthing me barely five months into the marriage. I was sent back to England with a wet nurse, where I was placed in an institution. By this time the bishop had met his maker and nobody knew about me except the reverend. He paid for my upkeep. Shortly after, he married Mrs Bryson, who'd been widowed.'

'How did you get the information?'

'The Church keeps meticulous records and I was good at picking locks. In fact, I considered taking up crime as a profession until I decided that making money honestly was just as easy and less worrisome. I don't want to spend my life looking over my shoulder.'

Ryder thought, if that was the truth, it would explain what was going on. If his own reported death had proved to be true, then Oliver Bryson would have inherited the title of earl. In line after him would be Luke Ashburn.

Ashburn gave a low chuckle. 'I can see you've reached the probable outcome.'

'I have, and it perturbs me, not the possibility of us being cousins but the means being employed to inherit my title. You know as well as I that some random shooting has taken place, and that makes me uneasy in case there was a sinister purpose behind it.'

'I'm almost certain the reverend was not part of that. He finds it hard to kill a rabbit or neck a chicken for his dinner . . . his wife usually attends to that task.'

'Does she wear a brown robe with a cowl attached on occasion?'

Ashburn's eyes shifted slightly. 'Good Lord, I've never inspected the contents of her wardrobe, but I have seen one hanging in the vestry. When I asked the reverend for the truth about our relationship, he held the earldom up as a prize in an effort to make me bow to his wishes. What he cannot understand is that I don't give a damn about anything I haven't earned.'

Ryder nodded. Luke Ashburn was a lone wolf who wouldn't be swayed by position. 'Nevertheless, if you prove to be an heir to the title and the need arises I will expect you to give a damn when the time comes, and accept the title with good grace.'

'If that time happens to come, you will no longer be around to enforce your expectations.'

'True.'

'I doubt if it will become necessary but remember how your father died and take care. I'll keep an ear to the ground while you're away. The reverend wants to acknowledge me as his son, since he has no heir.'

'And?'

'Mary Bryson thinks it will make a fool out of her since

they've already passed me off as her nephew. She is demanding, and unpredictable when her temper is roused, which makes life exceedingly uncomfortable. She seems to be unstable at times. Sometimes she's so agitated she never stops talking and at other times . . . well, let me just say that inheriting relatives at short notice can be a liability, especially when obligated.'

'What do you intend to do in the long run?'

'When I've paid off my loan to the reverend I intend to sell the Lawrence estate at a profit and leave the district. Pardon me, my lord, but you do understand that the price must include recompense for the Duck Pond acreage. We must sort that matter out soon because a lengthy delay could cost me more than I stand to gain. I have allowed myself eighteen months, by which time the sale of the corn crops followed by those of the estate should see me straight.'

'Weather permitting.'

'As you say, my lord. Rest assured, I will not leave the district while I'm responsible for a debt to anyone, for if nothing else I was raised to be honest. I do agree that Mrs Pelham seems to have an equal claim to the cottage and the land it stands on. I'll make no attempt to evict them while the problem exists, but if I am declared the legal owner then I will expect them to pay rent.'

The man rose a mile in Ryder's estimation. He was a good businessman. 'You won't have to worry about that. I'll offer you a proposition, Mr Ashburn. I'll buy the Lawrence estate from you, and will offer fair compensation for the perceived loss of the Duck Pond property, though I don't think you have any real entitlement to it.'

Ashburn's eyes widened. 'This offer is entirely unexpected. I will need to think about it. It was not part of my plan.'

'Plans can be changed. Mrs Pelham has the original deeds and her grandmother's will on her side. Sometimes life has its own plan to follow.'

'It certainly does. I shouldn't take too much time deciding, in case I begin to think the better of launching a face-saving solution. Such a proposition would help further my aims considerably, though I'm not entirely happy at being given an ultimatum. Will my terms of employment still stand?'

'As long as you remain competent . . . you specified a contract for two years, did you not? Why two years. I'm curious?'

'It will take that long before your land produces a decent corn crop, though I've made a good start with the ploughing, and the earth should be ready to seed come winter. Buying enough seed is a problem because your land has been neglected. I have recently made a contact with a merchant who has offered us a decent amount of superior seed, at a price.

'I could ride that out and I could also hire someone else to do it. What's the real reason?'

'I stand to lose what I've gained if I'm unemployed, since there is very little in the way of employment at this time of year.' A flush crept into Ashburn's cheeks. 'Also, by that time Miss Pelham will be old enough to wed and I'll be in a better position to support her.'

Ryder thought about that and didn't like it. 'So, you intend to pay court to the pert Miss Sarah Pelham. Has she consented?'

'She has not been informed of my interest yet but it's my intention to bring her round to the idea gradually, to learn her likes and dislikes. After all she has only just turned sixteen. I was going to ask your permission.'

Laughter huffed from him. 'Good grief! Are you always so cold-blooded? Besides, Miss Pelham is not my ward but is employed for clerical duties.'

'A word from you on my behalf might help her see me in a good light.'

'I would prefer a clean break, and for that reason alone I would not encourage a union of marriage between you.' Ryder's laughter had an ironic undertone. 'She is an intelligent young woman who will see right through that. If you wish to impress her you'd be better off stating your case for yourself, since Miss Pelham has a mind of her own. Besides, I don't seem to be doing too well in matters of the heart. The object of my desire is proving to be a little recalcitrant, but I intend to bring her to heel when the right opportunity presents itself.'

'You still intend to wed Mrs Pelham, then?'

Ryder gave a faint frown. 'Can you think of any reason why I shouldn't?'

'No, my lord. She's a lively, good-natured young lady, and will make a fine countess deserving of respect.'

Ashburn had sounded doubtful nevertheless.

'Make sure you remember that, and offer your assistance should she ever need it, that's all I ask. Think about the other matter, Mr Ashburn. If you decide to go ahead with the sale let me know the numbers as soon as possible. Do not mention the transaction to anyone, else the offer will be withdrawn and the matter will be put before the court. Out of curiosity, where do you intend to go from here if you sell?'

Ashburn shrugged. 'I haven't decided yet. I was thinking I might move abroad eventually. America perhaps, since Miss Pelham talks about the country with great enthusiasm and tells me it has much to offer settlers.'

Rising, Ryder ambled to the window and gazed down the long driveway, at the tender green colours washing across the land. This place was his home, his life and his future. Just across the distant woodlands, where the stream wound gently through the countryside, his love resided. Now he'd learned that love forgave everything, he wanted nothing more.

'I've heard that America is a young man's country and there is wealth for those who are not afraid to earn it. I don't envy your freedom to do as you please and be your own man. My days of adventuring are over. Army life cured me of any urge in that direction.' Though he'd had to admit India had possessed a colourful elegance and an exotic energy all of its own.

'The snake . . . was that a tall tale?'

'It was a python and it bit me on the ankle. We were bathing in a river and it was in the grass on the bank, minding its own business until I trod on it. At least it bit me on a respectable part of the body, since I was bare-arsed. For that I'm thankful.'

They chuckled at the funny side of what it might have been, or was it with relief that it hadn't been the disaster it could have been.

'Bear in mind I'm not in any hurry to lose you, or Miss Pelham come to that. In the meantime I'd be grateful if you kept the matters we've discussed in confidence.'

'If you will accept my hand on that assurance, my lord.'

Exchanging a handshake the two men parted company.

Ashburn took with him an aura of tension, and his laughter had been strained. For every plus Ryder seemed to unearth a minus. Something was bothering the man and Ryder wondered if his story was true.

After Ashburn had gone Ryder drew on his coat and set out. He intended to talk to the reverend next. After that he must go to the Antelope and confront James Pelham, who had contacted Adele and threatened her.

He found Oliver Bryson in the church and the man gave him a hard stare. Although Ryder had taken to Ashburn a little bit more, he liked the reverend less. But the man represented the church in the area and for that reason alone Ryder could not dismiss him out of hand. It had been obvious to Ryder that even if Ashburn was the reverend's son, Luke Ashburn owed no allegiance to the father, for he'd never been offered any kinship to him in his younger years, just spent his youth in the company of Anglican priests.

'My lord, to what do I owe this . . . pleasure.'

There was nothing humble about this man and Ryder wished he hadn't bothered to come. It was hard to offer an apology to an adversary who'd become little more than a thorn in his side . . . worse to allow his temper to suggest that the man give up his living.

'Can we please stop this sparring. I'm here to straighten matters out between us.'

'Very well.'

'I was hasty when I suggested you should give up your living. My temper got the better of me.'

'Yes it did . . . but I've been thinking on it, my lord. Perhaps I should depart, since it will have no effect on the eventual outcome of the Madigan inheritance.'

He was not going to get an admission of any responsibility from the reverend.

'May I remind you that will change when I marry and produce children.'

The reverend ignored that notion. 'There's a living becoming vacant in Hampshire and I was just about to write to the bishop about it. It's a larger parish and it pays more than this one.'

Ryder knew when he was being manipulated, and he

wasn't going to let his relative get away with it. He cancelled any apology he'd been about to make. 'As you wish then, Reverend. I came here in all good intention to retract my earlier comments regarding the position you currently fill and to take the matter of your income into my own hands. I intend to increase it.

'My one regret is that you are regarding me with hostility, and at every turn you seek to undermine me in the community. I understand the reason why,' and he threw a barb into the ring. 'The difference in our ages and the remaining length of our lives will decide for us. You might die tomorrow, and so might I.'

'Perhaps there's something you need to be made aware of, my lord.'

'You'd be a fool to imagine any past indiscretion of yours has remained a secret, if that's what you're referring to. One thing, Reverend, I understand you were called to missionary work in the past, I find it odd that you didn't tell me.'

'You were a child, and one doesn't discuss such matters with a child. Besides, there was no need for you to be informed of that which was my sole business.'

'When that business concerns the lineage of the Madigan estate, it does.'

An atmosphere of wariness suddenly surrounded them. 'My lord?'

'You know very well what I'm alluding to. If I'm wrong I owe you an apology. However, I intend to have any claim to the title and the Madigan estate lands investigated thoroughly, and will engage my former companion in arms, Hal Stover, for the task. It seems that a lie passed on by the tattletales is accepted as the truth in the district these days. Good day to you, Reverend. Do let me know your intentions, and in good time for the Church hierarchy to suggest a new man to me to take up the position, should I require it. We don't want the congregation to suffer from a lack of spiritual guidance, do we?'

Bryson looked as though he'd like to floor him, but he didn't have the courage. Mary Bryson edged through the door. A flush stained her cheeks and there was a fidgety look to her. She moved from one foot to the other.

She was a handsome-looking woman, except she was thin. Discontent had scored taut lines into her features and they looked permanent. Her skirts half-concealed a pistol as she went to stand by Oliver Bryson, the weapon ready to discharge. She couldn't miss at this range. He remembered she'd won the women's purse for shooting at the recent fair. Goosebumps raced down his spine. She wouldn't miss at any range!

The reverend turned and shifted into her line of vision. 'That pistol is not needed, Mary, give it to me,' he said gently.

'Then will you give me my medicine? The devils are inside me.'

When he gave a defeated sigh and nodded Mary did as she was told.

Ryder noticed that her eyes were light brown and the pupils were staring and enlarged, despite the dim light inside the church. He'd seen eyes like those before and he gave a swift intake of breath. 'I'm sorry . . . I didn't realize. How long has she been . . .?'

'On medication?' The reverend slid an arm around his wife's waist. 'Since the doctor prescribed it after she fell and banged her head. That was two years ago. Mary gets odd notions in her head, and the . . . *medicine* . . . helps to calm her.'

'Is there anything I can do to help?'

'We don't need your pity, my lord.'

'I'm not offering it. I was thinking of something practical . . . someone to look after her on a permanent basis, perhaps.'

'We can manage.' He was stiff-necked with pride.

Striding away from the pair with the woman's disconcerting glare boring into his back, Ryder thought: Ashburn had been right. Mary Bryson did show signs of instability, but she also displayed signs of laudanum addiction.

He stopped at the door and turned. 'I'm sorry, and I won't insist that you lose your living.'

'It matters not, if I can get the Hampshire position. It has a hospice run by the Anglican sisters of mercy.'

So it hadn't been bravado when he'd mentioned it before. 'I'll send a note of recommendation to the bishop if you decide that way.'

'Thank you, my lord, I know I can rely on your discretion.'

Mary said, 'Discretion? There's precious little of that in these parts. The Lord will bring fire and rain and only those without sin will survive. There's no place in heaven for sinners.'

'Hush, Mary,' the reverend said tiredly.

Mounting Henry, Ryder rode off towards Poole without a backward glance.

Ryder's anger at himself had abated by the time he reached the harbour town, due no doubt to the hustle and bustle of the crowds, the sea air and the piquant smell of the mud, for the tide was out.

He entered the Antelope Hotel and enquired if James Pelham had left town. The place was bustling. In the yard, luggage and parcels were being loaded onto a coach and the horses, muscular beasts, fretted to be off.

He didn't intend to stay here long, and left Henry in the charge of a lad, along with the promise of a ha'penny piece for his trouble.

'Not yet, my lord. Mr Pelham had some business to conduct about town, I believe. If you'd care to wait in the parlour I'll furnish you with a mutton pie and a tankard of my best ale to wash it down with.'

James Pelham walked with a long-legged stride. Under his arm he carried a satchel.

When the innkeeper spoke to him, he turned towards Ryder and nodded.

Ryder stood and the pair shook hands.

'I have only a few moments to spare before the coach departs, my lord. How can I help you?'

'Mrs Pelham received the remains of a pair of travelling trunks that had been stolen or mislaid. I'm representing her in the matter you raised.'

His smile faded. 'Forgive me for being frank, but I'm given to understand that you and the lady concerned are . . . involved.'

'From whom?'

'Someone who claims to be related to you.'

He didn't have to strain his mind to realize who that was.

'I have the utmost respect for Mrs Pelham. As for us being involved, *that*, sir, is a slanderous falsehood, along with the suggestion that she may have stolen from you.'

The man bristled. 'Nevertheless, items were missing that belonged to my family.'

'Stolen by Edgar Pelham in the first place, I imagine.'

'But taken from his estate after his death.'

'Surely his goods should go to his next of kin.'

'That woman is not his next of kin. They were not even wed. The Church advised me that a shipboard marriage is invalid in its eyes. I had already disowned him.'

'And the child . . . what about her?'

'Child?'

'Your granddaughter . . . Sarah Pelham.'

'Sarah?' He looked suddenly bewildered. 'Sarah is dead. We received a letter from Edgar a few months after he absconded with her. She died of a fever in Boston.'

'And what of Sarah's mother?'

'Gwen fell down a flight of stairs just before Edgar left . . . and she died from her injuries. She and Edgar never got on.'

'Is that why you disowned him?'

His voice became a whisper. 'No . . . yes . . . I couldn't be sure. Jeffery . . . it's hard when you suspect your own son of criminal behaviour. My younger son suspected Edgar of harming Gwen too. He accused him and they fought.'

Ryder began to stitch it all together. 'Allow me fill the rest of it in for you, Mr Pelham, because I want to get this straight. You suspected that your elder son, Edgar Pelham, killed his sister-in-law. Your younger son, Jeffery, who was her husband at the time, accused Edgar of the crime and threatened to have him arrested. Edgar fled, taking Sarah with him. She was only a child at the time.'

James Pelham nodded. 'That's about it.

Ryder sighed. 'Here's some information you need to be made aware of. Edgar Pelham came to Dorset, recommended as an architect for some restoration work by the reverend's wife, who is apparently a relation.'

'A very distant one. I can't say I ever met her but we have corresponded on ocassion.'

'I dismissed Edgar Pelham because his work was well below standard.'

'He failed his master's examination and obtained forged certification.'

'Later, and out of spite, I imagine, he tricked a decent young woman into leaving her bridegroom on the eve of their wedding and he used force to remove her from the care those who loved her.'

'Am I to take it that bridegroom was you?'

'It was. Your son shamed her, making it impossible for her to return home. That is the woman you now accuse of stealing from you. Believe me, she arrived back home with nothing to her name except the clothing she wore.'

'She should have left him?'

'She would have, except she feared for the life of the child he had with him . . . a little girl called Sarah.'

Pelham's eyes reflected his confusion.

'The coach is leaving in five minutes, sir,' the innkeeper called out.

'Tell it to wait!' Ryder ordered.

Looking anguished, James Pelham whispered, 'What mockery is this? Sarah was my younger son's child. Edgar stole her away and then wrote to say she'd died. My lord . . . you talk as if . . . does Sarah still live?'

'She does.'

'Oh . . . thank God!' and tears sprang to his eyes. 'Jeffery won't believe it until he sees her himself. He is married again and has a son. I don't know how his wife will take it. She's not much older than Sarah would be now.'

'The coach, sir?'

'Give me a minute.'

They rose together. 'May I see Sarah?'

'Not until she's properly prepared. Rest assured, she has been well looked after and loved all these years. Not by Edgar, I'm given to understand, though she thought he was her father. Can you return in a week with your son? It will give me time to prepare Sarah, and also the people who love her. By then I hope I can assemble enough evidence to convince you not to take this before a magistrate, because you will just be persecuting the innocent.'

'What's a week after all this time? There's one thing you should know, my lord. Mary Bryson contacted me recently. She made claims that need investigation, because if they are true the woman concerned must be brought to account for such a deed.'

'What deed is that?'

'That you can assess for yourself, my lord.' Fishing in his pocket he brought out a piece of folded paper and held it out. 'It relates to my son's death.'

Ryder was reluctant to take it. 'Mary Bryson is ill. Without her medicine she is liable to lose control of her emotions, and imagine things. Anything she says should be ignored.'

'A suspicious death cannot be ignored.'

'Suspicious death? I would advise you not to repeat such a scandalous proposition to anyone. In fact, the matter of your son's death has already been dealt with by a maritime board. Statements written by Mrs Pelham and two eyewitness accounts are on file in Bridport. Your son's death was an accident.' Ryder handed the man his card. 'I will see you in a week so we can get this matter cleared up.'

The innkeeper rushed in. 'Sir . . . you must come at once, the coachman said he is about leave, with or without you.'

'I'm coming.' The man nodded and Ryder took the letter. James Pelham strode to the coach and the fretting horses.

A crack of the whip and the coach and its passengers clattered away.

Ryder gazed at the letter in his hand with a strong sense of foreboding. He was not in the mood to read it. He folded it into its creases and slid it into his pocket. Then he strolled over to St James' Church to speak to the rector there, and was pleasantly surprised to find the bishop visiting.

'My lord, You are just the person I wanted to see,' Ryder said with an expansive smile.

Fourteen

My dearest Ryder. Please accept my sincere apology for my rudeness. Nothing you did or said warranted such a remark, which came from anger. Because I know you to be honest and sincere, I must believe you when you say you still love me, and on that premise you must forgive me. In return you must also believe me when I say there's a reason why I cannot allow myself to love you in return. Something so terrible happened it still haunts my dreams. Should it become common knowledge it would ruin every kind or romantic notion you have ever had of me. Ryder, friend of my heart, we must not see each other again. I'll always keep you close to my heart.

> *Forgive me.*
>
> *Adele*

Adele sealed the note with wax and handed it to Sarah. 'Make sure the earl gets it, but not until tomorrow.'

'He reads his communications over breakfast. They will mostly be acceptances for the social supper dance. We're all invited. I'm so looking forward to it. Mr Ashburn has asked me to put him down for the first dance.' Sarah kissed her. 'The aunts have gone to the market in Blandford and I'll be going to Madigan House soon. You won't mind being on your own, will you? Don't worry about the earl, I'm sure he will forgive you.'

'What I said to him was unforgivable, especially after his tolerance of my past actions towards him. I don't want to discuss it, Sarah, but I'd be obliged if you'd just put it on his message tray, along with my refusal to attend his social evening.'

Sarah stared at her in disbelieve. 'You're not going? But you must, it would be the height of rudeness to snub him in such a manner. He will want to know why you're not there.'

'If he does you must tell him I have a previous engagement.'

'He might ask what it is.'

'He won't. He'll accept the reason at face value and will not question it.'

'Lord Madigan is not that forgiving. If you push him too hard he might drop his pursuit of you altogether and find another woman to love.'

'Has it not occurred to you that it might be my intention?'

'What would you do if he fell in love with me?'

'Enough now, Sarah, you're being ridiculous. Stop meddling in my personal affairs.'

Frowning a little, Sarah picked up a white gown and held it against her. 'Why do you consider it ridiculous?'

'Because he's a grown man and you are still a child.' Adele gave Sarah a sharp look. 'Surely you don't harbour inappropriate feelings towards the earl.'

'Why would they be inappropriate? It's not as if his affections are claimed by another.'

Adele had to know. 'You don't entertain any tender thoughts towards the earl, do you?'

Sarah sighed. 'He's so handsome, manly and strong – and so impossibly wealthy. His eyes are so blue and dark, like the evening sky.'

'You must not allow your thoughts to dwell on such things. It's impossible. You can't marry Ryder, I forbid it. If he makes advances towards you . . .' It occurred her that Sarah was teasing her and she said rather sheepishly, 'Well, I think I might kill him.'

A giggle ripped from Sarah. 'For someone who declares herself not to be in love you're a dog in a manger where the earl's concerned. You say you don't want him yourself, but you don't want anyone else to have him either.'

'Because he's my friend from childhood, and I . . . well, I do have his welfare at heart.'

'You had mine at heart a few moments ago. Why are you in such a flap, Adele? Honestly, are you scared that I'll snatch the earl from under your nose when it's obvious he only has eyes for you?'

Reluctantly, Adele laughed. 'All right, so you've made a fool out of me. Shall we drop the subject now? I wore that white gown to my first ball. What don't you like about it?'

'The neckline is too low and it draws the eye. I feel embarrassed when men gaze at me there, especially older men.'

'It's because you're becoming a woman. I don't think you realize how lovely you are, Sarah. You'll have to learn to cope with it.' She picked up a corsage of silk flowers. 'I wore that white gown when I was your age. It's a tradition for young girls to wear white gowns. If you want to be modest, wear this across the neckline. We can sew it to the gown.'

The girl's smile returned. 'I can't make up my mind which of my two best gowns to wear.'

'You can wear any gown in my wardrobe.'

Sarah's eyes began to shine. 'Does that offer include the blue and white silk gown with the muslin overskirt and pearl drops on the bodice? It's exquisite.'

Tears pricked at Adele's eyes. 'I intended to wear that when Ryder and I were wed. It seems a long time ago now.' She would never wear it now. She'd been like any eager young bride and the dressmaker had fussed over her and presented her best work because she was to wed the earl and would become someone of importance in the district. How things had changed.

'You may have the gown.'

Sarah's smile faded and the girl gave her a fierce hug. 'I'd rather wear sackcloth than use your wedding gown. You only offered it because you're feeling sorry for yourself. All you'll achieve is to encourage everyone around you to feel guilty. You're plotting something, aren't you?'

Adele gave in to a moment of sharpness because she'd had enough of being the villain for one day. 'My goodness, you're becoming such a little busybody. Why should I be plotting anything? Truthfully, I'm tired of being the local pariah, and the subject of constant rumour. I just want some peace and quiet. Now, you'd better get yourself off to Madigan House.'

Sarah's eyes narrowed. 'I still think you're plotting something.'

'When you think of what it might be, do let me know. I need another plot in my life like parliament needs another Guy Fawkes.'

'Sarcasm doesn't suit you, Adele.'

'Nevertheless, it's very satisfying.' She laughed. 'Do you realize we're having our first argument?'

'And it's over the same man.'

Her heart wrenched. She hadn't thought that leaving behind those she loved would be quite so hard – and she hadn't even gone yet. Not only that, she didn't even know where she was going.

As soon as she had the house to herself Adele packed a bag. She pulled on her walking boots, donned her pelisse and bonnet, and set off for Poole.

She could hear Gypsy kicking up a fuss as she strode away. She had locked him in the laundry room so he couldn't follow her.

It wasn't long before she began to tire and the bag in her hand grew heavy. She struggled on for another mile then stopped to rest in her favourite place by the willow tree. The grass had been cropped and a new wooden seat placed there. Across the pond a small bridge arched.

It was the sort of surprise Ryder used to devise to please her with. As she drew closer she noticed something carved into the back of the seat. It was a heart pierced by an arrow, and under it, some words. *Constant Heart*. Ryder had made this little setting for her.

Pushing her bag under the seat with her foot she seated herself and ran her forefinger gently over the carving, thinking of Ryder, and of the portion of the childhood they'd spent together. It was peaceful; the air was a moist, but sultry breath against her face, as if the breeze skimmed the surface from the stream and turned it into whispers. Yet there was a bite to the air. She sat amongst leaves that roared in the tree canopy as they bent before the breeze like silver raindrops. Summer had come early and the earth was alive. Soon the land would be offering up a yield of hay, followed by the corn crops. Not at Madigan Estate though. There, the earth was being coaxed into production after its long rest.

Running away was a silly notion. She had no friends she could go to and it would serve only to worry the people she loved most. Ryder wouldn't appreciate it if she caused any more trouble. Using her crooked arm as a cushion she placed her face against the carved heart and closed her eyes, imagining it was beating. Gradually the world faded.

Something woke her. The air was still with a tense quiet that came before a storm. Between the trees glimpses of grey cloud piled one on top on the other. Cold began to invade her. Thunder rumbled in the distance and something in the copse on the other side of the path snapped.

Her eyelids flew open as she remembered that this was the place where she'd been shot at. A thin, clinging mist pressed in on her. She hoped her aunts had reached home before the storm hit.

Another snap!

Disorientated, she rose and panic set in. She grabbed her bag and began to run, the blood pounding in her ears.

It was a while before she stopped, brought up short by the whinny of a horse as it stood on its hind legs and pawed at the air.

She yelped and fell backwards into a patch of stinging nettles. A light sweep of the nettle over her hand and wrist brought the skin up in angry lumps and it began to itch. She scrambled to her feet, hugging her arm.

It was Ryder who voiced the curse when he was almost unseated. Succinct and to the point, it was followed by, 'Easy, Henry, we're not at war now. At least I'm not. I can't vouch for the lady's temper though, so you'd better watch out.'

Henry snorted disdainfully, as if on cue.

Adele wanted to laugh, and chided him with, 'Your language should have been left in the army, where it belongs.'

'It was a slip of the tongue, and besides, you're a woman and shouldn't be aware of its meaning.'

'Well . . . I am aware. Apologize.'

'Be damned if I will,' then he laughed. 'I'm sorry, my Del.'

'Why were you so vexed?'

'I've been looking for you and you've led me on a merry dance.'

Her hands went to her hips. 'That's not my fault. Why were you looking for me?'

'I couldn't find you at home and your aunts were worried about the approaching storm. Also I'd just returned from Poole, where I met James Pelham, so at least I could reassure them that you didn't get on a coach.' He'd never know how close she'd come and there was always tomorrow.

'Why should I have got on the coach?'

'You have your travelling bag with you. Where were you going?'

She discovered a dock plant nearby and applied one of its leaves to the flaming nettled skin while she thought of an excuse. After a few minutes the sting went out of her arm. She looked up at him, smiling, and decided on the truth. 'I was on my way into Poole to see if I could confront James Pelham before he left. I came across the little arbour you'd made and I sat down. I began to think about our childhood, when things were not so complicated, and I fell asleep.'

'You were running when I saw you?'

'I was trying to beat the storm.'

The darkness was deepening and she wondered how long she'd been asleep. For some time, she suspected.

A handful of rain hit them. 'Too late, I think,' he observed.

'I was touched by your message on the seat.'

'I should change it.'

'To what?'

'Something more appropriate. "Broken Heart" would fit the situation.' He reached down, his voice gruff. 'Pass up the bag, and then put a foot in the stirrup and take my hand.'

She folded her arms over her chest. 'I can walk.'

'If I hear one more squeak of rebellion, so help me, I'll beat the bounce out of you.'

'You wouldn't.'

His eyes lightened. 'You're much too sure of yourself . . . of me. Enough of these games now else I'll leave you here to find your own way home.'

She remembered what had caused her panic and took his hand. She didn't want to be alone here in the dark. Swung up in front of him she found herself seated sideways across his lap, as comfortably as such a position afforded them.

Henry tossed his head and grunted.

They looked at each other, and Ryder's eyes were bluer than blue when he smiled and placed her bag between them.

'Thank you, Ryder,' she cooed. 'You're so sweet, even when you're angry.'

'You can stop the toad-eating right now. I'm on to you.'

'What did James Pelham have to say?'

'I'll tell you when we find shelter.'

His smile became a grimace when several fat raindrops spattered over them. 'We haven't been this close since I found you on the heath. You were more dead than alive then, and certainly less trouble. I feared for your life.'

She sensed danger in his words since she was unaware of how physically close they had been on that day. She'd been unconscious and anything could have happened to her in that state. 'I'd better go home, else the aunts might worry.'

'It's too late for that,' he said and he choked out a laugh. 'Are you frightened you might lose your newly discovered virtue if you stay with me?'

A blush spread under her skin and she turned her face into his coat.

'Aw . . . Del, my sweet, look at me so I can see you blush. We're only human, and so are your aunts.'

'I'm not blushing. My face is inflamed where the nettles stung.'

'You were stung on the arm. Allow me to kiss you better.'

'The juice from the dock leaf is adequate.'

'But not so exciting, surely.'

'No, not half as exciting.' Waiting a few seconds for her blush to subside she turned her face up to his. He deserved a reward, and so did she. He kissed her, his mouth a tease against hers, and then his tongue curled. Like a cat he delicately took a lick, as if she was made of melting butter.

Her mouth joined with his and she purred with pleasure, almost experiencing her ears flattening against her head and her whiskers twitching. When she withdrew she saw a little dimple appear to dent his cheek. She planted a chaste kiss on the spot when he smiled. It was a small caress, mainly because she needed to touch him and that was the safest place in daylight . . . or what passed for it at the moment. The light seemed to be fading in the vanguard of the storm. A shiver ran through her. What a delight it was to be with Ryder – to be this close in mind and body, and to love him.

Henry's stomach rattled.

'Does this horse go anywhere, or does it just stand still and grumble?' she asked.

His laughter was lost in a prolonged rumble of thunder that vibrated all around them. She jumped when fat drops of rain spattered down through the trees. Lightning snicked and spat, like the wick of a candle drowning in molten wax. Ryder pulled Henry's head around. 'We can hide in the hay barn until the storm is over, the one that belonged to your family. Remember it?'

The place of their initial act of loving, oh so casually, dropped into the conversation.

'Of course I do.' How could she forget the place where she'd surrendered her innocence to him.

A dart of desire buried its barb into her soft, warm centre. It was insidious, like Adam and Eve's snake. Her internal muscles clenched around the bittersweet barb, savouring the feeling. No good playing the innocent here with Ryder, when the place held so many memories.

How tedious being a spinster was with its sudden urges, the outcome of which were usually fulfilled only in the imagination.

She had a moment of regret when she thought of her father and his disappointment in her. He'd been so willing to think the worst of her – to abandon her. That had hurt. She couldn't put matters right with him now.

But perhaps she could let Ryder know how much she loved him. Her travel bag kept them effectively apart, so she gently nipped his ear lobe.

A warm and tender kiss touched against her cheek and slid across to her ear. 'See that you do remember it,' he whispered, and it was as if he'd picked up her thoughts.

Fifteen

Henry was left in the company of two farm horses that moved their muscular rumps aside at the feeding trough, allowing him to share their hay.

Making their way through the flickering lightning flashes Adele and Ryder carefully mounted the ladder into the loft, and made a cosy hideaway between the bales. Even so Adele began to shiver from the sudden drop in temperature.

After a while the wind began to howl like a banshee and the barn door rattled and creaked. The horses shifted uneasily and then seemed to get used to the din and settled.

Ryder gazed at his drenched and bedraggled companion in the grey twilight. 'Do you have something dry to wear in your bag?'

She nodded.

'Then you'd better change into it, because it looks as though we'll be here overnight. I'll go down and relieve Henry of his saddle. I spotted a lantern we can use, as long as I can find a flint to light it with.'

'Be careful you don't set fire to the barn.'

'Credit me with some sense, my love.' He dropped a kiss on her mouth and descended into the gloom. After more complaints from Henry, Ryder got his saddle off and draped a blanket over him for warmth.

He found the lantern and flint, along with some candles in a cupboard.

There was a dish to spark the initial fire alight, deep enough to stop it from igniting any debris that might spark up and get out of hand. He sighed with relief when he put the flame to the spill, and the spill to candle wick. It flared up briefly, and then the candle flickered and settled to a soft glow, protected by the glass surrounds of the lantern. Grabbing another horse blanket he nimbly scaled the ladder again, and hanging the lantern on a hook he turned to her. 'You haven't changed.'

'I've found myself a skirt and bodice. I haven't had time for anything else. Besides, I can't reach the back buttons. You'll have to undo them for me.'

He laughed. 'I didn't realize you were going to subject me to torture?'

'Pretend you're a lady's maid for a few seconds.'

A lady's maid he wasn't. He was a full-blooded man lusting for affection, if one could use the gentlemanly word for what type of affection he had in mind. But having it in mind didn't mean he was going to act on it – or that she'd even allow him to, come to that.

He fumbled on her buttons. They were tiny things, slippery like pearls dug from the glutinous depths of an oyster. The top of her back was a graceful curve and his fingers began to walk down the ladder of her spine.

She made a little noise in her throat and trembled when he kissed the junction where her shoulder joined her neck. He recalled several of the sensitive and sensual places on her body, like this one, just behind her ear. He nipped the lobe and she leaned back and murmured, 'Stop it?'

'You want me to stop when we've only just started?'

'No . . . I was just seeing if you would. I want you to love me.'

A ridge in her flesh against his fingertips stopped his exploration. 'What made this mark?'

She clutched her bodice against her. 'Nothing . . . it's nothing. I fell and hurt myself. It's healed now.'

'You're lying to me, Del.'

'Yes . . . I'm lying. I don't want you to know what happened.'

Freeing the last of the buttons he pulled her bodice fully open and brought down the lantern, so her back was towards the light. There were other marks, old ones that had healed into threads, discoloured, so they could hardly be seen and barely felt. A whip had been used on her. He ran a finger down the longest one, anger growing in him. 'If that evil bastard wasn't already dead I'd kill him with my bare hands.'

She placed her hands over her ears. 'Don't, Ryder. I want to forget he ever existed.'

He hung the lantern back on its hook.

She lowered her head and her hair fell over her face, hiding her expression from him. Drawing her close he brushed her hair back and gazed at her. There were tears gleaming in her eyes but she wasn't weeping. Adele had never been inclined towards self-pity.

For a moment she stiffened, then she shrugged away from him and dropped the rest of her gown and her jaconet chemise into the straw. She stood at arm's length, naked, the flickering light from the lantern playing over the shadows and peaks of her body.

His mouth dried when she said, 'Is this how you want me, Ryder?'

He'd never wanted anything more, yet his anger grew at this blatant offer. 'You know I do.'

'Then I'm yours. Just take me and get it over with. It will help me forget . . . *him.*'

Get it over with? It was as though she was offering a reward for something he'd endured . . . or realized she owed him something. Didn't she know the difference between love and the act of expressing it . . . the slow build-up of tension before the urgency of a burning climax and the release?

It was as though she were offering a titbit to a dog. '*Here, Gypsy, good dog . . . catch the reward and be grateful for it.*' Except he wasn't any woman's dog.

Forget the man who had ruined her, she'd said. If only he could.

He saw the confidence drain from her before she hung her head. 'Don't you . . . want me then?'

He snatched up the chemise and practically threw it at her, followed by her dry gown. This one buttoned down the front, so she could manage it by herself. He was sharper than he'd intended. 'I don't want you like this. Cover your body and stop cheapening yourself.'

She did as she was told, and without a murmur, and then sank into the hay and covered her face with her hands. 'You've made me feel as though I'm worth nothing. I didn't expect that from you.'

'I'm the one person you should have expected it from. How do you think I feel? You're not a trollop so don't act like one.'

'I'm sorry . . . I wanted to put things right between us.'

'A tumble in the hay won't do it.'

'What will?'

'I'll let you know when I think of something suitable.' He removed his damp coat, draping it, along with her discarded gown and pelisse, over a bale of hay to dry. Then he drew the pungent horse blanket over them both and turned his back on her.

Sneezing, she emerged from under it. 'Ugh! That stinks.'

'Then stop breathing, it will solve both our problems.'

That hurt. After a while she murmured, through chattering teeth, 'You didn't really mean that.'

'Yes, I did.'

There was a stealthy movement and she inched closer. 'Don't be cross with me, Ryder. I'm hungry.'

'What do you expect me to do, catch a rat and cook it over the candle flame?'

A giggle tore from her mouth, and then she said, 'I'm cold as well.'

Sighing, Ryder turned and pulled her close, spooning her into his body. 'Do something useful, like going to sleep.'

'You were going to tell me what James Pelham said.'

The last thing he wanted to do was to discuss James Pelham. He could sort that out in the morning when he had more time. 'Tomorrow will do.'

He recalled the image of Adele naked, the lightning flickering over her body, her firm jutting breasts and the shadowy pelt at the apex of her thighs. She'd been his for the taking . . . and he'd turned her down. His body reacted and he could have kicked himself. He hadn't had a woman since he'd been home, and he was as horny as a March hare.

One thing was for certain – he was not going to be able to sleep while he was wrapped around Adele like a second skin . . . and neither would she, for he could feel the tension in her. He turned her towards him, smoothed the tumbled hair back from her face and saw uncertainty reflected in her eyes.

He didn't care what she'd done to him. He loved her . . . he'd always loved her and always would. There was no other for him. Adele would become his wife and bear his children, as he'd always planned. He just had to change the plan to suit the situation.

But for the present he had a clear choice. It was either discuss with Adele his meeting with James Pelham, which would probably upset her. Or he could ravish her!

It took him two seconds to decide.

When Ryder's cold hand slid through the aperture of her gown and his fingertips brushed over her warm breasts Adele jumped. 'Your hands are cold.'

'I know . . . and your breasts are warm.'

He nuzzled into the fabric and touched his tongue against her nipple.

'Make love to me, Ryder.'

'What do you think I'm doing? Be quiet, woman.'

Her nubs hardened and came erect, and then her breasts seemed to surge into his hands, as if eager to be handled. 'A moment ago you called me a trollop.'

'Damn it, Del, you know I didn't mean it in that sense.'

'What other sense is there?'

'You can't expect me to hold you like this and not go crazy. You don't seem to be aware of what feelings you evoke in me . . . or perhaps you incite me on purpose.'

'Like this?' She slid her hand down his body and then used her finger to play lightly along the outline of his sheath before she cupped her palm over the bulge that presented itself for her inspection. The instant rise of his body, stiffened and strained upwards against the breeches that confined it.

He scrambled to loosen the flap and managed to pull aside her skirts at the same time.

There was a momentary silence, during which she took his face in her hands and kissed his mouth. It was a moment when love became more than just a word – when she understood she wasn't trying to deny it, but rather to avoid the complications and the inevitable outcome of it.

His stomach, chest, and the smooth buttocks that curved beneath his breeches were shaped with a firm economy of flesh. He was the type of man who would avoid becoming portly in later years, and she remembered the portraits of previous earls on the staircase. They were graceful men, tautly muscled and confident in the positions they'd been born to. Ryder was made in the same mould.

'I know things can never be the same between us, but I want you to know I never stopped loving you.'

'Be quiet, woman,' he growled, and his mouth closed over hers. The man in him sprang firmly into her hands.

Silky.

Alive.

Sliding into her warmth.

Spreading her wide.

A pulsing living thing . . .

They rested, limbs entangled, she inhaling his manly smell and her ears filled with the sound of his powerful, pounding heartbeat.

She gentled him, caressed him with soft kisses on his eyelids, his lips, the palms of his hands.

Their eyes opened and each absorbed the other's being.

She gave an impatient little wriggle.

The sky roared, and then, after a moment of frustrated hesitation, her body arched to capture his powerful first thrust.

The wind increased in its rampaging fury and at one point gave what seemed to be a maniacal cackle of laughter that rose above the rest.

'Did you hear that odd noise?' she whispered against his ear.

'The one that sounded like a coven of witches flying past on their broomsticks?'

'Yes, that one.'

'No . . . I didn't hear it.'

'Neither did I.'

They looked at each other and laughed.

The barn rattled and shook, lightning renewed its flashy display of temper and the sky opened. Hailstones rattled on the roof, short, sharp bursts of ice.

Adele snuggled into Ryder's body and he laughed, though it was more of a triumphant cry of release that rose above the thundering summer storm, and he kissed her, and then, as the night progressed, neither of them noticed the weather.

Sixteen

When Adele woke it was to the sound of whickering horses and male voices. One of the voices belonged to Luke Ashburn.

'I'm relieved to find you safe, my lord.'

'Quite safe, though I had a rather disturbed night.'

So did I, but a very satisfying one, Adele thought, stifling her laughter at Ryder's smug observation.

'I think the sluice has become blocked with debris. There are a couple of trees uprooted, one of which landed directly on the sluice, and I've come for the horses and some rope to pull the trunks off the road if we can get to it. I've alerted the gardeners and issued saws from the house.'

'Has there been any damage to Madigan House?'

'Not any damage that's obvious . . . the garden is a mess, of course. Your valet and William Swift are doing a room by room inspection of the upper floors for signs of water intrusion or cracked windows.'

'You seem to have everything in hand, Ashburn.'

'The stream came up overnight. Duck Pond Cottage is flooded and the pond is three times its size. The stream has diverted into the meadow. It's well under water, and the stream is running fast.'

'We'll sort it out. I'll help you collar the horses and join you there.'

Adele quietly pulled her dishevelled clothing together, and then she ran her fingers through her tangled hair. There was nothing she could do to tidy it now.

Ryder was speaking again. 'Are the Manning sisters safe?'

'They managed to get to the church with the dog and a few other Brackenhurst residents. I dare say Mrs Pelham is with them, but I haven't seen her. Miss Pelham is still at Madigan House. The housekeeper found her a bed in the servants' quarters.'

'I see . . . there will be room for them all in my home until the cottage is repaired. You go on ahead, Mr Ashburn.'

'I need to get the ropes from the loft.'

'I'll get them. My coat is still up there.'

Ryder's feet clattered on the rungs and his head appeared, followed by his body. He offered her a wide smile and whispered, 'Good morning, my love,' then taking a couple of lengths of coiled rope from a hook he tossed it down to his manager and grabbed his coat.

When he got downstairs, Ashburn said, 'I'll take the loft ladder, in case some branches need pruning.'

'I'll bring that too.'

'No need, my lord. I can manage quite easily. I daresay you'd like to go home for some breakfast.' The ladder was unhooked.

From the small window in the loft Adele saw Ashburn move off, carrying the ladder, and with the two farm horses plodding after him. A coil of rope hung from their collars.

She called, 'Ryder, I can't get down.'

'Yes you can.' He stood under the lip of the loft with Henry and held on to the supporting beam. 'Use those wooden pegs; climb down to this beam and on to Henry's back. I'll catch you if you fall. Throw your bag down first.'

She did as she was told, though Henry turned his head and managed an exasperated sigh at being used for a stepladder.

She found herself safely on the ground. He placed her shawl around her shoulders and drew her closer by the ends. Eyes bluer than blue gazed into hers, and they had a teasing light in them when he enquired, 'How do you feel this morning, my shameless hussy?'

As if she could repeat what had taken place between them, right here and now. A blush seemed to spread from her toes and climb upwards throughout her body. It settled on her face. 'If you tease me I'll bite you.'

He laughed. 'I'll drop you off at Madigan House and I'll tell the aunts you're safe.'

For a moment or two she hugged him tight, and then she said, 'Everyone will suspect we were together.'

'Most likely.'

'You don't seem to mind?'

He cocked his head to one side and regarded her. 'It's different for men, my dove. While they congratulate their fellow men over the conquest, the woman is condemned for the same reason.'

'Do men talk about the women they've known, then?'

'Some do.'

'Did you talk about me?'

'No . . .' he said, shortly. 'You must realize that our aborted wedding wasn't an event I wished to remember with any pride.'

They fell silent, then after a while Ryder said, 'Would you rather wait at the church with your aunts?'

'And give Mary Bryson the opportunity to vent her spleen on me at every turn? She certainly has created a cause against me, though God only knows what I've done to personally upset her. I can't help that, but I do feel sorry for her. She is so nasty and sharp-tongued, she must be filled with the most unhappy of thoughts, and I think her mind is twisted in torment for most of the time.'

'It wouldn't surprise me.'

'Besides that, I'm hungry, and your cook will supply me with some breakfast.'

'There's that . . . an egg and a slice or two of bacon between two knobs of buttered bread will set me up for the day. As will a kiss from you.'

Rather it was a kiss from him, fierce and possessive and leaving her breathless.

She remembered the note she'd left for him and nearly panicked. She couldn't remember what it was about . . . an apology, she recalled. She would ask Sarah to retrieve it before he sat down for breakfast, since now they were reconciled she would no longer need to apologize formally.

Leading Henry outside Ryder lifted her up on the horse, closed the barn door and mounted behind her. They ambled through the countryside, relaxed with each other. The lanes were littered with bruised and ragged leaves and the grass stalks bent at angles against the ground. Limbs were torn from the trees and hung in awkward, splintered shapes – like shattered bones.

Yet the air had a clean, wet smell and a sharp silver bright-ness to polish the grey shreds of the morning. Over the hill Madigan House came into view.

Ryder reined Henry in. 'I can't believe it's almost six months since I returned home. It was a good storm, one I'll always remember.'

He sounded as though he was reading a journal entry rather than recalling a love affair, and she wondered if he would still pursue her now he'd achieved his desire. Had his remark about men talking about their conquests been a warning?

Oh Lord . . . she'd just remembered something! Her journals were missing as well as the will and the house deeds.

He said, 'Most of the men have gone to see to the storm damage and the women will be busy in the kitchen, I expect. If you don't want to be noticed, walk from here and keep to the shrubbery. I can keep the servants busy while you slip into the upstairs sleeping quarters and find a vacant room.'

She nodded, relieved by the thought. Her reputation wouldn't survive another onslaught, and Ryder obviously didn't want his association with her to become public knowledge.

'Someone might see me?'

'Use your imagination. Tell them you were walking in your sleep and ended up in my bed, where the evil lord of the manor ravished you . . . They might not believe it but they wouldn't contradict you.'

Laughing, he swung her down and handed down her bag. 'I'll wait here until you get to the house. See if you can find something to tidy your hair with, then you won't look so thoroughly rumpled.'

She didn't know how to take him. Last night he'd been so warm and loving. Now, in the light of day he was almost remote, as if nothing of importance had happened between them.

She headed for the house, keeping to the shadows. The front door was unlocked. Pushing it open she entered and fled up the wide, carpeted stairs. She'd just reached the upper landing when Ryder's valet, John Moore, came out of a room and called down. 'The earl is on his way.'

William Swift took up position near the front door to relieve the earl of his hat and cane.

Adele shrank into a dark alcove in the panelling that opened on to the servants' stairs. The staircase circled up where another door opened out to a floor of guest bedrooms, then carried

on up further. She stepped out onto a landing, still covered
with dust sheets.

She heard someone humming a tune, and it sounded like
Sarah.

Racing up a set of stairs to the servants' quarters, Adele
carefully opened the first door and nearly collapsed with relief
when Sarah said, 'So that's where you've been.'

Adele jumped, saying the first thing that came into her head.
'It was the storm . . . I slept in the barn . . . alone, of course.'

Sarah grinned. 'Now the foliage has been thinned by the
storm you can see quite a lot from here. Are you saying it
wasn't you I saw with the earl on his horse?'

Adele shrugged. 'I think I was saying something like that
. . . but there was no other choice. You know what people
are like. They would make more of it than it was . . . which
was a simple conveyance. So we decided to encourage the
servants to think I'd been here all night . . . with you.'

'Rather than have them think you were in the barn all night
with the earl? I suppose the most naive amongst us might
believe it.'

Adele's face warmed. 'There was nowhere else to go. The
countryside, and that includes Duck Pond Cottage, is awash.
People are gathering in the church because it's on high
ground. I heard Mr Ashburn and the earl talking about taking
a look at the sluice to see if tree debris has blocked it. They're
taking the farm horses to help clear some trees that have
fallen.'

'Hmmm . . . you learned a lot considering you were
supposed to be with me. Where did the earl sleep, I wonder?
I'll go and fetch a jug of warm water so you can wash, and
you'd better tidy your hair. It has pieces of hay in it.'

'Well it would have, wouldn't it?'

'Will you be staying for breakfast?'

She nodded. 'I could eat a plough horse. Besides, Ryder
had a meeting with James Pelham, and I rather wanted to hear
what he had to say about the return of the missing trunks.'
She removed her crumpled gown and pelisse from her bag and
began to shake the creases from them.'

Sarah took the garments from her. 'I'll use the iron on them.

There's a brush on the shelf. Try and get the knots out of your hair while I'm gone.'

And when Sarah returned with the water, she also carried a message. 'The earl requests your company for breakfast.'

Fifteen minutes later found Adele reasonably tidy.

There was a cheerful fire burning in the breakfast-room grate when she entered and took a seat.

Ryder handed her a plate of breakfast, picked from the variety of dishes on the sideboard, attended to by Mrs Betts. 'You look tired, my dear, perhaps this will replenish your energy.'

Lord, he was pushing it. He would expose their relationship if he was not careful. She gazed down at her napkin, twisting it in her fingers. 'I'm sorry I kept you waiting, my lord. I'm not hungry.'

'Under the circumstances your apology is accepted. However, Mrs Betts told me you didn't have dinner yesterday, which means you haven't eaten. I insist you do so now.' Taking the seat opposite her, he smiled. 'Apart from that I trust you enjoyed a comfortable night, Mrs Pelham. I understand you slept in one of the attic rooms.'

Where had love gone? He was goading her and she felt like kicking him.

'I didn't want to put anyone to any bother.'

'You're my guest, Mrs Pelham. My hospitality is yours at any time you have the desire to enjoy it.' He turned to the housekeeper. 'Allocate a permanent guest room for Mrs Pelham. One that overlooks the stream would be ideal since it catches the morning sun and gives a glimpse of the sea . . . the room across the corridor from mine, perhaps.'

Mrs Betts gazed at the ceiling and her mouth twitched. 'Yes, my lord.'

'And tell the staff Mrs Pelham is to be regarded as part of my family.'

Adele didn't want to look at the sea. What if Edgar's spectre rose from the deep and tapped on her window, his face half-eaten away by crabs and his eye sockets empty so his brains hung out? What if he dragged her from her bed and down through the copse by her hair and held her under water until that last breath escaped and the water rushed in to fill the space?

Dragging in a ragged breath she held it and heard Ryder say, as if he was far away, 'Prepare another room for the Manning sisters. I think they may need accommodation until their cottage has dried out.'

In the corner of Adele's eye the shadow moved and began to take on some substance. It couldn't be, she wouldn't allow it. She closed her eyes unable to breathe and made a little mewing noise to catch his attention. When she tried to stand the room spun and her knees gave.

Ryder caught her up before she hit the floor. Sweeping her up he carried her through to the drawing room and placed her on the chaise longue. 'There, I knew you looked tired,' but the edge in his voice was salted with concern when he said, 'Mrs Betts, do you have any *sal volatile* with you?'

The housekeeper hastily explored the depths of her apron pocket and handed over a small glass vial.

Adele revived in an instance and her eyes flew open as the smelling salts were waved under her nose.

The butler came in, silver salver in hand. He hovered, looking slightly unsure of himself, and then backed away.

'There, that's better, at least you can breathe now,' Ryder muttered, almost to himself, and then to Mrs Betts, 'Bring a small bowl of oatmeal and warm milk, then fetch Miss Pelham.'

Within moments it was placed on the table.

'I'm sorry, my love, it was all my fault,' Ryder said when the housekeeper scurried off.

The butler returned just as Adele touched Ryder's cheek.

Ryder covered her hand with his. Seemingly without care that they had an audience, he kissed her palm.

Adele hurried to reassure him. 'You weren't to blame. I have dreams sometime, about . . . about drowning. This one followed me into the day time.'

'When I mentioned the sea.'

He didn't miss much. 'Yes . . . I'm perfectly well now.'

'You're not perfectly well until I say so, though I have to admit you're perfect,' and he smiled and gently kissed her on the mouth. 'I love you.' The endearment had hardly left his mouth when he replaced it with a spoonful of oatmeal and bade her swallow it.

Her protestation fell onto deaf ears, and it wasn't until the bowl was empty that he said, 'Make sure you rest.'

Sarah dashed in, concern written all over her. 'Mrs Betts said you'd collapsed.'

'It was a faint, that's all.'

The butler gave a discreet cough while he had the chance. He was nothing if not persistent. 'Your messages, my lord.'

The messages were waved aside. 'They're mostly acceptances for the social. Give them to Miss Pelham. Perhaps you'd go through them and weed them out, later, Sarah. In the meantime persuade your stepmother to eat a little more, and then she must rest. Toast with a coddled egg, and some fruit wouldn't go amiss.'

Sarah sifted the messages around the salver with a forefinger. 'Yes, my lord.'

'Now I must go and see how they're getting on with clearing the flood.' He gazed at the butler, frowning slightly. 'Was there something else, Swift?'

'Can I be of assistance in any way, my lord?'

'Yes . . . Mr Swift. You can come and help to move the debris if you would. I dare say the women can do without you for a while. There should be some corduroy trousers in the storeroom. Ask Mrs Betts to get you a pair, and at the same time tell the cook to keep the breakfast on the hob, because I'll be sending the workers back to be fed when we've finished. And tell the coachman to put the horses to the carriage. We can use it for transport if we have to.'

After the butler had gone he said to Adele and Sarah, 'We need to have that talk when we're back to normal. I have something to say to you, as well, Sarah. And we'd better have your aunts there too, since, although it doesn't concern them directly, I don't want them to worry. There are too many lies and an equal number of truths disguised as secrets being bandied around. I'm about to squash them.'

'Is this about James Pelham?' Sarah asked.

'The appearance of James Pelham with your trunks has made the issue at hand imperative.'

'But there was nothing of value in the trunks.'

'Exactly. But the trunks no longer exist, and burning them might seem like a guilty act to some.'

Indignantly, Sarah stared at him, 'Guilty of what, killing my father and stuffing his body in the travelling trunk? They were full of woodworm, and we weren't about to store the trunks in the attic and allow the pests to munch their merry way through the house.'

Ryder gazed from one to the other and smiled. 'I'll make enquiries and we'll sort it all out, in case James Pelham decides to place the whole mess in front of the magistrate – and I wouldn't blame him if he did. But then, I've got the winning hand, and he knows it.'

Sarah's eyes widened. 'What is it, my lord? Won't you tell us, or are you going to make us suffer?'

'The latter.'

'Then I shan't tell you what I know.'

'Which is?'

She held up a folded piece of paper sealed with wax. 'This message is from Sergeant Stover.'

'Thanks.' Plucking it from her hand he opened it. 'It's to say he's on his way. Hmmm . . . he should have arrived last night. Perhaps the storm held him up.'

And thank goodness it had, else last night would never have happened. Adele thought. She was looking at Ryder through new eyes now, remembering his warm flesh, strong and fevered in his need for gratification, like a stallion put to a mare, or a much gentler way, a baby put to the breast. Her gazed followed the contours of his body, his riding breeches taut where they touched the muscles in his thighs.

For a moment she closed her eyes, and when she opened them again he smiled, blew her a kiss and left.

Seventeen

There was the flood, a sheet of dirty water that covered the road. No longer clear it carried the dirt and debris dislodged in its initial rampage down the bed of the stream.

Thank goodness the rain had stopped, though Duck Pond Cottage was under water to the height of the windowsills and the surrounding meadows were sodden. The cornfields were on higher ground so were unaffected. If anything, the rain would help wash the lime and manure into the earth.

If they were quick the rest of the potatoes and other root vegetables could be saved from rot.

Water lapped at the doorsteps of the village cottages, which were on higher ground.

'Is everyone accounted for?' Ryder asked Ashburn.

'Mary Bryson hasn't been seen but the reverend isn't concerned. He's convinced that she might be at home. She told him she had a headache and went to bed early. He didn't disturb her this morning, just came over to the church to see what could be done. The road is flooded on the other side of the church too. I checked the sluice last night and although it was running fast, it was clear. The damned ducks nearly pecked my balls off and I think they've hatched a gang of thugs.'

Ryder grinned at that, and then he gazed over the pond, at the disturbance in the water. It was not clear now. With the water coming in and the sluice blocked, left to its own devices the water would spread out over the village and the countryside. It would not reach Madigan House, which was on a rise, but would effectively maroon it.

He swore. 'I'll have to go in there and try to unblock the sluice.'

Luke Ashburn said bluntly, 'It's too dangerous. The water's murky and if you're able to free the tree, the pressure of the water suddenly escaping will drag you into the race. If that tree shifts it could easily pin you to the bottom . . . if it doesn't crush you first.'

'Do you have a better suggestion?'

'Not unless someone has a rowing boat; and I've already asked.'

When Ryder began to take off his boots, Luke swore. 'Let me do it.'

'It's my responsibility. Let's get a rope around the tree first and tie it to the horses. They can drag it onto the bank.' He took off his coat and handed it to the coach driver, along with his boots.

The mud oozed up between his toes. As he began to clamber over the branch it rolled under his weight. He held his breath, concentrating to keep his balance, though he felt like a tight-rope walker. Then he gave a sigh of relief when it stabilized.

A small group of men had gathered on the bank.

Taking the rope from about his waist he tied it between two branches so it couldn't slip off, and called out, 'It's secure, so you can haul her in.'

'Get off the tree first. We'll be pulling it into shallows and it will be unpredictable. The weight itself will be uneven since the ground is uneven. If it rolls on you, it will kill you.'

It wasn't hard to walk along the trunk because he'd always been surefooted, and he knew instinct would adjust his feet to any signals of danger they received.

He wasn't about to become reckless and die . . . not now, when Adele had become his. He grinned. That had been a night to remember.

Luke took his hand in a firm grip and dragged him to the bank. He clicked his tongue, and with the help of the men, who added a bit more power to the operation, the horses strained against the weight of the tree. Slowly it moved.

'You were right,' Ryder said as the tree began to drag then took a half-roll that would have killed him had he been on it. It came to rest with a sharply splintered branch pressed into the bank.

They turned and gazed at the sluice. It was still blocked.

Disappointed, Ryder sighed. 'I'll go down and have a look around.'

'Not without a rope, you don't. And it will be a grope rather than a look. The water has too much muck in it.'

'I caught a glimpse of something dark at the bottom. A deer might have been drowned and washed into the sluice. I'll go down keeping my hand on the walls of the sluice.'

Luke tied the rope round his waist and then took a flask of brandy from his hip pocket. 'Take my knife. You might need it, and take a swig of this; you're shivering.'

The brandy warmed Ryder's belly and gave him courage. The fact that Luke Ashburn said, 'Don't stay down there too long. I don't want to go in after you, since I can't swim very well,' did nothing to comfort him.

The water in the stream usually came to the bottom of his ribcage. It seemed colder this second time, and he estimated it was twice as deep as usual. He would be submerged in a bowl of soup. He drew in a deep breath and descended quickly. His feet touched against something soft. He groped on the bottom.

For a few moments the water cleared and he saw a body. It seemed to be weighted down with the stone he and Hal had removed from the sluice the last time it was blocked.

Shocked, since it had taken two of them to handle the stone comfortably before, he tied the rope to the body and pushed the stone off with his feet. His lungs ached from the effort to hold in the air when every instinct told him to breathe. The body moved upwards, the loose garment it was clad in billowing out with water like the sails of a ship fuelled by the wind.

Ryder tried to follow it but the rush of water was too strong and though he kept his feet against the sluice, his body seemed to have lost all its strength. Inch by inch he was being sucked into the foaming current – inch by inch he was losing his strength and his eyes were beginning to dim. Inch by inch he was drowning!

Would Adele mourn him? She said she'd mourned for him before. He didn't want to die with kissing her one more time. Didn't want to leave without saying goodbye.

He put up a desperate struggle, but tired almost immediately. Desperate for air he opened his mouth to let the stale breath out into the stream of bubbles. Water rushed to replace it.

Then the race of water gentled. Someone had thought to close the sluice gate. That same someone grabbed him by the hair and hauled him upwards. He crawled towards a bush, where he swooped in a deep breath and emptied the contents of his stomach.

Curiously weak he collapsed, and was turned on to his back. A seagull floated above him. He'd never seen a prettier bird or a more beautiful sky. The air had never smelled so good.

A face floated into his vision. It was Luke Ashburn . . . Oliver Bryson's son, a man of scrupulous honesty who didn't give a damn for anyone else.

'Are you still alive, my lord?'

'It sounds like it. Another tot of your brandy might help the situation.'

He went up on his elbows and gazed at the stream, now racing along its chalky bed with a dirty, but gushing flow. It would be back to normal by morning.

His glance went to the taller man standing behind Ashburn and he smiled. Hal was dripping wet and wore an ear-to-ear grin. 'You're drenched, Hal.'

Both of them were covered in slimy green weed.

'And you're a bloody fool. Why didn't you check if the sluice gates were closed before you went down into the water?'

'I forgot.' He was as weak as a woman and felt like crying, as he'd cried all those years ago when Adele had left him. He'd thought he'd never stop. He had faced death and won today. But his wasn't a victory because he'd had an irrational thought that Edgar Pelham had been down there, trying to snatch him away from Adele. No wonder she had dreams of the event. Drowning was not a pleasant way to go.

Hal pulled him upright. 'You owe me a new suit of clothing.'

'I owe you more than that. I owe you my life.'

'Yes . . . well, it wouldn't be the first time, but I think we're just about even on that score. Can you put a name to the corpse, it looks like a female?'

Ryder remembered the body and pushed through the gaggle of men who were gazing down at the limp, bedraggled figure lying face down in the mud.

Nobody had touched her.

'Not one of the Manning sisters, surely?' He turned the body over and gently cleared the mud from her features.

'It's Mary Bryson,' someone said. 'I reckon she was trying to open the sluice and got caught by her skirt just as the flood of water came racing down . . . see, she has a rip in it. Always interfering in things that didn't concern her, was Mary, and look where it got her.'

'Enough! Have some respect for the dead,' Ryder said sharply, acutely aware that he'd just missed a meeting with the Grim Reaper in the same manner.

Mrs Bryson was wearing only a nightgown and her legs were exposed to above the knee. She wore no stockings, and the sight of her thin thighs and her bare feet, the toes ragged and torn, touched Ryder's heart.

He adjusted her clothing and wrapped his cloak around her. She was unattractive in many ways, and he hadn't liked her, but she'd had her own demons to contend with, no doubt. So had her husband.

'The poor old crow,' someone murmured.

'Will someone let the Reverend Bryson know?'

Luke said, 'That duty falls to me. Go home, my lord. You need to rest and I can see to the clearing up and monitor the water levels at the same time.'

'I'll leave the carriage for the Manning sisters. Perhaps you'd tell them. And send the workers, or anyone else in need, up to my kitchen for breakfast, a few at a time.'

Luke gathered up the limp body of Mrs Bryson and said, but quietly so Ryder could barely hear it, 'There you are, old girl. You don't have to worry about anything any more.' He looked up. 'There's a handcart on the other side of that fallen tree. I'll put her body on that and take her to the church. I imagine that's where the reverend will be.'

Hal stepped forward. 'I'll help you carry her to the cart.'

'Many thanks. Would you allow me a private moment with the earl, Hal?'

Hal took the sodden body in his arms and moved out of earshot.

Ryder said, 'Offer the reverend my condolences and tell him I'll call on him in the morning about eleven. Tell him

Mary lost her life trying to open the sluice gate, and an enquiry is unnecessary.'

'He'll appreciate that. By the way, I've decided to take you up on your offer. Will you accept my hand on it?'

'You might like to take a few days to think on it, Luke.'

'I'm through with thinking.'

'Very well, then we will exchange contracts the day after tomorrow at Stephen Tessler's office.'

A handshake was exchanged, the purchase sealed.

Ashburn and Hal strode off with the body of the unfortunate Mary Bryson, skirting around the water. It was already beginning to recede, leaving a muddy rim around the edge.

Hal was soon back, bringing Henry to Ryder's side. 'You look exhausted. I'll help you mount?' He made a stirrup with his cupped hands and tossed him up, and then plucked his bag from the branch he'd hung it on.

On the way back to Madigan House, Hal said, 'You're too quiet, Ryder. What's bothering you?'

'The manner of Mrs Bryson's death. She must have been terrified. I was.'

Hal understood fear. 'It was an unfortunate accident.'

'Remember the stone that took two of us to lift from the sluice? I found it pinning her body to the bottom of the creek. Her feet were bare and she was wearing only a nightgown.'

'You were in no state to examine the scene, my friend, but I did, so you can lay your mind to rest. There were deep imprints of her feet in the mud and slide marks going into the stream. Remember that the stream wouldn't have been as deep as it is now, but it would still be too deep for someone of Mrs Bryson's small stature. After consideration it appears as if she tried to use the stone as leverage to regain her footing and her feet went from under her. She fell backwards. The stone followed and pinned her to the bottom. Perhaps she was walking in her sleep . . . some people do.'

'You make everything sound so simple, Hal. What if she was already unconscious and someone placed the stone on her to weigh her down, and then slid her over the mud and down the bank into the water?'

'Someone murdered her, you mean? Why should they?'

'Mary Bryson was a gossip, and was nasty with it. She was also addicted to laudanum.'

Ryder sighed. 'There will be no enquiry unless the reverend insists. Mrs Bryson was lying on her back with the stone on her stomach and chest, like a stranded turtle. What was she doing there in her night attire in the first place?'

'Trying to flood Duck Pond Cottage, as she had on occasions before. I imagine she was trying to further the petition of Ashburn, in trying to cause annoyance to the occupants. The lady was muscular, and the depth of the footprints, especially the heels, tell their own story — as one of the men there witnessed when I pointed it out. They are almost too perfect.'

'What if the coroner ruled that a crime had been committed? Who would they suspect first? Adele, I imagine.'

'You think the reverend did it?'

'Mary was becoming a nuisance to him but I doubt if he'd go so far as to murder her.'

'That leaves Luke Ashburn. For what reason?'

'Adele hasn't found the deeds to Duck Pond Cottage yet?'

'It matters not. I've bought the entire Lawrence estate from Ashburn. It will become part of mine, as Adele's father and I had originally planned. Ashburn has agreed to stay on and set the place to rights.'

'That's an odd thing for him to do.'

'Not when I tell you that Ashburn has his eye on young Sarah and intends to take her to America with him.'

'The devil he does!' Hal fell quiet for a moment or two, and then he laughed. 'I'm of a mind to settle down myself. Young Miss Pelham is a spirited little filly, and practical as well as fair. I might give him a run for his money in that regard.'

'Really, then you should be made aware that something has happened that might change the direction of her life entirely.'

'Which is?'

'Her father and grandfather have turned up.'

'But I thought . . . Edgar Pelham?'

'So did she, but it seems not. I haven't told her yet. I need to prepare her, before a meeting with the concerned parties, and see what emerges. I'll ask Stephen Tessler to co-preside over it with you, if you don't mind.'

'What does your lady love think of your machinations concerning her home?'

'Adele doesn't know.'

'And if her papers come to the surface?'

A grin spread across Ryder's face. 'All for the better since I won't have to explain myself. If Adele finds out first she will raise merry hell.'

'Am I to believe that Mrs Pelham has finally been conquered?'

Ryder's smiled faded. 'That subject is not for discussion. Let's say she is not some woman of convenience, but the woman I've loved all my life.'

'My apologies, Ryder, I wasn't suggesting otherwise.'

'Something is holding her back I feel . . . something I'm missing. I have the strongest feeling it's something to do with the late Edgar Pelham.'

Madigan House came into view, and Gypsy must have broken free from Duck Pond Cottage, for he hurtled through the door from the kitchen, throwing warning yaps left right and centre. Horses neighed, and chickens clucked their way around the stable yard.

It all seemed so normal and Ryder felt at peace as they unsaddled their mounts and let them into the stalls for the groom to deal with. He had everything he wanted in life – except Adele. She would come round eventually, he was sure of it, but he wanted her body and soul. He'd meant what he'd said about loving her for ever.

They went in through the kitchen, Gypsy sniffing at their heels. Mrs Betts looked shocked at their unkempt appearance.

'We'll clean ourselves up and then will have some tea in the drawing room.'

'You didn't eat much breakfast, my lord,' Mrs Betts pointed out.

What he'd had he'd left under a bush. 'I had a repast of pond water and weed with a couple of ducks hanging off my heels.'

'He will have coddled eggs, and toast, with a slice of ham, and so will Mr Stover,' Adele said from the doorway. Her glance grazed against his, and there was a shy awareness about her, so she could hardly meet his eyes. A smile edged along her mouth.

'We saw you coming past the barn so have prepared some hot water so you can wash. If you take the kettle with you there should be enough for two.'

He crossed the room and gazed down at her, quite willing to kiss her senseless in front of anyone who wanted to gossip about it.

She must have guessed it because alarm filled her eyes. To break the tension between them she took a step back. 'Tell me what happened?'

'I nearly drowned.'

Her face drained of colour and she whispered, 'You nearly drowned? It cannot happen again.'

His ears pricked. She must be referring to Edgar Pelham. 'I'm very much alive.'

'So you are, and thank goodness.'

Her colour began to return and as she took a visible grip on herself her smile returned.

Tremors ran through Ryder's body and he began to tremble, even though he fought to control it.

Adele gave him a quick look before she turned to gaze at Hal. 'Is that everything?'

'A tree was blocking the sluice and he went down to free it and discovered the body of Mrs Bryson.'

Adele gasped. 'How terrible a tragedy . . . poor Mrs Bryson.'

'Our host didn't have enough strength left to fight the sudden rush of water that occurred, so I went down and brought him up. Neither of us could see a hand in front of our faces.'

'Hah . . . then you were both addle-brained.' She gazed at Hal. 'Are you all right?'

He nodded. 'Just cold.'

Ryder's teeth began to chatter and she crossed to him. She took her shawl from her shoulder and set it around him, still warm from her body. He captured the faint, musky perfume of loving on her.

'There,' she said, and softly, as though she was comforting a child. He touched her hand for a moment under the shawl, and she smiled when her fingers slid through his, leaving behind a tingling awareness of him.

'The pair of you must go and change. It's important that you keep warm in case you catch a chill. No doubt you can fend for yourselves in the absence of a male servant. Is the fire lit in Lord Madigan's chamber, Mrs Betts?'

'Yes, Mrs Pelham, and the cook has a large pot of chicken broth simmering on the hob. That will go down a treat, I daresay.'

Hal smiled at the housekeeper. 'You're an angel, Mrs Betts. So is the cook.'

'Thank you, sir. Speaking for myself, I'd rather remain earthbound for the time being.'

'Very sensible, I'd say.'

The pair of them left, Ryder hugging Adele's shawl around him. He turned at the door. 'Can you manage by yourself, Del?'

'I'm not by myself. I have your entire staff at my disposal. Go, make yourself comfortable and rest.'

'Then I'll see you in the library about five. Ask Miss Pelham to join us if you would . . . for dinner as well, since it concerns her.'

Eighteen

It had been a busy day, with workers cluttering up the kitchen while they waited for breakfast.

The aunts had arrived, chattering with excitement and with a cat clutched to each chest under their shawls. Adele got both them and cats settled in a room with a cosy fire and a tray of tea.

Gradually everything regained a semblance of order. The workers left. The daylight faded into twilight and William Swift was lighting the candles. Madigan House resumed its normal background hum.

When the long clock in the hall chimed the hour, hair tidied and faces washed Adele and Sarah entered the library.

The men stood. John Moore had transformed the two formerly bedraggled men into lean and elegant creatures.

Goodness, there hadn't been much resting going on, Adele thought, eyeing the empty glasses and the game in progress on the chessboard. Both men were smartly turned out and she could smell the sharp lime scent of Ryder's soap.

Adele had also managed to wash, and she felt refreshed. Her gown still had the smell of rain lingering about it but had been dried and pressed, her shawl returned earlier by John Moore.

Her heart soared when Ryder smiled at her. Both men stood. All she could think of was the time they'd spent together in the barn, and her knees felt weak at the thought of repeating it. All those years she'd gone without the need for a man, and now she had cravings that were positively indecent.

Ryder indicated the chaise longue and they seated themselves. 'I've asked Hal to stay in case there's anything legal you don't understand, Miss Pelham. If you'd prefer privacy he will leave . . . and so will Adele.'

Sarah smiled at Hal. 'I missed greeting you earlier. Welcome back, Hal, of course you must stay. As for Adele, she knows everything there is to know about me. What is it you want to say, my lord?'

'What if I told you that your father was alive?'

Adele put her arm round Sarah when the girl moved closer to her. Only in her wildest nightmares had she imagined that Edgar could have escaped his fate and still be alive? She felt as though somebody had punched her. 'What sort of cruel trickery are you inflicting on Sarah?' she flung at him. 'Edgar drowned. I know he did. I was there, and I . . . I saw it happen.'

Sarah gazed at everyone in bewilderment. 'How can he still be alive when he's drowned? Do I have to go back to him?'

'No . . . I put that very badly, Sarah, I'm sorry. It's your real father who is alive. So is your grandfather. His name is James Pelham and he's the person who delivered the trunks. The man known as Edgar Pelham was actually your uncle.'

Sarah looked totally confused. 'I don't understand.'

'Your real father is named Jeffery Pelham. Edgar took you from his care, and then he wrote to him and told you'd died.'

'Why did he steal me in the first place?'

'I don't know. Perhaps he wanted a daughter.'

'He didn't act as though he wanted one. He scared me half
to death. He said I was a nuisance and knew too much. Sometimes
he hit me. He said he was going to sell us into slavery.'

'Perhaps he did it out of spite. I understand that he and
your father didn't get along.'

'I can't remember. The only thing I clearly remember from
that time was when he killed my mother. He put his hands
around her neck and he shook her backwards and forwards
and he threw her down some stairs. There was a snap and she
went all floppy, like a rag doll. My mother's eyes were open
and they were brown.' Sarah placed her hands against her face.
'He said he'd kill me if I told anyone.'

'Which is probably why he stole you from your family, so
you wouldn't tell anyone.'

'He said he had a legacy to collect, and when he got it he
was going to leave without us, and never return.'

'He said that?'

'He wrote it in his notebook.' Sarah lowered her voice. 'I
think my father – Edgar Pelham – was going to kill us.'

Ryder and Hal exchanged a glance, then Hal said, 'What
made you think that?'

'He put something in Adele's drink on the night he fell
overboard. I think it was laudanum, for she was sleepy.
He didn't like us talking to the other passengers or the crew.
We had to restrict ourselves to the cabin for most of the time.
Adele and I used to take a few turns around the deck in the
evenings when the water was calm. On that last night it was
rougher, so he took her. Adele was in pain that evening. She
said she was suffering from sea sickness, but I knew he'd hurt
her again because she had a bruise on her face and more bruises
on her upper arms, and she'd been weeping.'

Ryder gazed Adele's way and she grimaced. 'I'm not a very
good sailor. I fell over when the ship canted sideways.'

'That's what you always say. But this time you were quite
befuddled and didn't seem to know what you were doing. You
said you were tempted to throw yourself overboard and put
an end to it. I was so worried I confided in the watchman,
who promised to keep you in his sight.'

Sarah was peeling back the layers of something Adele didn't want to remember. 'Stop this at once!' and her voice was sharp enough to bring the girl to heel. 'You're here to prepare for the meeting with your relatives, Sarah, not to indulge in discussing my private business. It seems that gossip is catching, and I would be obliged if you didn't encourage her in the practice of repeating what is little more than supposition, my lord.'

'Forgive me, Adele,' he said, looking slightly abashed.

Sarah's eyes had widened at the rebuke and now she coloured. 'I'm sorry, I didn't mean to, but it's the truth. Ask the other passengers. They knew you were ill-treated by him, and most of them avoided us because of it.'

'Oh, God,' Adele groaned. 'Is there no end to this?'

Hal intervened with, 'Let's stick to the point of the meeting. Do you still have Edgar Pelham's journals, Sarah? They should be handed over to his father and brother. It will help them piece together what happened.'

'I can't, I burned them in the trunks.' Sarah considered for a moment, and then gazed at Ryder rather doubtfully. 'Thank you for finding my kin, my lord.'

'It was accidental, since they found us first. I believe you expressed a hope that you had family still living. Now you know you have.'

'What's your impression of them, my lord?'

Adele became the recipient of a raised eyebrow and a grin before Sarah said, 'May I ask him that Adele. They are my kin, after all. Or would the answer be classed as gossip too?'

Adele's annoyance faded. Sarah certainly knew how to snap back. Picking up a cushion she threw it at the girl and the chess pieces scattered.

'Damn, and just when I was in the winning position,' Hal muttered.

'I only met your grandfather. He seems to be a good man and he was overjoyed to discover you were still alive, and eager to see you. I believe they will have your welfare at heart. I wanted you to get used the idea first. Perhaps they would like to stay for a while. Do you have any other questions?'

William Swift entered. 'Supper will be served in ten minutes, my lord. Miss Manning and Miss Prudence are waiting in the drawing room.'

'Then let's not keep the ladies waiting any longer. And Swift. I have something I'd like to discuss with you later.'

'Yes, my lord.'

There was a hubbub of greetings when the Manning sisters set eyes on Hal and Ryder. They were the recipient of a kiss apiece, then hardly pausing for breath Prudence said, 'Such heroic gentlemen, and what a terrible day for some, though we must be thankful the flood was mostly held back, thanks to your bravery, my lord, otherwise it might have crept up and covered the village and drowned us all in our beds. It was such a fright to get out of bed and go down the stairs to find ourselves waist deep in water, and with the ducks clucking at us through the window. Noisy creatures.'

Patience took over the conversation. 'Poor Mary Bryson; how tragic an event to take place in our community. We will offer a prayer for her soul tonight. Is it true that she threw herself in the stream, I wonder?'

Prudence looked from one face to the other. 'Do you suppose . . . dare I say it?' And Prudence did dare. 'Will they bury her body in hallowed ground?'

'Oh, don't start that again, Prudence, nobody in their right mind would choose to die by throwing themselves into a raging flood. It is merely conjecture. Besides, the doctor has to examine her body first to establish cause of death. Then we shall see.'

'Such a pity . . . poor dear Mary . . . I heard . . .'

What Prudence had heard faded into the background. It was only words – words that were a ritual to be aired for such occasions. They fooled none of the company present. Mary Bryson and the aunts had been bitter adversaries in life. The aunts would go to her funeral, and because she was dead and no longer a nuisance to anyone, condolences would be offered to her husband, whose bereavement would probably be a blessing, and then she'd be forgotten.

Adele caught Ryder's eye and he winked before turning back to her Aunt Patience. 'May I escort you into supper, Miss Manning? Miss Prudence? And we shall think of a more pleasant subject to talk about.'

'Our pleasure, my lord.' Looking pleased because the earl had singled them out for the honour, the pair twittered and attached themselves to Ryder's arms, while Sarah and Adele shared the sergeant between them.

Sarah was reticent during supper, though Ryder gently tried to draw her out. The women retired to their rooms, leaving the two men to catch up with a decanter of brandy. Now and again Adele heard outbursts of laughter and smiled.

Some nightdresses had been borrowed from the staff for the aunts. The cats snuggled happily in the chairs on opposite sides of the fireplace as Adele and Sarah said goodnight.

Gypsy decided to guard his mistress and Sarah used the truckle bed.

'You were quiet during supper,' Adele prompted, for she needed to know if Sarah was worrying.

'I was thinking . . . I don't want to leave you and the aunts. I have a position in the earl's household, and I love it here. It will be like going to live with strangers if they make me go with them.'

'I think you are worrying unnecessarily, Sarah. All we can do is wait until the meeting. I imagine they will be a normal family with reasonable expectations. Through no fault of theirs they were deprived of your company. Were you my daughter I'd want you back, and even though you're not I will miss you most dreadfully.'

'Do you think that man who said he was my father was normal? Edgar Pelham was everything I hate. He was cruel and a liar and he hurt us both, but mostly you. I used to lie in bed and think awful thoughts, and hope he'd be dead when I woke. When it happened it was such a relief that I laughed and cried at the same time and ended up with a stomach ache. It is such a relief to know he wasn't my father. All the same, I don't want to go away and leave you.'

She drew the girl close. 'Perhaps you won't have to, because in the normal course of events you would be working for a living at your age. I'm sure the earl will put your case to your father and grandfather most reasonably.'

'What if the rest of the family is just like him . . . Edgar?'

Adele sighed. 'Then we'll pack our bags and run away and

find somewhere to live where nobody knows us. Perhaps we could travel with the gypsies.'

Sarah giggled. 'The earl would move heaven and earth to find you again.'

'That's not true, although he is the most generous of souls and I love him dearly, I also hurt him badly and he has suffered. Eventually he'll revert to convention. If he'd died serving his country I don't think I could bear the guilt it would bring me.'

'I'm sorry I hurt you by repeating gossip at the meeting. It was such a relief to tell somebody and it just came out.'

'You could have spoken to me in private about it.'

'I tried to, but every time the subject came up you began to talk about something else.'

'Can you remember the two brothers and your grandfather?'

'There, you see . . . you diverted the conversation. But oddly, now they have been mentioned I keep remembering little snatches.'

'I'm not ready to speak of what I went through, and doubt I ever will be. Tell me the snatches that you remember of the brothers.'

'They were alike in looks and build, almost like twins. Edgar Pelham used to come and go, and tease me. I knew something wasn't right, but he scared me so. I addressed him as uncle once and he flew into a rage and said he'd burn my eyes with a hot poker if I didn't address him as papa, and after a while I supposed I got used to it. We left in the dead of night and travelled a long way. I was tired, and he hid me in an old cottage and told me to stay there until he came and not make a noise, else the wolves would eat me. When he came it was just beginning to be dark and he had to hurry. Why did you stay with him, Adele?'

'Much the same as you . . . out of fear. I was tricked into going with him. He confronted my father and asked for my legacy in exchange for me. My father refused, but by then it was too late. I couldn't go home because of the scandal. Ryder wouldn't want me back because I'd shamed him so. And then we were on the ship and on our way to Boston. I wanted to escape the storm of scorn that would have followed me. I considered a shipboard marriage and a change of name was better than being considered . . . well, you know . . . shameless.'

'I don't remember much, except the death of my mother. And then you came and everything was better.'

'Go to sleep now.' Adele blew the candle out.

After a short while Sarah said, 'If you run away, I want to run away with you.'

With that solution looking more and more unlikely, Adele laughed. Then she remembered Ryder had warned her she'd be punished for how he perceived she'd treated him all those years ago.

Her smile faded. He'd always had a great deal of charm and the ability to manage any situation to his advantage, but he was stubborn and usually carried out what he said he'd do.

Now she was in his bed again, if you could describe a heap of hay in a barn a bed. It seemed as if their past plans had run full circle and they were back to where they'd started. Except, she was no longer a wide-eyed and innocent girl, and there was no Edgar Pelham to ruin her life. She had surrendered her body to Ryder, and apart from that she could only offer him her heart. Would that be enough to appease him for running away when he'd wanted her all?

'*I must tell him,*' she said. 'I'll send him a whisper in the wind.'

There was a sleepy murmur. 'Must send what to whom?'

'Nothing. Goodnight, Sarah, everything will look better in the morning.'

Nineteen

Duck Pond Cottage sat in a sea of mud and waterlogged vegetation.

A group of five men leaned on their shovels, three of them awaiting instruction.

The ducks paraded on the opposite bank, fluffed their feathers and quacked in consternation at the destruction of their home.

Ryder huffed with annoyance. 'It's a mess. Perhaps we should pull the cottage down.'

Head to one side, Hal said, 'Nonsense! The cottage is quite sound and will dry out given time.'

Ryder addressed the labourers. 'We need to clear everything out of the bottom floor and get rid of the mud. Anything that can be saved should be taken upstairs. The rest can go on the bonfire. Please bear in mind the privacy of the Manning sisters when you open the cupboards. Save anything loose such as ornaments, money, linens and general goods. They can be placed in that wicker basket. I'll take them to Madigan House to be washed and dried. Can I leave this mess with you then Hal? I must go and offer my respects to Oliver Bryson. Afterwards I'll come back and attach myself to the fighting end of a shovel.'

Ryder would rather not front up to Oliver Bryson at all, but under the circumstances he couldn't just ignore the man. From now on he must become the servant of convention expected of an earl, if he wanted people to respect him.

Adele popped into his mind and he grinned . . . in her case, perhaps not quite that conventional.

'Your help is not needed,' Hal said. 'You can go home and entertain the ladies. I'm going to pack a trunk so your guests have a change of clothing. I'll put it in the donkey cart and you can collect it on your way back, if you would.'

Luke Ashburn gave him entry to the vicarage, and guided him to the morning room, where Mary Bryson was lying in state in a satin-lined oak casket. She looked small and childlike in death, and wore an embroidered shroud of white linen. Her cheeks were sunken in slightly. Her eyes were closed and her hair tucked under a frilled cap. Her hands lay in an attitude of prayer on her chest.

'Will you take a glass of brandy, my lord?'

'Not at this time of day, Reverend.'

'Your father didn't drink to excess either. Very laudable.'

Obviously the reverend hadn't seen the state he'd been in

on the day Adele had spurned him. Hal had told him he was hanging on to Henry's neck, his reins in one hand while the horse walked patiently around in circles. Henry had been youthful then – so had he.

Ryder moved his full attention to the reverend when the man said, 'I believe you fetched Mary out from the pond and covered her nakedness.'

Ryder uttered a small lie. 'Your wife's clothing was in some slight disarray, but she was decently covered from head to toe with my cloak before anyone else saw her. Hal Stover helped Luke carry her to the cart.'

'Thank you for that. Mary would not have liked people gazing at her, though death tends to overrides such vanity. Two of the women in my congregation laid her out. The death has been recorded in the parish register. Luke told me there needn't be an enquiry.'

'Not unless you'd prefer one. There seemed to be no suspicious circumstances. Hal Stover found obvious signs that Mrs Bryson slipped in the mud where the flow of water had undermined the bank and she was pulled into the sluice by the force of the water coming down the stream.'

'The doctor said there were bruises on her stomach.'

'As to that, it wasn't my place to examine her. I imagine she would have got those from the branch that had her pinned against the sluice. I was trying to move it when I first caught a glimpse of her. The water was churned up and murky and I couldn't tell who she was, at first.' He crossed to where the reverend sat, a dejected figure in black. 'We pulled the branch away using the farm horses. Then I went back down for her. I'm so sorry, Oliver, is there anything I can do for you?'

'No thank you, my lord . . . Luke is being a great strength to me. Though Mary was troubled in many ways and I did care for her . . . I wondered . . . was it deliberate?'

'Is there any reason why it should have been?'

'Sometimes her behaviour was erratic. I imagine that thought must have crossed your mind, my lord.'

'Not at all. My first thought was that she may have walked in her sleep and become disorientated, since her feet were bare and she was wearing only a nightgown. When Hal pointed out the signs to me it became obvious it was an accident.'

Oliver Bryson looked relieved. 'I was never able to give her a child, you see, and she had these turns. When she learned about Luke's existence it turned her head, and her mind began to play tricks on her. The doctor prescribed laudanum.'

'Perhaps if you'd discussed it with her a little earlier?' Ryder didn't want to be the recipient of this man's confession, or hand out advice like slices of stale bread, and the hands on the clock on the mantelpiece ticked away time with an irritating slowness. He could not spare much pity for this man's loss, when the pair had treated his Adele so badly.

'Matters are always easier with hindsight. I daresay you wouldn't have returned to the responsibility of home had you known the problems awaiting you. Rather you'd have been gadding about, like most young men of your age.'

Ryder didn't have to think about that. 'I was being of service to my country, which involved very little *gadding about.* Returning home was always my intention, and the estate was in a better condition than I expected due to your diligence and management.'

'I always thought . . . well, Mary and I both hoped it would become mine one day. I was doing it for myself . . . and Luke.'

'Yes . . . I know.'

'He's a good boy.'

That was debatable, for Luke was a man not a boy, and knew right from wrong. Ryder didn't offer an opinion.

There was a short, tense silence then the reverend said, 'Mary must have slipped out during the night, for I found the door unlocked this morning. I thought she had woken early and gone to the church, but only a few people were there. I thought . . .' Tears began to trickle down his cheeks and he suddenly looked old. 'I thought she was out visiting the sick perhaps. Was it God's punishment because I was too lazy to put a stop to her foolish prattling?'

'I'm certain you did your best, Reverend. Best not to dwell on it, but allow bygones to be bygones.'

The reverend gave a faint smile. 'A common platitude, one

easier to spout than put into practice, wouldn't you say so, my lord.'

The reverend was referring to his relationship with Adele, and Ryder had no intention of engaging him in a conversation involving her. Also he was not going to allow his private business affairs to be picked over by this man. 'I decline to argue the point with you on that,' and he managed to refrain from looking at the clock. 'When will the funeral be held?'

'Two days hence; it will be conducted by the bishop.'

'I'll be there.'

A knock at the door brought relief in the shape of Luke Ashburn. 'Mr and Mrs Wilson are here to offer their condolences.'

Feeling like a hypocrite Ryder patted his uncle on the shoulder. 'I won't monopolize your time, Reverend, and will see you later in the week.'

He nodded to the couple coming in on his way out.

'My lord,' the man said and the woman bobbed him a curtsey.

'Can you get away for a short time?' he said to Luke Ashburn, after he'd shown the couple into the drawing room.

'The housekeeper will be here in about half an hour.'

'Good . . . then we'll go and see Stephen Tessler and get our business over and done with. I'll wait for you in the Antelope if you still want to go ahead with the sale.'

The business didn't take long and Stephen had made sure that the sale was properly receipted.

Afterwards, Ryder said. 'You will regret selling it? It's a good piece of farming land.'

Luke shrugged. 'But then, so might you regret buying it . . . especially if Mrs Pelham's deeds turn up. The past should be left behind and forgotten, my lord.'

'I have something to say to you now, Mr Ashburn.'

'I hope it doesn't take too long. I have to get back to my father. He has moments of remorse and melancholy.'

Ryder placed a purse on the desk. 'I'll be quick. Here is your wage for the coming two years.'

The man gazed at the purse, slightly bewildered. 'I don't understand, my lord. I thought . . .'

Stephen leaned forward. 'Come, come, Mr Ashburn. You are being released from your obligation on full pay.'

'I don't understand.'

Ryder rose to his feet. 'Then allow me to spell it out for you. Firstly, I will say I have no dissatisfaction with your work, for which a reference will be provided.' He nodded to Stephen, who slid a folded paper across the desk.

'Secondly, there is such a thing as loyalty, and you have been playing one against the other. You know nothing of my past except that which has been gleaned from gossip. Neither are you qualified to give me advice. I have bought the Lawrence property so Mrs Pelham will have the security of knowing she still has the home her grandmother left her. Duck Pond Cottage and the acres of land it stands on are also hers. I have employed another man to replace you.'

Ashburn's smile faded. 'Hal Stover, I suppose.'

'You suppose wrong. Hal has made his own plans.' And Ryder hadn't been made party to them so far, so he could only assume the legalities hadn't been finalized.

'William Swift has agreed to take over. He grew up on an estate in Yorkshire.'

Ashburn said nothing. Just dug the toe of his shoe into the rug, which seemed reminiscent of schoolboy behaviour when caught out in a lie.

Ryder's suspicion of this man grew. There was something Ashburn wasn't telling him.

'Adele never lost the deeds to the cottage did she, Mr Ashburn? They were stolen and you know who by. Why didn't you tell me? By claiming the cottage, you and the Brysons robbed the woman I love of the little security she had left. I have treated you more fairly over this matter than you actually deserve, Mr Ashburn.'

Ashburn didn't say anything to that, but he nodded slightly. 'I thought the sale was above board at first and closed my eyes. The man who inherited the Lawrence estate was keen to get rid of it . . . he had debts. The reverend overruled Stephen Tessler's protest, which fell on deaf ears. He bought it for me out of conscience I think. It has not been easy to be passed off as Mary Bryson's nephew.'

'No, I don't suppose it would be,' and Ryder reflected that he'd been lucky that Adele's father had become his own guardian. He had raised him to fit the plans their fathers had made for them. Neither of them had counted on Adele being abducted by another man. Her father's anger and grief had influenced Ryder's own behaviour at the time, but he couldn't blame anyone but himself for the way he'd acted. Adele had been young, hardly a woman, and he'd deserted her at the very moment she'd needed him. He should have gone after them.

Ashburn gave a triumphant little grin as he turned away.

Ryder administered the coup de grâce. 'And Mr Ashburn?'

The man turned, not one shred of respect in his eyes. 'Yes, my lord.'

'I will expect the missing papers, plus the other items stolen from Miss Pelham's trunks to be returned. Otherwise charges will be brought against the pair of you.'

'I didn't steal them.'

'But you know who did, and so does the reverend. Mary Bryson stole them and you both knew about it. That makes you culpable in my estimation.

Ashburn's eyes widened in shock and a smile shadowed Ryder's face. He hadn't expected to enjoy this denouement, but he had. 'That will include the original deeds, the silver buttons, the purse with its contents, the pocket watch and the tools of his trade, of course.'

The man found some courage. 'I always intended to give them back. What if I can't find what Mrs Bryson has done with them?'

'Try asking the reverend. If the items are not returned I will certainly inform a magistrate of my suspicions, and I might even hunt you down and kill you. By the way . . . I will be meeting with Edgar Pelham's father and brother at the end of the week. You could attend the meeting too, and explain where those valuable goods have gone. You have made enough money from the estate sale to make reparation for the missing articles.'

'You think you have it all worked out, don't you?' Ashburn sneered.

'I hope not, because you know, Ashburn, I'd begun to like you. I thought you were honest.'

He shrugged. 'Old habits die hard, I'm afraid. And if I apologize?'

'It's too late for that since there's no trust left between us.' Ryder gazed at Stephen and nodded.

Stephen said, 'As for your hand in Mary Bryson's death . . .'

Luke Ashburn turned pale as he stared at him. 'What are you saying?'

'We're suggesting that, were we to consult a coroner, the most likely verdict would be that one or both of you fed her some laudanum until she didn't know what she was doing, and you then carried her down to the stream and pushed her in.'

'She fed herself the laudanum and then she walked off into the storm, raving like an old witch. She said she was going to confront the Manning sisters.'

'And you didn't try and stop her?'

'I followed after her, but I didn't lay one finger on her. I didn't have to. She closed the sluice herself, I think. It was too dark to see anything properly and I didn't know it had been closed. There was a bit of a splash, and then a cracking noise as the tree fell. I was lucky it missed me, because it was heavy. As far as I could see, the stone was amongst the roots and it slid on top of her and took her under the water when it sank.'

'And you didn't try to help her?'

'I leave the heroics to people like you. I crept along the tree trunk but it began to move and I went back to the bank. I called out for her, but she'd disappeared and I can't swim. I waited for ten minutes, and then I knew it was too late because nobody can last that long under water. I returned home and stayed there until one of the estate workers knocked at the door and told me about the flood.'

'Why did you wait?'

'I thought someone might try to blame it on me, because I forgot to open the sluice, I had too many other things on my mind. I wanted someone else to find her first, so I could be witness to it.'

Ryder sighed and put himself in Ashburn's shoes. It was a

lame excuse, but on examination it would hold up in an enquiry. 'I will accept your version of events. Three days after the funeral I'll call on you and the reverend, and we will settle the matter at hand. After that I hope never to see either of you again.'

The knock at the door caused the man to jump, but he had an expression of relief on his face.

Hal Stover stuck his head around the door. 'Have you finished your business?'

At Ryder's nod the rest of Hal followed through.

'Mr Ashburn is about to leave, after which the clerk will attend us.'

When the door closed on Ashburn, Hal said to Tessler, 'Where are those papers you want the earl to countersign?'

'Papers! What's going on, Hal? Stephen, you didn't mention any papers.'

'Mr Stover wanted to surprise you . . . such a childish notion.'

Hal grinned at that because Stephen was looking almost as excited as Hal. 'You're looking at Stephen Tessler's new associate. Halifax Stover.'

Two days later Mary Bryson was buried. The day was windy and carried the salty smell of the sea inland. The event was well attended by most of the villagers, some out of respect, and others who hoped to catch a glimpse of the earl, or his paramour, the widow, Mrs Pelham.

Reverend Bryson looked old and grey, and Ashburn avoided Ryder's gaze.

Ryder felt no remorse. The pair of them had sought to defraud Adele, and himself come to that. They were lucky to have escaped prison, or worse. He'd heard that the reverend had been offered a posting to a parish in Hampshire, so Ryder didn't feel too guilty about his loss. It was far enough away to not be a bother to him.

As he'd promised Luke Ashburn, he visited at the end of the week to clear up the outstanding business.

The housekeeper answered his knock at the door, and she bobbed a curtsey. 'The reverend asked me to dispose of all the personal items belonging to Mrs Bryson, poor soul, and to give the place a thorough clean for the next tenant. My husband will tidy up the garden at the weekend, like he usually does at weekends. He'll prune the roses and dig some horse manure around for winter. Roses like plenty of manure.'

'So I've heard. Did Mr Ashburn pay you?'

'No, my lord . . . he said you would.'

Ashburn had bounced back quickly, he'd give him that.

'Mr Ashburn left a satchel for you. He said it belongs to Mrs Pelham, and he found it under the wardrobe in one of the servants' rooms. At the last minute, and just before I closed the door behind them, he remembered the Pelham girl had stayed the night before she was sent off to the workhouse, and thought it might be hers. "Off you go and look for it," says he. "I wouldn't want anyone to think we'd stolen it." I told him it wouldn't be there, how could it be. I would have seen it when I cleaned the room before. But there it was – in full view. You could've blown me down with a puff of wind. He told me there was probably a reward.'

She accepted a florin and Ryder took the satchel home. He went into the library and set things out on the desk. The purse was weighed down with sovereigns and everything was as it had been described. He put the will and the cottage deeds to one side.

His gaze went to the three journals and he smiled. Adele had kept a monthly journal since she'd first learned to read and write. He recalled that her first entry had stated emphatically, *Rida wuz nortee.*

He was tempted to read the journals. She would have mentioned the child she'd lost . . . their child. He sat for a long time gazing at the little pile of valuables, and thinking of Adele and the child. Then he raised the book to his nose and thumbed quickly through the pages. There was a short, elusive drift of perfume – roses, perhaps. Adele liked roses. The temptation to know what was in her journals almost overwhelmed him and he flipped open to a random page.

Sarah was punished for making friends with the deck boy. He was a nice lad of about twelve years, who was teaching her to tie knots. Edgar hit him with his cane. Sarah and I have a plan

What the hell was he doing! Throwing the book down he scrambled to his feet, crossed to the bell pull and gave it a jerk. After a while Sarah came in.

Her glance went to the objects on the desk and a smile lit her face. 'You've found them . . . thank goodness. Adele had almost given up on the cottage. Now I can give them back to her. Where were they?'

Sarah was too sharp to be lied to and get away with it. 'Apparently, Mrs Bryson stole them from your bag when you stayed overnight there.'

She looked troubled. 'It had crossed my mind, so it doesn't surprise me, though she denied having them when I asked her. It appears now that the woman has become a convenient scapegoat, since she can no longer defend herself. She was inquisitive nevertheless. Have the Reverend and Mr Ashburn gone?'

'Yes.' He noted the relief in her eyes. 'Did he bother you?'

'Sometimes, when we were working together . . . I was conscious of him watching me, and it made me uneasy when he stood too close. Then once, when I asked him to step back, he just laughed and kissed my cheek.' She lifted her hand and unconsciously scrubbed it. 'Then he said he might steal me and take me to America, just like my fath – uncle did to Adele . . . and that if he did that nobody else would want me because . . .' She blushed. 'I just didn't like him. He was a bully, just like—'

Ryder cut in, 'Was he indeed? You can stop worrying about him now, my dear.'

Her glance went to the journals. 'It occurs to me now that he must have read Adele's journals to know such details.' Her gaze came up to his, shining with the honesty of her own innocent conviction about gentlemen, until her hand came down on the books. 'A gentleman wouldn't stoop so low as to read a lady's journal without her permission. You wouldn't do such a thing, would you?'

He tried not to look guilty. 'Indeed I would not. I'd rather like to give them to her myself. Ask her to come to the library. As for the other things, I'll put them in the strongbox until tomorrow. Oh, by the way,' he said as she turned to leave the room. 'Hal has become a partner to Stephen Tessler in his legal practice. I have suggested you work for him two days a week, and the other three days for me.'

'What if my family objects?'

'I daresay we can talk them round. It's not as though you'll be far away. You won't mind working for Hal, will you?'

A little blush of colour touched her cheeks. 'Oh no. He's such a pleasant man and I've . . . I mean all of us, and especially the aunts, have missed him visiting us at the cottage.'

'Good . . . off you go then, Miss Pelham.'

Hal would have no trouble plucking this little peach from the branch when she was ripe, he thought with satisfaction.

A little while later, Adele came in. 'Sarah said you've found my papers.'

'They're here on my desk.'

'You haven't read the journals, have you?'

'Of course not.'

He basked under the warmth of her smile. Four steps brought him close to her. Cupping her face with both hands he tilted up her chin and kissed her soft mouth, shaping it to his so the natural pout of her bottom lip was full, ripe and moist, like a juicy cherry hanging from the tree in the orchard.

'Do you remember when I carved "I love, you, Del, marry me" on the trunk of the cherry tree?' he said. 'You told me you'd sent me a whisper on the wind. What did that whisper say?'

She picked up the journals, holding them defensively against her, and backed warily away. 'It was a childish game.'

'I know what you whispered. You said you were too young to get married, but would love me for ever.'

'Then you know what I said.'

'You're not too young now, so I'm asking you, and most humbly. I'll beg you on my knees if you want me to.'

Tears filled her eyes. 'No . . . you mustn't be humble, it's not in your nature. Besides, it will do you no good. Don't ask me again . . . please, Ryder.'

There was something in those damned journals she didn't want him to see. 'What's in those books that's so important?'

'Nothing.' She slipped through the door and was gone, her feet pattering up the stairs.

Twenty

As best as she could, Adele tried to avoid Ryder for the rest of the day. He carried on as normal . . . as if what had occurred between them hadn't happened.

Ryder asked the aunts to help pick half a dozen oddments of chairs from the Madigan House attic to replace the ones that had been soaked through. The maid gave the chairs a thorough pounding with a paddle to remove any dust. They were tied on to a wagon and would be pulled to the cottage by one of the farm horses the next morning.

First though, they must assist Sarah with her reunion. Ryder took the Pelham men into his library and introduced Hal. 'Mr Stover will assist Miss Pelham, should she need his legal advice. I have spoken to Sarah about the circumstances of her abduction. She remembers very little of her childhood and is naturally quite reluctant. She is used to us, especially to Mrs Pelham, who had an important role in her upbringing.'

'The woman lives here . . . with you?' the elder man said, sounding rather taken aback.

'May I remind you that you're a guest in my home, sir.'

'Your pardon, my lord.'

Ryder nodded, and addressed the younger man. 'You may have noticed the damage done by the flood. Mrs Pelham's cottage was flooded, and I offered Mrs Pelham, her two aunts and your daughter accommodation until it is dried out and they can all return home. Miss Pelham is usefully employed by me for three days a week, and Mr Stover intends to employ her for the other two days in his legal chambers in Poole.'

'Doing what, my lord?'

'In both instances she's employed as a clerk. She has a good hand for copying documents and the like and is clever with numbers as well as having a sensible head on her shoulders. You can be proud of your young relative, sirs. Naturally, we will be sorry if you decide she must leave our midst.

'We will show you the cottage later, so you can satisfy yourself that all is above board. In the meantime . . .'

He rang the bell and the housekeeper came in. 'Are the ladies in the drawing room?'

'Yes, my lord. I was about to serve tea.'

'Then we will join them.'

As they crossed the hall, Ryder told them, 'You will be pleased to know that the missing valuables have been found. They were mislaid in the home of the Reverend Bryson, who accommodated your daughter on her first night here. Mrs Bryson has since passed on in regrettable circumstances, otherwise I'm sure she'd have been happy to explain how they came to be in her possession.'

The drawing room was pleasantly warm. But Sarah began to tremble when the door opened.

'Courage,' Adele said.

Ryder took Sarah by the hand. 'Sarah. May I introduce you. Mr Pelham. This is your daughter, Sarah.'

The pair looked at each other. Adele noticed that the looks of Sarah's father was similar to those of Edgar, but different. Where Edgar had smooth, handsome features that were slightly feminine, his brother was rougher.

'Sarah, my dear child, you're so much like your mother,' he said, tears seeping into his eyes.

'Papa?' Tentatively Sarah reached up and touched his cheek. Then his arms went round her and she hugged him tight and began to cry.

Ryder rode Henry. Adele came behind driving the donkey cart, piled with useful bits and pieces of china.

The workers respectfully snatched their caps from their heads when they saw Ryder leading the little procession. They soon relaxed when he began to laugh and joke with them.

Inside, the floor was now dry though some damp still seeped along the bottom of the walls. They had taken the curtains and linens to Madigan House to be washed, and they were rehung under Adele's direction. The rugs hung limply over a hedge waiting their turn; they looked like gaudy sheep, worse for wear with drying mud. Their bald patches were evidence of the many feet that had skipped and walked the fluff from the surface over the years.

'Allow me to supply you with some new rugs.'

'We're used to these, Ryder. They tell me I'm home. When the mud is dry I'll give them a good beating and it will soon brush off.'

The ducks watched all the activity from a safe distance, making little quacking noises.

'I hadn't expected the cottage to be ready so quickly,' she said, not knowing whether to be happy or sad about it.

'We've had dry weather and the wind has been blowing through during the day and we've had the stove going all the time. The water went down quickly. The garden's still a mess, but it will recover with a bit of pruning. It's a pretty and solidly built cottage. I always felt at home here.'

They sat on the stairs to keep out of the way while the furniture was brought in, and she thought about it. 'My father always wanted a son. I had a happy childhood here, but when you went away to school I was lonely. I was sorry I upset my father. I've always thought love had no limit, and it was not something that could be switched off the first time something went wrong.'

He took her hand in his and kissed her knuckles. 'When did it go wrong for us?'

'The day . . . I left.'

'It wasn't your fault. We'll do it properly next time. I'll arrange it. We'll wed in the church in Poole. Instead of running away you'll arrive in a pretty gown and I'll give you emeralds instead of pearls. If you don't turn up, bear in mind that when we're old and wrinkled I'll still be there, a skeleton to be pitied, waiting on my bony bent knees in my best hat and breeches for my true love.'

'Oh, Ryder . . . you haven't listened to one word I've said.'

He tossed a laugh her way. 'I most certainly have. I do know that we love each other, so can you give me a good reason why we shouldn't be wed?'

'Because I wouldn't be good for you.'

'Allow me to be the judge of that.'

She had to tell him . . . she had to! But the words

strangled her throat, paralysed her tongue and wouldn't leave her mouth.

He'll be horrified.

You know him better than that.

What she did know was that she had an uneasy feeling that matters were about to come to a head and everyone would learn of her crime. Her journals could have been read by anyone over the course of the last few months, and could soon be made public knowledge. If the Pelham men learned of it they were bound to prosecute her, and if she were found guilty they would hang her.

Her blood ran cold. The thought of being removed from those she loved was painful. Ryder would turn away from her. He would marry another and he would have children to love, despite his denial to the contrary. He would have to, unless he was prepared to hand his estate over to Oliver Bryson and Luke Ashburn, and he wouldn't do that if he could prevent it by keeping the family name and bloodline intact.

If he married and had a family they would learn to despise her eventually. 'I . . . I have . . . dreams.'

'We all do.'

'You don't understand, Ryder. They are dreams about something that actually happened . . . a crime . . . a horrific crime.'

'Tell me.'

Her voice dropped to a whisper and something inside her froze. 'I cannot tell you . . . I cannot.'

'Why not?'

'Because the words won't come out.'

'Let me help them along,' and he kissed her so tenderly she wanted to die on the spot and take that moment with her into heaven.

She pulled away. 'We'd better get back to Madigan House since Sarah is expecting another visit from her family,' she said.

If he was angered with her response he didn't show it. 'Her family isn't expected until this afternoon. After all this time you haven't learned to trust me, Adele, and that saddens me.'

He was persuasive . . . too persuasive. She wanted to throw herself into his arms, declare her love and beg him to forgive her. Life was too cruel sometimes, and she wanted him to be happy. 'I'm sorry,' she whispered.

'Not as sorry as me, my Del. It seems as though I shall have to find another lady to love. Perhaps I shall meet someone eligible at my social evening.'

The thought almost desiccated what was left of her.

Standing, he pulled her to her feet, his eyes as fierce as those of an eagle. 'Remember how much fun we used to have together?'

She remembered.

'You've turned into a sad mope now. You rarely laugh. What has that man you ran off with done to you to cause this change?'

'Nothing . . . everything.' She thumped a fist against his shoulder and he winced and took her fist in his palm, uncurling each finger with a kiss. 'He humiliated me at every turn, made me feel as though I was nothing . . . a dog in the gutter to ill-treat, a slave to wash and cook for him . . . someone to abuse.'

She had never been this open before and he encouraged her with, 'You should have left him.'

'I couldn't, he would have killed both of us.'

'He said so?'

She nodded, fatigue creeping over her like a grey tide. 'I hated him almost beyond reason and there was nothing I could do about it except—'

'Except what?'

'I'm tired, Ryder . . . I need to sleep.'

Breath hissed through his teeth and he pulled her close, holding her as she slumped against him. She seemed close to fainting, and that concerned him. 'I'll take you upstairs.'

Adele felt like a pent-up ball of emotion that needed to be expressed, though she was sure she'd explode if she didn't keep a grip on herself.

Hefting her into his arms, he carried her up the stairs and into her bedroom.

She was closer to laughter than tears, horrible laughter, bordering on hysteria rather than light-heartedness, closer to frustration than to rage, and totally aware the workmen might hear if she raised her voice. She lowered it. 'You know I didn't run off with him by choice . . . you said you believed me.'

He lifted her onto the bed. 'I do believe you. If it's not what he did to you, then what? Tell me, so I'll understand.'

One of the workmen gave a gruff shout, 'We've finished bringing the furniture in, my lord.'

'I'll be there in a moment or two.'

'It's something I did to him . . . to Edgar.'

His eyes narrowed in on her in speculation. 'Stop playing games, Adele. What exactly did you do to him? Tell me.'

'I . . . I killed him.' She began to tremble and forced the words out again. 'I killed him before he killed me.' There, she'd said it.

He pushed her to arm's length and she watched the expression in his eyes change from annoyance to disbelief, then puzzlement. It was followed by a dawning horror and then an agonized acceptance. 'Oh God, you don't mean it. I won't praise you for such a confession since it's not true.'

She'd rather have his scorn than his lopsided pity. 'You practically forced it out of me. Now I've done what I vowed never to do. I've ruined your life just by telling you. If this gets out I'll be imprisoned, or worse . . . they'll hang me. I'm so scared—'

A finger over her mouth stopped her rush of words. 'Do you still love me, my Del?'

'I've always loved you. You'll never know how much, and I'll feel guilty about the way I've treated you, for the rest of my life.'

'Then my life will be all the better. A worthy cause, to embrace, my dearest Del.'

She felt numb and without purpose in her life when she was away from him. 'I've never stopped loving you, even when I thought you were gone, though I couldn't bear the thought I was living in a world where you no longer existed. If I hadn't had Sarah to care for I don't know what I would have done.'

'I do . . .' He began to open drawers and throw garments on to the bed . . .

She didn't know whether to laugh or cry. 'What are you going to do?'

'Everything I should have done all those years ago. Didn't you get all those whispered messages I sent you?'

'I guess we grew out of such childish games.'

'You think so? Close your eyes now.'

He whispered something against her ear . . . something that sent suggestive messages through her body. When she shivered, he laughed and so did she. 'See . . . it does work.'

There was the sound of him opening and closing her dressing-table drawers. Was he packing her travelling bag so he could get rid of her?

Curiosity got the better of her and after a short while she opened one eye and found him looking her!

They smiled in mutual recognition of a childhood spent together, and then he indicated the garments he'd laid out on the bed.

'This looks pretty, just like your eyes.' He indicated a gold, fine silk pelisse with pale green padded trim on the sleeves and shoulders. A matching bonnet flaunted pale green ribbons and feather trim. Taking her hand in his he kissed it. 'Whatever I do will only be for your own good, so promise you'll trust me.'

'I promise.'

He took her downstairs, saying to the workmen, 'We've got some business to conduct in Poole. I'll be back in a short time. Perhaps you could put the men to tidying the garden.'

'Yes, my lord.'

'Why are we going to Poole?' she asked when they were underway.

He gave a barely discernible grin. 'You promised to trust me.'

'Damn you, Ryder, you tricked me into saying that. You've always been stubborn about keeping secrets . . . I couldn't get one out of you if I used a hammer and chisel.' She sighed. 'As you will. I hate it when you don't tell me anything, and hate it even more when you sidetrack.'

'And what have you just done? For months now you've had me on tenterhooks, braying like a donkey following after a carrot on a stick. When were you going to tell me about that particular misdemeanour?'

'Never . . . I suppose. I thought it might ruin your estimation of me if you found out the truth.'

'My darling, Del, you should know me better than that. You'd better tell me about it now. And don't leave anything out.'

Dismounting, he lifted her down from her cart, hitched Henry and Daisy to a post and then turned to her, his eyes softening. 'Now would be a good time, my love.'

He listened to her faltering account of what had taken place and took her hands in his.

'That's not what the witness accounts revealed. They state that Edgar Pelham trod on a piece of holystone left there by the ship's boy, who was cleaning the deck, and he fell and went over the side. As he slipped Pelham grabbed you for support and his strength pulled you over the side with him. The seaman on deck duty managed to throw a drag net over the side and you became tangled in it.'

'I remember . . .' and her eyes were swimming in tears. 'It was so hard to breathe.'

'Pelham tried to climb over your body and he grabbed a fistful of your hair and you struggled to free yourself from the net. You banged your head on the side of the ship and became unconscious. Unable to help yourself you began to slide back into the sea. The seaman could only save one of you, so he cut you from the net and dragged you on board. He said you could have both been saved if Edgar Pelham hadn't been such a craven coward, trying to save himself instead of helping you.'

'So I didn't kill him?'

'The seaman couldn't manage the weight of both of you together, and he was forced to take a knife to the net and cut you free. He pulled you on deck and when he turned to get Edgar, the man had gone. That version was verified by the deck boy and by Sarah, who was up on deck with you.'

'But . . . the dreams . . . I pushed him in. I wanted him to die.'

'That I can understand after all you went through with him.' He shrugged. 'You always had a vivid imagination, my sweet, and you'd had a hard bang on the head that knocked you out. That probably concussed you. Whatever your dreams tell you, you didn't kill anyone.' He placed a kiss on her mouth.

She gazed at the building. 'This is a church!'

'How clever of you to recognize that, ouch!' he said to the finger poked in his ribs. 'They open for weddings between the hours of eight a.m. and noon. I've booked ours for ten thirty.'

'But how could you when you didn't know for certain.'

'I simply made several appointments over several likely days, when I knew we'd be in Poole.'

'I'm awed by your efficiency.'

'I live only to please you. My love, you've confessed to a serious crime that might, or might not, become public knowledge, since Mrs Bryson wrote to the Pelhams with her poisonous suggestions. If you marry me nobody will bother you, because nobody in their right mind would believe that my beloved countess, Lady Madigan, would stoop to such a thing.'

Lady Madigan! She grinned despite her need to cry.

'I have a bishop's licence, which you must sign if you agree to become my wife.' He ignored her snort. 'This is a matter of trust between us, Del. We can exchange vows now and announce it at the social next week.

'I'm going inside the church. I'll wait fifteen minutes for you to decide.' He held up his hand when she was about to speak. 'We have reached a point in our lives where we must fulfil the promise we made to one another. As far as I'm concerned you either love me enough to become my wife, or you don't love me at all.'

She hadn't expected an ultimatum.

As he strode towards the church grounds she called out, 'I forgot to mention that I hate it when you walk off in the middle of a conversation.'

His footsteps faltered and he turned and came back, his eyes gathering the dark blue of a summer sky before a storm. 'You don't mean it, Del . . . I couldn't live with the thought that you hated me.'

'It's for your own good.'

'Don't ever do anything that's for my own good again. You've put me through hell.'

The vulnerability in him was endearing, and it softened her. 'I didn't say I hated you. How can I when it's not true? I absolutely adore you – and you know it. Besides, we can't get married without witnesses.'

He turned, and smiled, held out his hand. 'I'm sure we'll find someone. Are you coming? I'm not going to ask you again.'

'Are you sure about that?'

'No . . . I was lying.' Two steps took her towards him and she found herself drawn into his arms.

A man and a women walked by and the man whispered, 'It's the earl.'

'And he's kissing Mrs Pelham in public . . . how shocking.'

'Oh, I don't know. I wouldn't mind kissing her in public myself.'

'Joseph Braithwaite, you behave yourself.'

Laughing, they sprang apart and Ryder managed a sweeping bow for their audience. 'May I shock you even further by asking you to witness our wedding? It will only take a few moments of your time, and I know I can trust you to keep it a secret before we announce it at the social next week.'

'Don't you fret sir, my wife and I can be as quiet as the grave when the occasion arises.' Laughter boomed out of him.

The woman tittered and curtseyed. 'Take no notice of his silly jokes, my lord. It will be my pleasure to attend your wedding, my lord, Mrs Pelham.'

Joseph mumbled with a gruff sort of laugh, 'This will tweak a few noses in the district.'

'Do be quiet, Joseph, undertakers should keep a suitable mien on their faces at all times. They're not supposed to be amusing.' She turned, displaying an ingratiating smile. 'It was such an honour to arrange the burial of Mrs Bryson, especially with her being so closely attached to nobility.

'It was my pleasure to attend her funeral, Mrs Braithwaite.'

'Quite,' Braithwaite muttered under his breath, and the two men exchanged a faint smile of agreement.

'Ah yes . . . about the social,' Mrs Braithwaite cut in smoothly. 'I don't think we've received our invitation yet, have we, Joseph?'

Smoothly, Ryder said, 'An oversight by my clerk, I would imagine, for I'm sure your names were on the list of businessmen.' Taking out his card, Ryder handed it over. 'Give this to the doorman and he will announce you.'

Joseph slid it into his pocket. 'That's settled then. Shall we go and witness the gentleman handcuff himself?'

A clock chimed the half hour and Ryder picked up Adele's hand and kissed it.

'Are you ready?'

She nodded. 'I sent a whisper on the wind.'

'You said that you love me, and hope we'll always be happy together. We will be.'

'I love you, Ryder.'

'And I love you.' When he kissed her again she had never been happier in her life.

Somehow, Ryder had managed to hire some more staff. Adele's maid, Elsa, was one of them. She was comfortably built, and creative.

Adele had decided against wearing the gown that had been fashioned for their former, doomed union. It would remind both of them of the past, when they should be looking to the future. She wore a new gown of white silk with a diaphanous overskirt of pale green with puff sleeves and touches of sage.

They had managed to keep their wedding a secret except for informing Hal and Sarah. The Braithwaites walked around with smug expressions on their faces. Most rumours were dismissed, since the supposed bride was still living in Duck Pond Cottage with Sarah and her aunts.

Elsa curled the last ringlet around Adele's face and threaded ribbons through her coppery hair, catching it at the nape of her neck with a posy of green silk leaves. 'There, my lady, it's a simple gown that makes you look every inch the bride.'

'But how did you know Elsa? I didn't tell you.'

Elsa's smile was suitably mysterious. 'It was a whisper in the wind, my lady. His lordship will fall in love with you all over again.'

There was a knock at the connecting door and Ryder entered, splendid in dark blue breeches and satin coat over a silver brocade waistcoat and lace cravat. He carried a jewellery case. 'I have something for you.'

The something was a string of emeralds. He settled the glowing green jewels in their place and then leaned forward, kissing her behind the ear. 'Are you ready, my sweet?'

She drew in a deep breath. 'I'm ready.'

They went down the stairs together, Adele's hand resting lightly on Ryder's arm.

The new butler bowed to them and called out, 'Please clear the stair and stand for your hosts, the Earl and the Countess Madigan.'

The room fell silent as they descended, until Joseph Braithwaite called out, 'I can vouch for that since I witnessed the ceremony. Congratulations, my lord. I hope you will allow me to bury you when the time comes, only with a little more ceremony.'

There was a hubbub of laughter, then cheering, led by Hal.

'Oh my, I didn't even know about it,' Patience was heard to exclaim above the crowd. 'I don't know what to say.'

'That's a blessing. I won't have to put up with your prattle then,' Prudence retorted.

'I love you so much,' Adele whispered, and Ryder whispered, 'I love you too.'

'I was whispering to my aunts.' They grinned at each other, and in case anyone thought they weren't serious he drew her into his arms and kissed her, to the cheers of the men and titters and loud gasps from the women. She emerged from it blushing. He was certainly rubbing people's noses in it.

Sarah stood with her father and grandfather, shining with the excitement of the moment. They had come to an arrangement, where she would spend every sixth week with her kin. Ryder had offered the Madigan carriage and Hal had promised to act as escort.

Hal stood behind them, tall and handsome, and totally reliable. His eyes were on Sarah and he had a faint smile on his face. Adele wouldn't be surprised if something developed between them.

Her aunts wore new gowns and they both smiled the same smile at her.

Ryder had worked his way around the hall, making introductions, collecting curtsies, bows and best wishes to leave in their wake, and then he signalled to the orchestra and the music began.

Adele's gaze met Ryder's and was pulled into their depths and she didn't have to guess how much he loved her.

'It seems as though we've reached an agreement at last, my Del,' Ryder said, and they began to laugh.